CA
PA

For Tim Palmer, the best husband a woman could ever want, with thanks for all you have taught me and meant to me during our marriage.

Love's Haven

CATHERINE
PALMER

Steeple
Hill®

Published by Steeple Hill Books™

STEEPLE HILL BOOKS

Steeple
Hill®

ISBN 0-373-78538-0

LOVE'S HAVEN

Copyright © 2005 by Catherine Palmer

www.SteepleHill.com

Printed in U.S.A.

ACKNOWLEDGMENTS

My thanks to Karen Solem. Your faith in my writing ministry is a gift I treasure always. Thank you for all you mean to me both professionally and personally.

To Joan Golan, I'm so grateful to you for believing God can use me at Steeple Hill, for having the vision and the perseverance to bring me back to my roots and for using your wisdom and insight to help me hone my craft.

May God bless both of you with a full measure of His richness. Anna Cory-Watson and the staff at Steeple Hill, you are wonderful. Thank you for all you do on behalf of the Kingdom. Great Holy Spirit, my Comforter, how thankful and amazed I am at the path down which You guide me. Isaiah 55:8–13…oh, glorious God, lead on.

Chapter One

✤

"I'm going to marry you, Mara."

"What?" The word didn't make a sound. "What…?"

He placed a finger on her lips. "I'll marry you and give Todd's baby a home, medical care, college—whatever both of you need. I'll pay the bills, the insurance premiums, the creditors. I'll put the baby in my will. I'll do everything. Whatever you want."

"You're crazy."

Balanced on a scale in her tiny bathroom, Mara stared up at the man in the doorway. Brock Barnett looked as he always had. Six feet, four inches tall. Two hundred pounds. Black hat. Black hair. Gray shirt. Wrangler jeans a little worn at the knees. Black boots. Nothing about him had changed.

He even acted the same. Moments ago, he had barged into her apartment and demanded to know why she hadn't told him about her pregnancy. When she mentioned the difficulty of seeing over her stomach to weigh herself, he had propelled her into the bathroom and onto the scale.

"I went to the county clerk's office this morning to check on the license," he informed Mara. "I've already been to the lab for my blood test. Now we have to get yours, and we're set."

"But that's...that's—"

"I'll manage Todd's company until we find a buyer," he went on. "I've already talked to the project director at the Bureau of Land Management. Dr. Long said the restoration of Fort Selden is on hold while they iron out the legal details of Todd's contract. I told him I'd find a capable person to take over."

"In Las Cruces, New Mexico?" she snapped, suddenly furious at his cockiness. "You think you can find somebody around here with the experience to run a historic restoration company?"

"Sure. Why not?" His brown eyes, like dark, wet oak, searched her face.

"You're nuts. Get out of my bathroom."

"The moving company gave me a date to box up your stuff. You can live in the west wing of the ranch house. There's a room for the baby, and you can use the Lincoln—I'm always in either the pickup or the Jag. We'll fence the swimming pool, and I plan to turn the weight room into an indoor playground with a seesaw and one of those nifty little—"

"Brock!" Mara pushed his chest. It felt like a granite wall. "Stop. You're rambling. You're scaring me."

"Scaring you?"

"I'm not going anywhere. This apartment is my home. This is where Todd and I...we..." She couldn't start crying. Not in front of this man. She had the horrible realization she might want him to hold her. "Just move, so I can get off this scale."

"I'm not going anywhere until you listen to me."

"You can't trap me in my own bathroom!"

"Looks like I already did." He gave her a smile more tender than brash. "Come on, Mara. Hear me out."

"I heard you, Brock. You're talking nonsense."

He propped one booted foot on the edge of the bathtub beside a novel she had been reading, and then he lifted his eyes to Mara's face. "You'd give up the chance to drive a brand-new car?"

"Of course I would."

"How about a big house with two maids and a French chef?"

"Forget it. Look, I told you—"

"Free medical care?"

"I can take care of… I can get help." She searched for an escape, just as she had every day in the past months. Only blunt reality emerged—haunting her, nipping at her heels like a hungry wolf.

Orphaned at six, Mara had been raised in a series of foster homes until she turned eighteen. During her teen years, the Division of Family Services had placed her with a godly family who had taken her to church on Sundays and to youth group meetings on Wednesday evenings. This family had been different from the others she had lived with, and Mara came to understand why. Soon, she committed her own life to Christ, clinging to Him through the upheaval of the ensuing years. But never had she experienced anything like the turmoil and pain of her husband's death. Consumed with grief, Mara took comfort in only one thing. Todd had been a faithful Christian, a true man of God. Now he was in heaven. Though she missed him terribly, Mara knew he was where he had always longed to be.

She and the baby would learn to make do without him. Childhood as a ward of the state had taught her to treasure independence. For several years, she had supported herself and her husband as a history teacher at a private academy. But when Todd's restoration company began to be successful, she had resigned her position in order to help him with research. They had purchased insurance that Mara could no longer afford, and the company held contracts that now could not be completed. With the school year well under way, she wasn't likely to find a teaching position. History teachers who filled the few slots available rarely gave up their jobs until retirement. And what principal would hire a pregnant teacher who would need a substitute almost immediately?

Though Mara rejected the idea of welfare, she tossed it at Brock anyway. "The government," she said. "They have programs, you know."

"You'd turn down life insurance? Health insurance? The best medical care money can buy for you and the baby?"

"Oh, Brock, don't be…" She couldn't finish. What was he? Irrational, ridiculous? Or a taunting temptation sent to lure her off the straight and narrow path she was trying to walk? For months, Mara had prayed that God would help her—that He would show her a way out of the mess that entangled her.

But Brock Barnett? Surely God hadn't sent *him*.

"How about a college fund? I can send your son to Harvard, Mara."

"Harv—" She caught herself and stared at him. Who could think of college? "But he's not even born yet. And what makes you think it's a boy?"

"Boy or girl, that kid's going to grow up. He'll need things—clothes, toys, education, summer camp, a car. I'll make you the beneficiary of my estate. Both of you—you as my wife and the baby as my child."

She drew back and wrapped her arms around her middle. Everything unbearable that had happened in the past five months went back to this man. "My baby will never be yours!"

He sucked in a breath at her vehemence. "Look, I am the baby's godfather. Todd wanted me to be."

"Who told you that?"

"Your friend Sherry Stevens. We met at your wedding. I saw her again at Todd's funeral, and I've called a few times to check on you. She let it slip that you were pregnant." His eyes went dark. "And she told me Todd wanted me to be the godfather. You'll honor that wish. I know you will."

Furious at her best friend's betrayal, Mara lashed out. "You're trying to buy me off so I'll release you from your guilt."

"Wrong!" He lowered his head until his mouth was an inch from hers. "That is wrong!"

"You think you can walk out of this with a clear conscience."

"Never." He swallowed hard, as though a fist had formed in his throat. "If you think I won't live with this for the rest of my life, you're the one who's crazy. Todd was my best friend."

"My husband!"

"I know!" His voice boomed off the tiled walls in the tiny bathroom.

For a moment Mara thought she saw the ropes that held him in control start to unravel. He stared, breathing like a locomotive, eyes of molten bronze. And then he leashed the anger— visibly took it, folded it and stuffed it away. His brown eyes turned to wet oak again; the corners of his mouth turned down.

"I know he was your husband," he whispered.

Mara bit her lower lip as she watched pain write messages across his face. For the first time in all of this, she felt the urge to reach out, to comfort, to console. She had tried so hard to forgive him. Tried to let go of her resentment and anger. To give it all to God.

But how could she allow any tenderness toward this man? It was him. *Him!*

"Mara," he said gently. "I'm not trying to buy your forgiveness. I'm doing what I can to honor Todd and take care of the people he loved."

Her shoulders sagged as the breath left her chest. "Oh, Brock, I'll be all right."

"You'll be better than all right once we make it all legal." He set his hands on his hips. "Come on, let's go get that blood test."

"No."

"Yes, Mara."

"No!" She grabbed his sleeves and twisted them in her fingers. "No, Brock! I'm not going with you. I'm not going to marry you."

"Why not?"

"Because it's… You're… I don't want to marry you!"

"Yes, you do, for the child's sake."

"I don't like you!"

He caught her shoulders. "What does that have to do with it?"

"It's your fault! Your fault!"

"Listen, Mara, don't make me—"

"I hate you! I hate—"

He scooped her up in his arms, turned to the door and carried her down the narrow hall. "I don't care how you feel about me, Mara. You *will* marry me. It's the only way."

"The only way for you to soothe your guilty conscience!"

"It's the only way out for both of us. For all three of us." He carried her across the threshold and kicked the door shut behind him.

"You didn't lock—" She twisted in his arms, her bare feet flying, kicking. "My stuff, my things—"

"We'll buy you new stuff."

"I don't want your money! Put me down. Brock Barnett, you put me down this instant! I'm in my nightgown. I'm pregnant!"

At the Jag, he cocked one leg and balanced her on his knee as he jerked open the door. She fought him, but it was useless. He set her down and grabbed the seat belt. As he fastened it around her swollen stomach, she hammered his back with her fists.

"Just a blood test, Mara!" he growled, snapping the buckle. "You can have the next two days to try to talk me out of the marriage."

By the time she could respond, he had slammed her door, opened his, climbed inside and started the engine. He managed to drown her words as he gunned the Jag out of the parking lot.

"Coming through!" Brock shouldered open the door to the small clinic and carried Mara inside. "Somebody point me toward the lab."

So furious and upset she couldn't even speak, Mara looked over the lump of his bicep as the waiting room erupted with cries of surprise, dropped magazines, a scramble of children. The receptionist gawked. A nurse threw open the door to the examination section of the clinic.

"Sir, you'll need to take your wife to the hospital. We're not equipped—"

"You have a lab, don't you?" He frowned. "I know you do, because I was here this morning."

"Is this an emergency, sir?" The nurse attempted to keep her voice low. "Has her water broken?"

"Water? No, it's blood—"

"Blood? She shouldn't be miscarrying at this stage!" The nurse touched Mara's arm. "Ma'am, can you tell me when you began to feel contractions and how often—"

"We need a blood test," Brock interrupted, his voice loud. "We want to get married."

The commotion in the room evaporated. The nurse's face drained of color. "Oh." She pursed her lips. "I see."

Brock squared his shoulders. "Just give us that little twenty-dollar blood test so we can sign the marriage license."

The nurse leaned toward Mara. "Ma'am, are you all right?"

Eyes shut, Mara couldn't respond. All the way across Las Cruces the clenching intensity had built—a spasm in her back, a hard band across her middle. Brock had been unaware, of course.

For the last two months she had been plagued by false labor. Though she took medication, each time a contraction began, she worried. What if her water broke? What if the baby came? It was too early!

Absorbed with her discomfort, Mara knew vaguely they were in a clinic somewhere. A nurse asked questions. Brock rambled as the contraction began to slink away like a naughty child. It left her legs, then released its hold on her abdomen. She let out a breath.

At the gently rocking motion of Brock's stride, a scent drifted around her head. Clean, starched denim and leather. She allowed her head to roll against his arm and pressed her cheek against the contracted muscle. This arm felt strong enough, more than strong enough.

"You're sure about this?" The lab technician eyed Brock.

"We're sure," he declared as he set Mara on an examining table.

The technician looked at Mara for confirmation. "Are you feeling all right? A physician could speak with you, if you'd like, Miss Rosemond."

"Mrs. Rosemond," Mara corrected her softly. "I'm married."

"Oh, but I thought…you were going to…with him…"

"My husband died."

"I'm so sorry. We have counseling services here, Mrs. Rosemond."

"She doesn't need counseling," Brock cut in. "She needs a blood test."

"I'm concerned about her mental and physical condition, sir."

"She's been through the mill, ma'am. What do you expect? Mara…" He laid his hand on her shoulder. "Mara, are you okay?"

"I'm waiting for the next one."

The lab technician caught her breath. "Contractions…she's in labor!"

"No, I'm not," Mara said calmly.

"Take her blood," Brock bellowed. "I want to marry the woman before this baby gets here. Do it. Now."

The technician tied Mara's arm and flicked the tender skin inside her elbow. In a moment the needle stabbed into her vein. Mara squeezed her eyes shut. Here we go again. The place in her back began to knot.

"Done!" the technician muttered, removing the needle. "You may sit up now, Mrs. Rosemond…Barnett."

Mara bit her lower lip. The contraction hammered through her pelvis. She reached out and found a hand. She squeezed, dug her fingers into flesh. Breathe, breathe, breathe.

"Mara, Mara!" The voice at her ear sent a trickle of calm down her spine. "Easy now, Mara."

The hammering began to shrink into a gentle thud, the sound of her own heart. She could hear in snatches. "Eight months…widowed…fell off a cliff…marry me…blood… Barnett…"

Another voice. "When was the last?…stay with her…delivery…" A bright light flipped on overhead. "Mara, I'm going to examine you now…"

She gripped the fingers she held, felt cool lips on her forehead, her hair. The constriction crept from her stomach into her back, where it held on for a moment. Then it vanished.

"Mrs. Rosemond?" An image appeared in the space above her head. An old man with white eyebrows drifting off the sides of his face. "I'm Dr. Brasham. Delivered hundreds of babies. When was your last contraction?"

"The car," she managed.

"In the car!" Brock Barnett's face emerged, eyes flashing gold sparks.

"How long ago? Ten minutes, would you say?"

"Maybe…seven."

The doctor frowned. "Any contractions before the one in the car?"

"It's false labor…Braxton Hicks contractions. I'm taking ritodrine."

The doctor regarded her for a minute, his eyebrows like angel's wings. "I think perhaps…not this time. You're dilated to three."

"Three!" Her gasp brought her back to reality.

"Would you like to rest here at the clinic while I contact the hospital? I think you're going to have a baby—you and your…fiancé."

Chapter Two

❧

Brock sat on a low stool beside the examining table, Mara's fingers clenching his. The doctor and two nurses hovered around her, taking her temperature and blood pressure, asking questions, checking everything.

Mara Rosemond looked as beautiful as he remembered. Soft, straight blond hair spilled across the pillow. Set above high cheekbones, her gray-green eyes tilted up at the corners. Pale pink lips had always curved easily into a smile. She wasn't smiling now.

Another contraction absorbed her, demanding all her energy and concentration. She squeezed his fingers, stopping the blood. Her teeth clenched and a sheen of perspiration appeared on her forehead.

Then, just as quickly as it had come, the contraction slipped away. Mara closed her eyes and drank down a deep breath. A strand of her hair draped over the table. Brock studied it, wondering at the natural curl that turned up the end of each yellow-gold thread. His gaze shifted to her stomach. Its canopy of white sheet rose like a mountain in winter. Surely the mound beneath it wasn't all baby.

But it was. And that baby intended to be born.

As the certainty socked him full force, Brock's hands went damp. He hadn't planned this part. Holding the reins of control meant everything to him. Early in his life, he had learned the hard lesson that he couldn't rely on anyone or anything. When his parents divorced, he was left on the ranch to be raised by his father. His mother moved away, and she rarely saw her son. Now she lived in Argentina with her third husband. Brock's father had been too engrossed in the ups and downs of his oil business to pay much attention to his only son. On the senior Barnett's death, Brock had inherited oil wells, stocks, a large bank account and the ranch. From that moment forward, he had seized his own destiny, taken charge of his future and mapped out his course for success.

Everything had gone according to plan until that day on the cliff with Todd. When his best friend had slipped and fallen, Brock's life had come unraveled. And now he was doing everything in his power to weave it back together. He intended to fix it all—to repair not only the shreds of his world but Mara's, too.

On learning of her pregnancy, he had mentally outlined everything. He would cover Mara's health insurance premium until after the baby came, then he would register her and the child on his own policy.

The Bureau of Land Management didn't like his plan to continue the operation of Todd's restoration company. But the BLM had its hands full coordinating the needs of private land owners with state and federal agencies managing New Mexico's seven historic forts. Protection and preservation was their priority. Restoration was a luxury made possible only through funding by private foundations. The cost of rebidding the job and hiring an out-of-state firm would be prohibitive.

Brock had covered all the bases, even in his own house. In recent days, his maids had aired out the west wing and put fresh linens on the beds. The French chef planned menus. Brock had bought a crib that now waited like an empty sentry box for pink fingers and tiny toes…a little rosebud mouth…a wisp of hair….

Blast it all! He hadn't thought about the actual baby. This had been another project to tackle and put in order. But there lay Mara with her round stomach and her hand gripping his….

"Let's get this woman to the hospital," he commanded the doctor. "Get a move on here."

Dr. Brasham laid a hand on Brock's shoulder. "Babies are unpredictable, Mr. Barnett. Right now, Mara's contractions are sporadic. True labor involves regular contractions that dilate the cervix. We'll keep you here for a half hour, Mara, and if your labor continues, we'll send you to the hospital to check in."

She nodded as the doctor and nurses left the room. From across the room, Brock watched her place both hands on her abdomen and run them gently around the dome of her baby. The gold wedding band Todd had given her shone in the soft light.

Brock studied her carefully. He didn't know the first thing about fatherhood or marriage. After his parents' divorce, Brock grew up with horses for company and oil pumpjacks setting the rhythm of his life. Carpentry fascinated him. Even now he worked in his shop nearly every evening.

But you couldn't call horses, books, adzes and lathes a family. You couldn't call housekeepers and ranch hands a family. No, Brock didn't have a clue how to be part of a family.

Well, Mara could take care of the baby herself, he decided. It was her baby, after all. Hers and Todd's. Brock had nothing invested in the whole process except the responsibility to meet the child's basic financial needs. That, he could do.

"I want to go home," Mara said softly. "I'm tired."

She turned her head to see Brock around the side of her stomach. He was leaning against the bunny-and-carrot-strewn wall, his brawny arms folded across his chest, his Stetson pushed down on his brow and his usual swarthy tan faded. Well, what do you know? The man was shaken up.

Good. Mr. Fearless Confidence deserved a little anxiety. Someone needed to teach Brock Barnett he didn't run the world. Those broad, squared shoulders announced the man as a tough, stubborn bull. Mara had to smile. Leave it to a tiny, fragile, unborn baby to throw the ol' bull off-kilter.

"Oh, Brock, when the doctor does that episiotomy," she said, sprinkling a dose of concern into her sigh, "I don't know how I'll be able to endure the pain…the contractions…the pushing. The baby is already so big, I'm afraid the stitches will be awful. And if my water breaks before I can—"

"Your friend Sherry'll get you through," he spoke up. "She took the classes with you, right?"

"Classes can only do so much. I'll be so stretched with the baby's head pushing—"

"You'll be fine. Sherry'll be right beside you."

"The doctor will take his scalpel and—"

"Excuse me a minute." He bolted for the door. "Nurse?" he called. "Isn't it about time you checked on…"

Brock's voice faded as he headed down the hall, but Mara could hear him issuing commands. She smiled. Thank goodness that when the time came, she wouldn't have to rely on Brock.

Mara had been right about the false labor. By noon that day the doctor had confirmed her suspicions, and Brock drove them back to her apartment. At the front door she ordered him to leave her alone, to refrain from calling Sherry and to forget his crazy idea of marriage.

Brock had regained his color, and with it his stubbornness. "You think over my offer before you turn me down, Mara. I never claimed to know about babies, but I do know how to keep a bank account in the black. I can keep you off welfare and give that kid of yours a future."

"This baby is Todd's, and she has a future."

"Not the one I could provide. What would Todd want, Mara? You think about it."

He did leave her alone, but Mara felt his presence. His offer was tempting with the reality of her situation so dim. The following week brought Mara a flood of bills, a notice that the checking account was overdrawn and a cost estimate from the hospital for labor, delivery and postpartum care.

She knew she could never give up her insurance. Even a normal birth was financially impossible. Then the credit card company wrote to warn her that legal action would be taken if she didn't pay Todd's bill in full immediately. A lawsuit! If she couldn't afford to pay off the debt, how could she afford a lawyer?

Thursday evening, Sherry Stephens stopped by after her work at a downtown clothing boutique. The two young women had met in a Bible study class several years before, and they had formed an instant bond. Mara's sober outlook helped keep Sherry's spontaneity and wackiness grounded, while Sherry provided Mara with a strong dose of optimism and fun. Petite, with dark brown hair and a pert nose, she perched on the edge of Mara's couch. Her sharp brown eyes missed nothing as Mara finally poured out the whole situation—her financial straits and Brock's offer.

"What would Todd want?" Sherry posed the same question Brock had. "Mara, he would want Brock's help for his wife and child. Todd put his own life in the hands of his best friend. Of course he would place his family there."

"Oh, right. Brock Barnett can take care of everything." Mara grabbed a tissue and stared at the pink wad through blurred eyes. "Sometimes I actually pick up the phone to accept his offer."

"Maybe you should."

"I can't bear the thought of relying on that man."

"Brock is a responsible person, Mara. He runs his ranch. He has lots of money. Let him help you."

"He's responsible, all right. He's responsible for Todd's death!"

"You don't know that for sure."

"He asked Todd to go with him to Hueco Tanks, didn't he? They were the only two climbers up there that evening, so they were responsible for each other's safety. Todd fell, and Brock didn't. Why on earth should I trust him with my child's future?"

"But to go on welfare? Would Todd want that?"

"Of course he wouldn't. I just don't see any other way out."

"Brock is a way out. He wants to take care of you, Mara."

"He wants to buy his way out of his guilt."

"So let him."

"And be stuck with him as my husband for the rest of my life? Todd told me he didn't think Brock was a Christian, and you know how I feel about that, Sherry. It's important to me to follow the Bible's teachings. We're not supposed to be unequally yoked with an unbeliever. How can I blatantly disregard that?"

"Oh, Mara, you don't expect this arrangement to last forever, do you? It's for now, for the baby. You don't have to have a religious ceremony. The marriage would be like a contract—without any emotional or physical union. Just an arrangement."

Mara dabbed the tissue in the corner of her eye. All week her emotions had pulled her this way and that. She told herself she missed Todd, but in truth her husband seemed far away. His memory had been buried under stacks of bills, his voice stilled by ringing phones.

"A man like Brock Barnett," Sherry continued, "is too attractive to live celibate the rest of his life. You know women are after him, Mara. Look at him! I mean…those eyes and that mouth. The shoulders. Some woman is going to snag him, and he'll want to get married for real. You just make sure you get a prenuptial agreement so you're legally able to take care of yourself and the baby in the years to come. Brock will use marriage to you to relieve his guilt, and you can use it to take care of your needs."

"Both of us using each other? That's a cheerful thought."

"Get real, Mara. People negotiate marriages all over the world—dowries, bride prices, the whole thing. It's just here in the States that we think love has to be a part of the picture. And as for the Bible, it's full of arranged marriages. Abraham's servant chose Rebekah for Isaac. Ruth's mother-in-law fixed her up with Boaz. Only when emotional desire got in the way did people have real trouble. Look at David and Bathsheba or Samson and Delilah. The truth is, Mara, you're a lot better off marrying someone because it makes sense. You and Brock and especially your baby all need this right now. So why not?"

"Because I despise Brock Barnett."

"Then you shouldn't have any qualms about tapping into his money."

Mara shook her head. "You're as crazy as he is, Sherry."

"I'm looking out for your interests." She paused for a moment. "They're going to take your truck, you know. They'll claim all your assets. You won't even be able to stay in this apartment."

"I know," Mara whispered. "What about those Scriptures that say Christians are to take care of widows and orphans? How much more could I fit that picture? Surely our church would help me out."

"For a while…in some areas. But church is basically a place of worship and teaching. Our church is big on evangelism, but it's not a charity service. That's the government's job. Do you really want to be homeless, Mara? Do you want to live in a shelter? Do you want to have supper in a soup kitchen every day? Do you want your baby to grow up eating groceries bought with food stamps?"

"Well, Sherry, thanks for the uplifting talk."

"Hey, what are friends for?" Sherry stood to go. As she picked up her purse, she regarded Mara. "Maybe I should keep my mouth shut, but you know me. You grew up in foster homes—paid for by the government. I know you don't want to go back to that kind of welfare. So, do what you have to do to stay free."

As Sherry walked to the door, Mara tossed her tissue into the trash basket. "If I marry Brock Barnett, I won't be free," she said softly. "I'll be living on *his* welfare system…under his terms."

"But he owes you, Mara. The state doesn't." Sherry opened the door. "Let me know what you decide. Meantime, I'll be praying for you, girl."

Brock shoved a log onto the fire and watched as sparks shot up into the stone chimney. The spicy scent of piñon smoke drifted into his cavernous living room. He took a deep breath.

A wispy curl of ash danced out of the grate and pirouetted onto the black, gray and red Navajo rug where he knelt. He let out his breath, brushed his palms on his thighs and hunkered into a more comfortable position.

Two weeks and Mara hadn't called. The deal was off, and he should be glad. He wasn't used to having people around, anyway. He studied the orange flames licking against the blackened wall of the firebox. Todd's kid would grow up just fine without Brock Barnett around.

He stretched his legs out and eased down onto the old wool rug. Hands behind his head, he stared up at the vigas that crossed his ceiling. Yep, Mara was definitely gone. Oh, he might run into her some day. He'd catch a glimpse of blond hair. Then he'd see those gray-green eyes and pink lips. He'd know her right away. She'd be thin again, but not as angular. Motherhood would have made her a little rounder, softer, fuller.

Brock tried to shut out the picture. He'd been seeing Mara in his thoughts too often. She was Todd's wife. She didn't belong in his mind at all. Squeezing his eyes closed, he reminded himself that Mara was a mother, not some long-legged beauty. She wanted a warm teddy bear like Todd for a husband, not a tall, hard man with callused palms and sunburned lips.

"She probably didn't give my offer a second thought," Brock muttered as he stood, giving the logs in the fire a nudge with his boot. Well, so what? He had his own life to live.

Chapter Three

❧

Mara rolled over in bed and squinted at the alarm clock. Six-thirty in the morning. Groaning, she groped for the covers. The bed was a mess, blankets on the floor, sheets pulled from the mattress.

She had been in labor all night. Braxton Hicks contractions again, she felt certain. Her water hadn't broken, and the discomfort had come and gone at random intervals. Now her bones ached, her stomach rolled, her legs trembled. She had debated calling the hospital, but she knew there was no point.

Her hand brushed across the familiar cool rectangle of her paperback novel, and she picked it up with a sigh of relief. At least she could drift into some other world for a few minutes. The false labor had to be the result of the previous day's stress. First her landlord terminated her lease. Then her insurance company phoned to give her two days to pay before they canceled her policy. The bank had already claimed the pickup, and she'd been forced to turn in her credit card and close her savings account.

This morning she would have to take a taxi to the family services office. Mara gritted her teeth as another pang swept through her. The last three contractions had been ten minutes apart. She gripped the sheets as her abdomen tightened in an unbearable constriction. Welfare was the last thing in the world she wanted! Every time she thought about walking into that building in downtown Las Cruces, she cringed. Could she actually do it?

Dear Lord, I need a way out, she lifted up. But hopelessness weighted her prayer like a sandbag.

When the compression of muscle and tissue finally began to subside, Mara opened her book. With a shudder, she stared at the black script on the creamy white page. The words swam, meaningless and disconnected.

She let the book fall onto her face. What was the point of reading about some far-off place where the world was rose-tinted and people fell in love and rode off into a happily-ever-after sunset? Mara couldn't imagine such a thing ever happening to her again. If she thought of men, she could see only Todd, the man she had always loved. Now Todd was dead, the apartment was lost, the money was all spent and—

Another contraction clenched her abdomen. From under the pages of her novel Mara peered at the clock. Ten minutes. Not today! Not now. She brushed the book aside. She needed to get busy. Take a shower. Fix a bowl of cereal. Pack those last boxes.

When the pressure subsided, she slid off the edge of her bed and stood on wobbly legs. As she made her way to the bathroom, she reminded herself the baby wasn't due for three weeks, and first babies were almost always late. Sherry had driven to Albuquerque for Thanksgiving, but she'd be back in time to coach Mara through labor.

In the bathroom, she pushed aside the shower curtain and turned on the water. As the tiny blue-tiled room filled with steam, she allowed her one escape to filter into her thoughts. Brock Barnett. She wondered if his offer still stood. A house to live in, food to eat, a car to drive, insurance…

She snapped up the chrome shower pull. Absolutely not! She would never rely on that man. God would help her. He would provide a way out of this—and it wouldn't be Brock Barnett!

As water spattered into the tub, Mara lifted her leg over the side. A dull ache poured into her back and tightened into a belt of steel around her belly. Fighting to catch her breath as the contraction hammered through her, she glanced out at the bedside clock.

Nine minutes.

Brock grabbed the phone on the second ring. Who would call him at this hour? "Barnett," he barked.

"Brock?"

He knew her voice immediately. "Mara? What's wrong?"

"I'm calling to let you know I've made a decision. I will marry you, and I'd like to get it over with this morning. Tomorrow's Thanksgiving, so I want to take care of it today. I've called the courthouse, and it's first come, first served at the county clerk's office. We'll meet at nine."

Brock dropped into a chair by the door. He drew his hat from his head and set it on his knee. The kitchen suddenly seemed uncomfortably warm, and he ran a finger around the inside of his collar.

"Look, Brock," Mara said, "you made an offer, and I'm accepting it."

"Yeah...but nine this morning? I need to check on my—"

"Look, either you marry me this morning or you don't marry me at all. Which is it?"

Brock studied the gray felt Stetson on his knee. "I'm in the habit of planning things out, Mara. What's the status on the baby?"

Her breath caught. "It's...it's not due for three weeks. I have to be out of my apartment by noon, so bring your pickup to town when you come. You can load my boxes and take them to your house."

Brock smoothed the brim of his hat as he listened to the emptiness on the other end of the line. Mara had been forced out of her apartment, and she must have lost the truck. Only this much loss, this much fear, had driven her to accept his offer. She must despise him more than he knew.

"I'll meet you at nine," he said.

As she hung up, he stood and settled his Stetson on his brow. He was going to marry Mara Rosemond, a woman who hated his guts. What a wonderful beginning.

Mara could feel Brock's eyes on her as she waddled down the sidewalk from the taxi to the courthouse. She knew she looked awful. The mirror in her apartment that morning had told her that the tight bun at the nape of her neck made her cheekbones stand out against the hollows of her eyes. She didn't care. This was an arranged marriage, merely an agreement between two parties. It wasn't anything like the blessed union she had shared with Todd.

On her first wedding day, a long white gown and veil had spoken of Mara's purity and innocence. Flowers, candles and a church altar had announced that the marriage was something special, a holy ritual dedicating the couple to the Lord. Today, Mara's black coat—obviously not maternity wear—covered nothing more than her arms and back. Her blue dress clung to her swollen stomach, its hem sweeping up into a curve at her knees. A bulky purse over her arm took the place of a bouquet.

"Did you bring the blood tests?" she asked Brock as she climbed the stairs.

"Good morning to you, too, Mara." He took off his hat, but she brushed past him into the warmth of the building. "Is Sherry coming?" he asked, matching his stride to hers.

"She went to Albuquerque for the weekend." She pushed open the door to the county clerk's office and stepped inside. Brock handed over the blood test results and twenty-five dollars. He and Mara presented their driver's licenses, signed a form and were told to wait.

They sat on a long bench, and Mara glanced at her watch. Six minutes since the last contraction. She'd barely made it into the courthouse. She shut her eyes and leaned her head back against the wall just as the ache swept into her back. Hands inside her coat pockets, she squeezed their polyester linings.

Lord, help me, she prayed silently. *Please help me to make it through these next few minutes.*

"I reckon we'll have a turkey and trimmings at the ranch tomorrow," Brock said. "Pierre's the best cook you ever saw. My dad brought him over from France years ago, and I kept him on even though I don't eat enough to make him worth what I pay him."

Struggling to steady her breathing, Mara fought for control. Brock's voice floated somewhere beside her. "One time I put everybody on a health kick, the whole staff. Pierre had himself one royal French hissy fit. So we're back to eating his sauces and fresh butter every day."

Mara took a deep breath as the contraction began to slip away. She glanced at her watch. She had at most six minutes to get through this. "Now," she croaked. "Let's do it now, Brock."

At her tone, he slipped his arm around her waist and lifted her to her feet. She leaned into him, aware that the man felt as warm and sturdy as a big oak tree in the summertime as he led her into the office.

As the clerk flipped through a book, she took off her glasses and studied the couple. "You are Mara Renee Waring Rosemond?"

Mara nodded, fairly sure of her name. The familiar dull ache had begun edging across her abdomen. It had been five minutes since the last contraction. As she listened to the clerk, she allowed her eyes to slide from her rounded stomach to Brock's flat one. The white cotton fabric of his shirt, clean and freshly ironed, smelled of starch. At his waist, a heavy silver buckle fastened a leather belt that held up a pair of black jeans.

"Mara?" The woman's voice barely penetrated.

Mara lifted her head and nodded, a monumental effort. Her voice sounded hoarse and distant. "Yes, I will. I do…of course."

She knew Brock was studying her, unable to suppress the frown that crept around his mouth. He probably thought she'd gone bonkers—turning down his marriage offer, then agreeing to it. Telling him she hated him, then deciding she wanted to get married after all. Now here she was, still wearing Todd's wedding ring, dressed more for a funeral than a wedding.

"Yes," he said firmly as the clerk finished with her questions. "I will. I'll do everything in my power to take care of Todd's widow and baby."

His power, Mara thought. That was Brock Barnett, all right. Total faith in himself, none in God. She shouldn't be doing this. No way.

"Brock and Mara," the clerk interrupted her recrimination, "I pronounce you husband and wife. Brock, you may kiss your bride."

"What?" he asked.

"I said, you may kiss your new wife."

"Wife…"

Mara held her breath, hoping he wouldn't. But that wasn't Brock Barnett. He would kiss her whether she liked him or not, whether she was Todd's widow or not. He slipped one arm around her shoulders and lowered his head.

"Brock," she gasped in a whisper. "We've got to get out of here right now. I'm about to have this baby."

Chapter Four

❧

Brock threw the pickup into gear and stomped on the gas. The truck spun out of the parking space and into the early-morning traffic. Mara curled into a ball on the seat.

"Get me to the hospital," she puffed, her face bright red. "Ohhh! Run the traffic lights if you have to, Brock. I mean it."

For the first time since he'd climbed down the cliff face after Todd had fallen to his death, Brock knew true fear. He glanced from side to side, pushed the gas pedal to the floor and sped through a busy intersection. Horns honked and tires screeched. "If Sherry's in Albuquerque—" Brock raised his voice above the racket "—how's she going to get here in time?"

"Just drive!" Mara snarled. "I called her at eight this morning, and she promised to leave right away."

"Eight! Albuquerque's a four-hour drive." Growling in frustration, Brock floored the truck through a red light. "Why didn't you tell me you were in labor?"

"It's none of your business."

"None of my b—" He cut himself off, gritting his teeth as he

glanced at the woman beside him. Though it was a chilly morning, perspiration beaded her temples. Her eyes were squeezed
shut, and her mouth formed a tight white line. She had
sprawled out on the seat, no belt around her middle, her legs
spread and her feet propped on the floorboard.

Alarmed, Brock grabbed her arm. "Put your legs together!
You're going to have the baby right here! What if it…falls out?"

"Don't be ridiculous," Mara snapped. "I'm not pushing yet."

"Pushing? Don't push, for crying out loud!"

"It's a stage. You can't help it."

"Great! You should have told me, Mara. A person doesn't get
married when she's in labor. And she doesn't have a baby in a
pickup. There's a right way and a wrong way to do things."

"Shut up, Brock!"

"Here's the hospital. I can see the sign."

"Go to the emergency entrance. Ohhh, no!" Mara curled into
a ball again, and Brock could barely hear her moans through
the fabric of her coat. Her bun had come apart like a haystack
in a twister. Wispy strands of blond hair scattered across her
shoulders as she jabbed at the air with both fists.

"Hang on, Mara," he advised, forcing calm into his voice.

"Get…me…something for pain!"

Brock threw open his door and lunged out of the pickup. He
ran around the vehicle and practically yanked her door from its
hinges. He lifted her against his chest. The emergency-room
doors slid apart as he hurtled toward them like a fullback headed
for the end zone. "It's a baby!" he roared. "We're having a baby!"

Two nurses at the reception desk dropped their charts. One
ran for a wheelchair, the other pressed an alarm and dashed toward Brock. In seconds, he and Mara were surrounded by
nurses. Questions flowed.

Brock tried his best with the answers as they bundled Mara
into the wheelchair. "She's preregistered. Mara Barnett. My wife."

"Rosemond!" she groaned. "I'm registered as Rosemond."

"We just got married," he clarified.

"Then you'll have to start over." The nurse grabbed his arm.
"Go down that hall to the first window."

Brock's boots pounded on the slick floor. He skidded to a stop and hammered on the window. "Mara Rosemond's here!"

The registration clerk nodded and turned to her file cabinet. Brock glanced down the hall in time to see orderlies wheel Mara along a corridor and out of sight. "What are they doing with her?" he demanded of the clerk.

"Your wife will need to be prepped for delivery. Don't worry, you'll get there for the birth."

"No, you don't understand. Sherry's coming here to—"

"Your insurance company?" the clerk cut in. In a daze, Brock rattled off what he knew. Before he could finish, the nurse appeared at his side again and ordered him to follow her right away.

"Where are we going?" Brock hollered as he jogged down the hall.

"Labor and delivery." The nurse pulled him into an open elevator. "Mr. Barnett, your wife is dilated and in transition. You shouldn't have waited this long. I'd advise you to monitor her more closely next time."

"Next time?"

The nurse marched out of the elevator, Brock in tow. "Since we haven't had time to fully assess the baby's position and vital signs, we're going to gown you, too, in case your wife needs an emergency caesarian section. Put these on."

She handed him a stack of blue paper clothing. Feeling uncharacteristically awkward, Brock jerked on the flimsy gown and tugged the cap over his hair. The nurse tied the mask to his face while a second nurse held the booties as he stepped into them.

"Let me explain," he tried. "There's a woman named Sherry—"

"Follow me, Mr. Barnett," the nurse ordered.

The doctor in the labor room looked as unrecognizable as Brock did. He was a pair of bright blue eyes, a pair of gloved hands and a voice that bespoke calm and confidence. "Your wife is doing beautifully."

"Not my doctor," Mara moaned from the bed beside him.

"Dr. Meacham has been notified, and he's on his way."

Brock stared in dismay at Mara's ashen face. She was lying on a gurney with a flimsy calico gown over her chest and thighs. A monitor showed the rise and fall of two lines of light. One tracked Mara's contractions. And the other line, Brock realized, was the baby's heartbeat.

He reached for Mara's hand. "Can you see that?" he asked, leaning near her ear.

She turned her head, and a wan smile tilted her lips. "Oh, it's so… Ohhh! Here comes another one!"

Brock stiffened as Mara's monitor line shot up at a steep angle. Her face went rigid; her fingers clenched his. A low moan started in the depths of her chest and grew louder as the contraction intensified.

"Do something," Brock commanded. "This woman is in agony here."

"Actually, she's doing very well. Breathe, Mara," the nurse said gently. "Not too fast. Slowly, slowly. That's great! Mr. Barnett, you should be very proud of your wife."

Goose bumps skittered like spilled marbles down Brock's spine. He was a husband. A married man. He looked down at Mara, whose silky blond hair spread across her white pillow. She smelled like talcum powder. While the nurse coached Mara to the end of the contraction, Brock tentatively stroked his hand over her abdomen. It was so hard, so firm and solid with undeniable life.

He swallowed, pent-up and confused. In some strange way, the moment stirred a whirlwind of emotion in his chest. He wanted to be near Mara like this forever—wanted her to care about him and need him. He longed to protect her from pain. And he wanted to kiss her, an expression of tenderness and compassion. Maybe even desire. Why shouldn't he kiss her? She was his bride, and he had every right.

"Oh, Todd," she moaned as tears slid from her eyes. She was gazing at the nurse. "I miss Todd. I loved him so much."

Brock grimaced. Mara was Todd's wife. She could never forget that, and she wouldn't let him forget it either.

But how could they go on with Todd's memory tormenting both of them? Why hadn't he thought that through more clearly beforehand? Still, in spite of another man's rings on her finger, she was Brock's wife now.

At rest for the moment, she looked across at him. Through tears, her gray-green eyes studied him. Her lips were pale pink as he let his focus trail across them. So soft and pretty. He could hardly breathe.

Yes, he wanted to kiss her. His bride.

And then she sucked in a breath, clenched her teeth, turned bright red and let out a yelp.

"Breathe, Mara," the nurse urged. "Breathe through the contraction."

"Forget breathing," Brock snapped. "Give her morphine."

The doctor looked up, his eyes narrowed. "We don't give morphine for labor, Mr. Barnett. The birth is still several minutes away. Maybe you'd like to step out into the hall and try to calm down? There's only one person in charge—and it's not me or your wife. It's certainly not you, so you'd better get used to that. From now on, the new boss in the Barnett family is this child."

As the contraction consumed her, Mara became nothing but the sum of constricting tissue around her midsection. She drifted above herself, staring at the suntanned fingers gripping her white hand and pressing Todd's gold ring into her flesh. Whose hands were they? One so frail…and the other winding through it like an oak tree's roots around a marble statue. She loved those two hands.

But now someone was touching her shoulder, stroking her face. She couldn't bear the sensation. "Don't touch me!" she growled. "You…you…you…"

The word became a part of her puffing. She stared at the man behind the blue mask. Who was he? She'd seen him before. Those deep brown eyes. She knew him…knew him well… didn't like him.

"Mr. Barnett, come and take a look at your baby's head," the doctor said.

"Brock!" Mara exploded. "I hate…hate…hate…"

"Don't worry," the nurse told him. "This kind of outburst is very common in the transition between the stages of contractions and pushing. She's not completely aware of what she's saying."

But Mara was aware. It was *him*. Brock Barnett. She watched him walking to the end of the gurney. He couldn't be here! She didn't want him!

"Can you see the baby's head?" The doctor showed Brock where to look.

"Oh, wow! Mara!" Brock leaped to her side and grabbed her hand again. "I saw the baby! It's right there, the head!"

"Really?" Mara heard her own voice filled with tired elation. A baby! That's what this was all about, wasn't it? The contraction had faded a little, and she wondered who she'd been barking at. This man in the blue mask? But he was so wonderful…standing there with her, holding her hand, helping her through. "How much can you see?"

"A circle about the size of a dime. And hair. Blond hair!"

"My baby has hair. I feel so…ohhh…"

"It's another contraction," Brock announced as he focused on the monitor's rising line. "Help her, doc!"

"Why don't you help her, Brock?" The doctor laid a hand on his shoulder. "Help Mara maintain the rhythm of her breathing."

"I have to push," Mara puffed. The sensation came over her like a rush of floodwater from a broken dam. And it felt wonderful to turn the contraction into something productive!

"Push!" she groaned.

"Not yet, Mara," Dr. Fielding warned. "Try to hold back for me."

"Hold back?" Her voice came out in a squeak of dismay.

"We need just a minute to get ready for the delivery." As he spoke, a nurse wheeled a cart of silver bowls and instruments beside the doctor. An anesthesiologist wrapped a cuff around Mara's upper arm to read her blood pressure.

Mara flung her arm out toward Brock, her hand open wide. A tear squeezed out of the corner of her eye and slipped down her cheek and onto her earlobe. "Brock," she moaned.

He hesitated briefly, then he leaned forward and dabbed the tear with his finger. "It's okay, Mara," he murmured. "You can push in a minute."

The words swirled around inside her head as she fought the flood tide urging her forward. She had to push! There was absolutely no way to hold back. A warm hand brushed the side of her cheek. It was Brock's hand, and she was so thankful for it. She turned her face into his palm and pressed her lips to the callused flesh.

"We're ready for delivery," he was whispering against her ear. "You'll be fine."

"I'm scared. Please don't leave me, Brock."

"I won't. I'll stay right with you, Mara. You can do this."

"Oh, Brock, I'm so…ohhh…"

The nurse flipped on a light above the gurney. "It's okay to push now, Mara," she said gently.

Mara hardly needed permission. Gripping the handholds at her sides, she summoned more strength than she had ever known she possessed. The core of her body seemed to glow as she strained toward it. The room around her vanished, all but the ultimate focused urge to push.

And then the contraction waned. Her head fell back, and she drank in a breath. She stared at the end of the gurney, at her legs draped in a green sheet. But before she could even begin to relax, another wave began. Brock stood at her side, holding her hand as she poured her energy into the effort.

"Brock," she whispered through panting breaths. "Don't go away."

"Never, Mara."

"Stay with me."

"I'm right here."

She felt as though her face were about to explode. The skin over her knuckles went white as she drove all her energy into the push. At this moment, she could move a mountain.

"Mara, look up into the mirror," Dr. Fielding instructed. "Brock! Come see!"

"I'll be right back," Brock told Mara.

At the foot of the gurney, he let out a cry. "Mara—it's the forehead! Tiny eyes…a little nose…two ears…a mouth. It's a—a baby…."

"Once more, Mara," the doctor told her. "Let's get this little one out into the world."

She watched in the overhead mirror as Dr. Fielding cradled the precious life. She pushed again. A shoulder emerged, then another, so small and delicate they hardly seemed real. And she pushed again. The infant slid into the world, a perfect jewel.

"It's a girl!" Brock shouted.

"A girl!" Mara's echoing voice wavered between laughter and tears. "Thank You, God! Is she all right?"

A sudden piercing cry announced that Mara's newborn daughter was indeed fine. Her vision swam with tears as Dr. Fielding handed Brock a pair of scissors to cut the umbilical cord. Mara had never seen anything in her life as beautiful as that tiny, precious baby.

"She's a dandy," the doctor remarked. The baby's holler faded to a whimper as he laid her on Mara's chest. Tears rolled down the new mother's cheeks at the sweet, soft pressure of her daughter's body against her own. She touched tiny arms and tinier fingers.

"It's okay, sweetheart," Mara whispered against the child's delicate cheek. "Mama's right here."

"She's a little early, but she's plenty big enough," the doctor said. "She'll be fine."

Mara tried to smile, but she couldn't work her way past the tears. She was holding her baby! A daughter…a baby girl… She wanted to share this, wanted someone special….

"Brock," she called.

"Mara." He was instantly at her side. "She's perfect, Mara."

"She is, isn't she?"

"So are you."

"Brock, I miss Todd."

"I know, Mara."

"I love her so much. God gave her to me…but He took Todd away. Why? Oh, Brock…"

The nurse touched his arm. "We need to warm up your daughter now. And the doctor wants to finish with you, Mara."

The baby was whisked away, and Mara felt the greatest emptiness she'd ever known. "Where is she?"

"They've put her in a warming bed," Brock explained, still at Mara's side. "They're weighing her. Now they're putting bands on her ankle and wrist. They're stamping her foot with black ink."

"She's crying!"

"She doesn't want anyone messing with her. She's like her mama."

Mara laughed. Brock took off his mask, and she could see the sparkle in his eyes. Well, it was done. She let out a deep breath—half in relief and half in trepidation.

"I'm a mother," she murmured. "My baby has a mother."

She studied the man whose hand she clasped. Your baby has a father, too, she could almost hear him thinking. But those were words she couldn't bring herself to say. The child belonged to Todd. She always would.

The recovery room was small, with only a single bed. In delivery, Mara had been stitched and pushed and manhandled more than Brock thought was necessary, but what did he know? Now in the narrow bed, she was shivering like a puppy in an ice storm.

"All right, Mara," the nurse said as she opened the door. "You can hold your daughter for a few minutes before we take her back to the nursery."

Feeling superfluous, Brock stood to one side as the nurse laid the tiny blanketed bundle in Mara's arms. He could barely see the top of the baby's head, and that white cap covered all the skin. Mara cooed and clucked as her lips trembled with emotion.

In a moment, Dr. Fielding, the doctor who had delivered the baby, stepped into the room, followed by Mara's physician, Dr. Meacham, who had finally arrived. Brock shoved his hands into his pockets and thought about heading outside to look for a snack machine as everyone laughed, offered congratulations, admired the baby. He edged toward the door.

"And you must be Mara's new husband!" Dr. Meacham, baby in his arms, swung around and gave Brock a warm smile. "This must have been quite an experience for you."

"It sure was." Brock tried to get a glimpse of the baby's face. He could just see the tip of a small pink nose.

"Here, take a closer look." Dr. Meacham held out the bundle. "Haven't you held her yet?"

Brock took a step backward, his eyes darting to Mara. She was talking to a nurse. Brock looked at the physician again.

"Wouldn't you like to hold her?" Dr. Meacham asked.

His mouth as dry as dust, Brock stared at the blanketed bundle. "I better not," he mumbled.

"I think you'd better. Might as well get used to it now."

The doctor set the baby against Brock's chest. As he gazed down at the miniature face, Brock slipped his hands around the blanket. The baby's weight, solid and undeniable, tightened his forearms. In the crook of his elbow, her round head nestled contentedly, her eyes shut tight and her pink lips making little O's.

"What do you think?" Dr. Meacham asked.

For a moment, Brock couldn't speak as emotion flooded through him. He touched her tiny ear, stroked a finger across her petal-soft cheek, then kissed her forehead. The strangest emotion was tugging at his stomach and swelling his heart. He'd never been in love before, but he'd have sworn this must be the feeling. At the present moment, he would do anything for the baby he held. He'd lay down his life for her.

"She's incredible," he whispered.

Mara smiled at him as he settled the baby into her arms. He'd never seen anyone so beautiful as this woman looked to him right now. He told himself it was just the intensity of the moment, but he couldn't deny a feeling he'd never known in his life. Somehow he had become attached to Mara. A thin silver thread connected them. It was a filament that might become tangled or frayed or stretched to the limit. But he didn't think it would break.

Chapter Five

M̲ara had never seen such perfection. Maybe the infant in her arms was a little bit pink and wrinkly, and maybe her eyelids puffed out and her head was slightly lopsided. So what? She was the prettiest, sweetest little girl Mara had ever laid eyes on.

"You planning to let Daddy hold her one of these days?" the parent educator asked as she wheeled in a cart of supplies. Before Mara could protest, the woman swept the baby out of her arms and into Brock's. "Now, Mrs. Barnett, you said you intended to nurse your daughter?"

Mara nodded. "I'm going to try."

"You'll be fine. It's the most natural thing in the world."

As the woman set out pamphlets and materials, Mara studied Brock. He was holding the baby as though she were a precious gem. His brown eyes had melted into pools of chocolate fudge, and the expression on his face spoke volumes. For the first time in his life, Brock looked…gentle.

How could that be?

Mara didn't want such tenderness from him. It made her feel somehow connected to the man. True, Brock was her husband—but in name only. And he wasn't the baby's father. He really had no right to look at her daughter that way.

But he had helped through the birth. He had laid his money and his reputation—even his future—on the line for this child. He'd done it out of guilt. Mara had to remember that. Yet she had a sinking suspicion she couldn't have gotten through the birth without him. She had wanted him. Needed him.

Did she want him now?

"All right," the parent educator began. "Let's get started."

"I'd better go." Brock held out the baby to any takers.

"No, it's okay," Mara said without thinking. "You can stay." And before she could change her mind, the baby was lying in her arms, and Brock was seated on a chair in the corner while the nurse untied the strings of Mara's gown.

"Now, you'll want to find a comfortable position," the woman said. "I recommend holding the baby at several different angles during each feeding."

At the intimacy of the moment, Mara could feel the heat flush through her cheeks. She glanced over the nurse's shoulder to see Brock, elbows on his knees and chin propped on his fist, staring at the floor between his boots.

"Now, first place the baby right here," the nurse suggested, deftly tucking the little bundle into Mara's lap. "All babies have a natural sucking instinct, so the moment you touch the side of her face, she'll turn toward you."

Again, Mara glanced at Brock. Head down, he was still intently concentrating on the floor. She focused on her baby. Tiny mouth pursed, the little one didn't seem to have the slightest interest in nursing. Mara knew she would have to forget about the man in the room and concentrate.

"How can I get her to open her mouth?" she asked.

"Stroke her cheek with your finger," the nurse said. "See? There you go. Oh, she's hungry all right. Look at that!"

Mara smiled with satisfaction as her daughter settled comfortably. A sweet contentment filled Mara at the thought that she was nourishing her baby. In the past nine months, God had provided a precious bond between mother and child. To Mara's joy, she realized that bond had not been severed by birth. In fact, she felt closer to her baby now that she could look into her daughter's tiny face and could see she was actually giving a part of her physical self to sustain this tiny, amazing life.

In a recent Bible study, Mara had learned the names God gave Himself through the ages. One name—*El Shaddai*—referred to a nursing mother's breast. God saw Himself as nourisher, sustainer, fulfiller, the teacher had explained. And Mara now saw that in somewhat the same way as God cared for His people, she was tending to her child. The realization made her feel closer to her Lord, and to her baby, as well.

"This liquid is called colostrum," the nurse spoke up. "It's the first, most nourishing fluid. The colostrum helps provide natural immunities for your baby."

"What about milk?"

"Your milk will come in by tomorrow, I imagine," the woman answered. "But you want your daughter to take as much colostrum as possible."

"This feels…all right."

"*Today* it does. But tomorrow may be a different story. Most women experience quite a bit of soreness in the first days of nursing. I'm going to give you some special cream. I recommend you rub this in several times a day. Maybe your husband could do it for you?"

The nurse swung around to look at Brock, who jerked his attention from Mara to the window. He appeared to be fascinated with a tree that still had a few golden leaves clinging to it.

"I don't think so," Mara whispered to the nurse. The baby had dropped off to sleep, her eyelids as delicate as rose petals.

"Whatever is most comfortable for you. I'm going to take her back to the nursery now, Mara, but I'll come around later in the day to see if you need help again."

"Thank you." Mara pulled her gown together and tied the strings. "I'd really like to keep her here with me."

Mara heard the longing in her voice as the baby was lifted from her arms.

"She needs to be warmed up again. It won't be long before you're in your own room, and you can spend all the time you want with her."

As the nurse walked toward the door with the baby, Mara turned toward Brock. At this moment of loneliness, she couldn't help wishing for her husband. Then she remembered she had Brock Barnett. He certainly wasn't Todd, but he was all she had. He would have to do.

"Stay?" she asked him, suddenly exhausted again.

He nodded.

"By the way," the nurse asked. "What's your daughter's name, Mara?"

"Abigail," Mara said softly. "I'll call her Abby."

"That's a beautiful name."

As the door shut, Mara studied her hands as they lay limply across the empty space where her baby had nestled. The wedding ring Todd had given her circled a pale finger. She felt tired and alone.

"Abby," she repeated, lifting her focus to the small window. "It means, 'Her father was joy.'"

Brock nodded, his face solemn. "Todd would like that."

For the next three days, the hospital became the whole world as Mara adjusted to motherhood while little Abby got used to life outside the womb. Neither transition was easy. Mara's milk did begin to flow, but it took Abby quite a while to figure out how to nurse effectively. In the meantime, Mara grew tender and sore, and she seemed to have either too much or not enough milk.

The hospital room itself was pleasant enough, pale blue walls with a pastel border around the ceiling. A window looked out on the streets of Las Cruces, placid and cold for the Thanksgiving holiday. A clean bathroom provided a warm shower. A sofa catered to the guests who came to visit—her pastor and his wife, neighbors from the apartment complex,

Mara's former coworkers at the private academy where she had taught some years earlier, members of her Bible study group. Bouquets of pink carnations and white roses jostled for space on the wall shelf, while boxes of tiny ruffled dresses gathered in a corner. Mara couldn't imagine her baby getting big enough to wear them.

Little Abby hated bath time and diaper changes, and Mara wasn't crazy about them, either. Her stitches and tired body made movement difficult, though she spent a good bit of time walking the floors of the neonatal unit. She showered and changed into a gown Brock brought in a suitcase, and once or twice she almost felt normal again. Then she would begin to ache or her chair would require a doughnut-shaped cushion, and Mara remembered that she had changed forever.

Her entire life felt new, different, and in some ways, unpleasant. When Sherry had arrived breathless and apologetic an hour too late for the delivery, Mara was basking in the afterglow of Abby's birth. But two days later when her friend breezed into the room with a meal of leftover turkey, a spoonful of stuffing and a bowl of cranberry sauce, Mara stared at the paper plate as if it were the saddest thing she'd ever seen.

"I'm married to him," she said. "Brock Barnett."

Sherry set the plate on the rolling tray and perched on the edge of Mara's bed. Her dark brown eyes sparkled as she waved a hand in dismissal. "Not that I would know—since I've never strapped the bonds of matrimony and motherhood around my own neck—but I'd guess it's just your hormones talking, Mara. You've heard about the baby blues? You know, post-partum depression? They say you feel sad for no reason at all."

"No reason! Sherry, I'm a widow who married a man I don't even like."

"You like Brock."

"How could I? Thanks to him, I don't have a husband."

"Brock *is* your husband," Sherry countered firmly, "and you do like him. When Todd was alive, you got along with Brock."

"I tolerated him. He's so self-assured and smug. Like he's king of the world. Strutting around in those jeans and boots. Driving a fancy car. Trying to buy off his guilt. I don't know…he's just so cocky."

"Who wouldn't be? Brock Barnett is rich and handsome and educated and successful—"

"Please, Sherry!" Mara groaned. "Spare me the buildup. He's been so unbearably nice these past few days. It's almost sickening. He packed all my stuff and moved me out of the apartment. He brought over lotion and shampoo and a new box of talcum powder. Expensive, designer-brand talcum powder, Sherry. He's bought Abby everything from diapers to booties to a velvet Christmas dress she'll probably be too big to wear by December. This morning it hit me that I was actually looking forward to seeing him walk through the door. You're right. I don't hate him as much as I should. And I hate myself for that."

"Let it go, Mara."

"I'm trying. But when I look into Abby's eyes, all I can think about is Todd. He was so excited about the pregnancy. He couldn't wait to be a father. He talked about holding her and teaching her things, you know? Three months of my morning sickness…that's all he got."

Sherry pulled a tissue from the box by Mara's bed. "Here you go. You can't wish this sadness away, so you might as well feel it. I think it's part of grieving for Todd."

"It is, but I can't forgive Brock for what he did, even though I know I should. I've heard countless sermons on the topic, and I never thought it was that difficult. If we want God's forgiveness, we're supposed to forgive others. But this is so different…so hard. I'm not even sure I know how to forgive Brock, Sherry. Besides, I can't let go of Todd. Not now."

"Abby is Todd's daughter, Mara. Of course you can't let his memory go. You never will, and you never should." She paused a moment. "But you're right about Brock. You do need to forgive him."

Mara stared at the door through which Brock had come and gone at least twenty times since Abby's birth. Half the time, he was wheeling the baby into the room in her bassinet. He rarely stayed while Mara nursed, and they barely spoke to each other. When they did talk, they discussed only the most mundane, factual matters. But he was there, consistently there, as though he belonged.

"If I shouldn't let go of Todd," Mara said, fingering the ring on her hand, "and if he'll always be Abby's father, how can I forgive myself for marrying Brock Barnett?"

"Because you know why you did it."

"I don't want to live in his house, Sherry."

"Why not?"

"Because…" Mara conjured the image that had been bothering her all morning—Brock at the breakfast table, freshly showered and dressed in a denim shirt and jeans. She could almost smell his aftershave. "Because I don't want to see him."

"You won't see him. He's a rancher. He'll be out feeding cows or whatever. You know, up at sunrise and to bed at dusk. Besides, you'll be busy taking care of Abby."

Mara pondered this for a moment. Sherry was probably right. Todd had told her Brock's home was a sprawling adobe ranch house with two separate wings and a courtyard in between. She and Brock probably could live side by side without ever setting eyes on each other. Just as well.

"I can't believe I'm going to add an annulment or a divorce to my résumé," she said with a long sigh. "Married, widowed, married, divorced. Good grief. How long do you suppose Brock will want to stay married?"

"Given what you've told me about his track record with women, what do you think? I imagine he'll decide he's had enough domesticity after a month or two, and he'll want to go back to having fun." Sherry shook her head. "Please don't worry so much about it. The Bible allows divorce."

"Because of the hardness of our hearts. That's what Jesus said about it. I don't want to become a hard-hearted, unforgiving, bitter woman, Sherry. What am I doing?"

"Just relax. You're in God's hands."

"This can't be part of His plan for me. I asked Him for help—not for Brock Barnett!"

"Well, he's who you got. Just make sure Brock signs everything, so your baby is legally protected the way he promised."

"He brought the papers in and showed them to me yesterday. Things couldn't be better for Abby."

Mara tried to project the future Sherry had outlined. She and Abby would live alone in the big house until Brock's hormones came calling. Then they would move out, the marriage would be annulled and Mara would fend for herself, as she had before and could again.

"Brock married you out of a sense of obligation, Mara," Sherry reminded her. "He feels it's his duty to keep Todd's daughter out of the welfare system. He knows he was responsible for Todd up on those cliffs at Hueco Tanks, and now he's responsible for you two."

"He thinks he can buy my forgiveness. And God's."

"Why not? He can buy everything else. Brock Barnett's wayward soul is not your responsibility right now, Mara. The only thing you need to be thinking about is Abby. Brock can take care of himself. As soon as he's figured out a way to settle you and Abby into some other satisfactory situation, you'll be able to walk away. In the meantime, why not take advantage of his remorse?"

"Oh, Sherry!" Mara had to laugh at her friend's cynicism. "I'm not as mercenary as you."

Sherry shrugged. "Maybe not, but a big house, two maids, a swimming pool and a car of your own are nothing to sneeze at. You're getting a cushy ride on ol' Brocko's guilt trip."

Mara touched the white silk bow on her new nightgown. At the time Brock had given it to her, she had sensed a genuine generosity in his eyes. He had carried the pink-papered box into her room early on the morning after Abby's birth. After laying it on Mara's bed, he had waited in silence for her to open it.

"It's got hidden slits in the front," he had explained as she drew the satiny garment from the tissue paper. Then he shoved his hands into his jeans pockets, and Mara would have sworn he blushed. "Well, it's a special nursing gown, so you can feed Abby in it. The lady at the store told me it was just the thing."

Mara had softened at the thought of the tough cattle rancher searching for just the right kind of gown. Now, she wondered if the gift had been merely another token to ease Brock's guilty conscience.

"I imagine he'll start to resent the situation after a while," she said. "Abby and me living in his house and all."

"As I keep saying, Mara, so what? Let him resent it. He offered to do this, and now he can just deal with it."

Mara knew Sherry was trying to comfort her, but somehow she felt worse than ever. Could she live with a man who resented the very sight of her? Could she live with a man she could never forgive? Did she have any choice?

Only the appearance of a nurse wheeling Abby's bassinet through the door lifted Mara's spirits. As the woman stopped the plastic-sided cart next to the bed, Sherry pulled back the edge of the blanket that covered Abby's face.

"Oh, Mara, I've never been the mommy type, but she's precious."

"She certainly is," the nurse concurred. "And she's a pretty good little sleeper, too."

As Mara read out the code on her wrist bracelet, the nurse checked the matching codes on Abby's arm and ankle tags. Then she lifted the baby out of the bassinet and laid her in Mara's arms.

"This child is all that matters," Sherry said softly. "Focus on her, Mara. Abby is all you need to be thinking about."

Mara gazed down at the tiny pink face and tried to make herself believe Sherry was right.

"Your rooms are in the west wing," Brock said as he drove Mara and Abby across the metal cattle guard between the highway and the dirt road that led to his house. Though only fifteen miles outside the city limits of Las Cruces, the ranch felt to Mara as though it was light years away.

"The courtyard is right outside the door to your suite," Brock said. "It's a good place to watch the sun go down."

Mara studied the man beside her. His tan Stetson shaded his eyes from the late-afternoon light that gilded his straight nose and firm, unsmiling mouth. These were the first words he had spoken since they left the hospital, and she wondered if Sherry's prediction had come true already. He certainly didn't seem thrilled to be transporting Mara and her baby to his house.

So what? Mara told herself, repeating Sherry's refrain. She didn't have to please Brock Barnett. All that mattered was Abby. She glanced behind her at the infant carrier strapped into the back seat of the car. The sleek purr of Brock's Jaguar had lulled the baby to sleep the moment they started on their way.

Abby and her needs. The baby was all that mattered in Mara's life.

"Is there a place at the house for Abby to sleep?" she asked. "The cradle…it isn't…well, Todd didn't finish it."

Brock worked the gears of his bronze Jag with a leather-gloved hand. "I bought a crib."

"You did?" She couldn't hide her surprise.

"There's a swing, too. It winds up. And one of those molded bathtubs. Yellow, I think."

"Oh." Mara tried to picture Brock walking through a department store selecting baby furniture.

"I reckon Abby won't need a high chair for a few months yet, but I got her one of those, too."

Mara stared at the endless barbed-wire fencing that slipped past her window. A high chair meant Brock expected to have Abby around when she was big enough to need one. Maybe he really did intend to continue the arrangement, at least for a while. Did she want it to last beyond the time it took to get back on her feet? Could she handle being there with him for one day, let alone weeks or months?

She allowed herself another look at the man. Dressed in a chamois-colored shirt that clung to his shoulders, a pair of faded jeans and the low-heeled brown leather boots New Mexicans called ropers, Brock scanned the terrain. He was tall, lean, fit and suntanned, and his black hair curled just a little beneath his hat. Again, Mara recalled the time Todd had introduced his best friend to her at an art gallery, and the way Brock's deep voice had slid into the pit of her stomach. He truly was a sight that would stir any woman's soul. Any woman but this new, utterly maternal Mara.

She turned back to the window. Truth be known, she felt more like a punching bag than a woman. She had been poked, prodded and stitched until her whole body ached. Worse, she had been forced to admit her figure was a long way from its former shape. A long, long way.

No man was likely to take a second glance at Mara—not that she wanted anyone to. But she had been appalled to discover that her stomach was almost exactly the size it had been before she gave birth. Only it was no longer hard and sleek with its cargo of baby. No, this stomach sagged like an old, half-full laundry bag. She had been assured she would firm up quickly, but she felt repulsive.

"It's too cold for the pool these days," Brock remarked. "But you can use the hot tub in your wing. Might help with those stitches."

Mara suddenly flushed. For the first time since Abby was born, she flashed on the moment of birth. Brock had been watching, hadn't he? He'd seen her body—seen the doctor cut her, seen how she was formed and shaped. He had seen her at her most raw and elemental moment.

She leaned her cheek on the cool window and shut her eyes in embarrassment. *So what?* Sherry would say. So what if he saw you, and so what if you look like the Saggy Baggy Elephant?

"Come summer, the pool is nice," Brock said. "I swim laps, myself. You swim, Mara?"

She nodded, at that moment resolving she would not be caught dead in a bathing suit—ever.

"Abby might like the water, if we watch her close," he continued. "I learned to swim when I was just a pup. Rode horses, too, but Abby won't be ready for that for a few years. Still, it never hurts to start kids out young. I was roping by the time I was nine or ten."

Mara forced herself to listen. Again, Brock was talking about the distant future—and Abby was part of his plan. She needed to focus on the present situation and turn off the inward microscope. It was just the baby blues again, she told herself. She had never been one to allow negative thoughts to rule her life, and she wouldn't start now.

Recalling her conversation with Sherry, Mara thought about how forgiveness had seemed a fairly simple act—until Todd's death. But she had to try. Even if it didn't do a thing for Brock, it would help her heal from the terrible loss of her husband. As she breathed up a prayer for help, she decided that if Brock wanted to chat as they drove the long road up to his house, she would join in the conversation. The least they could do was be civil to each other.

"Who taught you to swim?" she asked, seizing on the first thing that came to mind.

She saw his jaw tighten. After a long pause, he spoke two words. "My mother."

Mara let out a breath. Great. She had put her foot in her mouth on the first try. Todd had told her Brock's parents had divorced when he was ten years old. His mother had moved to the East Coast, and now she was living somewhere in South America. Brock had grown up with his father—a man too busy with his oil business to pay much attention to his son. Todd's happy childhood stood out in stark contrast to that of his best friend.

"I learned how to swim at the city pool," Mara tried again. "There was a special program. We swam and did crafts, that kind of thing. It was fun."

From under the brim of his hat, Brock gave Mara a skeptical glance. Though they hadn't been close, Mara realized that each knew about the other's past. No doubt Todd had told his best friend how chaotic Mara's childhood had been. *Fun* was rarely part of the picture.

"Ever ride a horse?" he asked as he swung the Jaguar onto the gravel driveway of his house.

"Never."

"Too bad."

"I don't think so." Mara leaned forward, trying to keep her mouth from dropping open at the sight of the massive adobe home looming before them. "I don't know the first thing about horses."

"You'll learn, once you've been here a while. I'll take you out one of these days when you're feeling better. Nothing like a good long ride to take your mind off things."

He pulled the car around to the side of the house and pressed the button that lifted the first door of his three-car garage. As the vehicle slowed and came to a stop, Abby woke with a start. The baby began to whimper, and Mara unlatched her seat belt.

"Oh, you're awake," she cooed as she leaned between the seats. "It's okay, Abby. Mommy's here."

As Brock switched off the engine, Mara climbed out of the car. She unfastened the baby and lifted her from the carrier. "She's probably hungry."

"Yeah." He was standing nearby as she straightened. "Listen, Mara. About Abby's birth…I didn't plan on being in there, you know."

"I know."

"The nurse just—"

"Thank you. I mean, I'm glad. You helped."

"It was an amazing experience. Wonderful. But you don't need to worry. I won't intrude again."

"Oh, good." The words were out before she had time to retract them. "You've been great, Brock. Really. Todd would appreciate it."

Todd, she thought. *You* appreciate this, Mara. Words seemed to whisper in her heart. Tell him. Tell him how thankful you are. Forgive him, Mara. Set him free.

"I think Abby's hungry," she said. She gave him a quick shrug and then turned away.

Chapter Six

❧

"I'm Rosa Maria Hernandez, and this is Ermaline Criddle, and, oh, my goodness! Would you look at this baby? How darling! How beautiful! *¡Que linda!*"

Brock stood beside Mara in the grand foyer as his house-keeper and her assistant pressed close for a better look at the household's newest member. Rosa Maria, a small, round woman with bright black eyes and black curly hair, fairly bubbled with joy as she oohed and aahed over Abby.

Beside her, Ermaline gushed with equal ardor. She was tall, almost gaunt, and she looked as though she hadn't eaten in a week. Her teeth were two sizes too big for her mouth, but Brock had always thought her face was genuine and kind.

"She's a doll," Ermaline said. "Three days old? I tell you what, me and Frank, that's my husband, we've got four kids. Every one of them's been three days old, too, but I'd swear I can't remember them ever being this small."

"They grow so fast!" Rosa Maria tapped Abby's cheek. "So fast! One day you can hold them in your arms, the next day they're getting a driver's license. Oh, my goodness, you better enjoy this one, Mrs….um…"

"Mrs. Barnett," Brock said as he set Mara's suitcase on the floor.

"You can call me Mara. Really, that's…that's fine."

"Mrs. Barnett," Brock repeated. "We try to keep things a little formal around here."

Mara hugged Abby tightly as though she was almost frightened by the reality of his world—a world that now had become her own.

"You have two housekeepers?" she asked as the women hurried away. Ermaline vanished down a hall, and Rosa Maria went back to polishing the mirror in the foyer.

"The house is huge." Brock looked around him as he stated the obvious. Her awe wasn't lost on him, and he felt a surge of pride at all he had accomplished in the past few years.

"How messy can one man possibly be?" Mara whispered. "And who is this?"

A man wearing a tall white hat, white apron and white cravat knotted at his neck stepped forward and bowed.

"Pierre Britton," he announced in a clipped voice, "at your service, Madame."

Mara glanced at Brock. He winked. "Just tell Pierre what you want to eat, and he'll fix it for you. As long as it's not hamburgers. Pierre doesn't do hamburgers."

"I am a chef, Madame, not a fry cook. I have trained with the finest in France."

"I'm looking forward to experiencing your cuisine," Mara said.

Pierre beamed. "The boy grew up with my food, and see how he is? Very healthy."

"I'm healthy, all right," Brock said, "as long as I head for the bunkhouse once or twice a week to chow down on grilled steaks and beans with the hands."

"*Oui!*" Pierre exclaimed. "Terrible, the things our boy does."

"Man cannot live by cordon bleu alone."

"Steaks half-burned and half-raw. Potatoes fried in fat. Beans laced with lard. *Mais oui,* terrible, terrible!"

Brock gave Mara a lazy grin as he brushed past her. "I love to goad him," he said in a low voice. "Come on. I'll show you the house."

"Tacos, he eats!" Pierre was exclaiming as Brock led Mara and Abby across the warm terra-cotta tiled floor of the foyer. "Tamales, refried beans, nachos and *menudo!*"

"And what's wrong with *menudo?*" Rosa Maria snapped as she turned from the mirror she had been shining.

"Cow's stomach!"

"You feed him snails!"

"Your hot chiles will burn his intestines!"

"And your eclairs will give him a heart attack!"

Brock chuckled as he beckoned Mara into the spacious living room. "They've been fighting for twenty-five years. They're happiest when they're at each other's throats."

Silent, Mara carried her daughter into the place that was the heart of his home. Brock watched her face register admiration and wonder as she gazed up at the huge, rough-hewn beams that crossed the twelve-foot ceiling. Each viga was supported by an intricately carved corbel buried in the wall. The adobe walls had been smoothly plastered in a rosy-brown color, even around niches that contained New Mexico artifacts.

As though seeing his own home for the first time, Brock took in the fragile beauty of baskets woven by Mescalero Apaches, clay pots shaped, painted and fired by Indians of the Santa Clara and San Ildefonso pueblos and kachina dolls carved and decorated by Hopis. Old Navajo wool rugs were spread across the tile floor, their patterns evoking spirit gods and their colors of white, gray, black and brown reminiscent of the landscape.

"I keep a fire going even in summer," Brock said as he pointed to the colossal fireplace that was an unusual combination of stone and sculpted adobe. "Hope you don't mind."

"No," Mara whispered.

Brock recalled the furniture he had removed from Mara's apartment and taken straight to the thrift store—snagged plaid sofas, garage-sale lamps, cheap curtains. Todd had been a great friend, a superb athlete and a trusted confidante. Brock had supported his decision to major in history and to start an architectural restoration company. But it hadn't provided much more than the basics for Todd and his young wife.

To Mara, Brock's long, buttery leather couches, wool-upholstered pillows, Mission-style cabinets, silver-inlaid tables and wrought-iron lamps must seem like utter luxury. "This part of the house used to be all there was," he explained as he led Mara and the baby past windows that faced north toward the vast plains that stretched to the San Andres Mountains. "The great room is more than a hundred years old. On the other side of it there, you can see the courtyard with the new swimming pool and the gardens. What are now the kitchen, dining room and library used to be bedrooms. My father bought this land from a descendant of the original Spanish land-grant owner. We moved into the house when I was six."

Mara followed Brock out of the great room and down a long hall lined with Native American and Hispanic art. "So, your father collected New Mexican artifacts?"

"Nope, these are mine," Brock replied. "I pick up things wherever I go. I particularly like the native crafts: baskets, pottery, silver, weaving. I'll buy a painting if it's one I'm partial to."

Mara gaped at the collection of originals by Peter Hurd, Henriette Wyeth and Gordon Snidow. A large framed Amadeo Peña hung on one long wall, an R.C. Gorman on another.

"If I can find an authentic Hispanic religious artifact," he was saying as she readjusted Abby on her shoulder and hurried to catch up, "you know, a *retablo* or a *santo*—I'm as happy as a skunk eatin' cabbage."

"I didn't realize you were so religious," Mara remarked.

Brock swung around, surprised at the question. "It's art. These things come out of old churches. They're hand-crafted folk art. That's why I collect them."

"I thought your interest in Todd's work was just a whim. He said you liked to try new things all the time. Let's see…parasailing, hang-gliding, whitewater rafting…rock climbing."

Brock stared at her, feeling the emotion behind her words. "I've collected art for years."

"Todd never told me."

"I don't know why not," he said, angry with Mara for some reason he couldn't quite pinpoint. The climbing accident wasn't her fault. It was his.

"I guess you and Todd covered more ground than I realized." Her voice was softer now. "You knew him longer."

"We liked exploring. I'd be hunting something every time we went off someplace together. Todd was looking at the architecture, and I was searching for folk art or paintings."

She nodded and turned her focus to the beamed ceiling. "So, did your father add the two wings onto the house?"

"I did."

"You?"

"Sure. Are you surprised?"

"I guess so."

Brock knew most people thought he lived solely on his father's coattails. "I took over the ranch about six years ago, after my father died. He founded Barnett Petroleum and turned his attention to the oil leases he owned over in the southeastern part of the state. He pretty much let this place go. I was kind of steamed about it. Then, when the bottom fell out of oil, Dad sort of dropped out of life. Tipped the bottle, you know?"

"I do know. One of my foster dads had a drinking problem."

"When I was in college," he continued, "I'd come home on weekends and try to put things back in order around the ranch. Dad died shortly after I graduated, so I moved back in and took over."

"What happened to the oil business?"

"A management group in Artesia takes care of things for me there. I look in on the operation regularly just to keep my hand in. The oil pays for itself and a little more. Well, a lot more, but the money goes into stocks and other investments. I let some boys in New York play around with it."

Mara focused on the tiny bundle in her arms, and Brock allowed himself to study Mara. Her hair, brushed shiny-smooth and gleaming, lay like scattered wheat across her shoulders. Mesmerized by her gray-green eyes and her pink lips, he took in her soft curves. Nothing like a long-legged lady in blue jeans, he thought. Mara was definitely beautiful to him—even more so since he had experienced the miracle of Abby's birth. But this was the last time he would study her this closely, Brock instructed himself. Every time he permitted himself to really look at Mara, it shook him to the core.

Satisfied the baby was sleeping, she faced him again. "Stocks and bonds, art, oil, cattle," she said. "It's all pretty foreign to me."

"Some of the money goes to causes I support. Charities, foundations." He knew Mara was religious, and she might not think too highly of his interest in acquiring stuff. Brock had gone to church as a boy, and he believed in God and Jesus—all that. But he had learned that money, and not religion, turned the world.

Brock had hated the loss he'd experienced when his mother moved away. His life felt upside down, and nothing he did could right it. Only financial success seemed to give Brock the feeling of control he craved. Until Todd's death, he had been sure he held the key to power. Nothing had prepared him for the emptiness and guilt that assailed him afterward. His only hope was that taking charge of the lives of Todd's wife and baby—salvaging something out of the future he had destroyed for them—would relieve his pain.

Brock led Mara down the hall toward her rooms. "I've always wanted to get this place back on its feet. Last year the ranch turned a profit for the first time since the seventies."

"So, you decided to use your cattle money to improve the house?" she asked.

"Afraid this is oil money." He pushed open a heavy door. "The ranch keeps itself going, but we're not setting the world on fire. I'm still working on that. This is the west wing. Here's where you'll stay."

Mara stepped into the huge room and squeezed Abby so tightly the baby whimpered in surprise. Her whole apartment could have fit into this place. And the decor! Thick wool rugs covered the oak floor. A large old bed with enormous posts anchored one wall. Two huge chairs flanked a beehive fireplace that filled a whole corner.

"A fireplace!" She tried to bite back her gasp, but Brock heard it and his mouth lifted in a pleased grin.

"I built one in every room."

"It's…nice," she said as she walked toward the windows that lined an entire wall. *Nice* was not an adequate word. The windows faced the plains at the base of the San Andres Mountains, now robed in shades of purple and indigo. Two tall French doors opened onto a deep porch on which sat wicker chairs and tables. A swing hung from the beams, its seat drifting back and forth in the slight breeze.

"Your sitting room opens onto the courtyard," Brock said as he stepped through a doorway.

Startled from the spell the scene had cast over her, Mara followed him into the other room and peered into the dimly lit garden. She could just make out the faint outline of the swimming pool and covered terrace.

"I put a little waterfall by the pool," he told her as he moved to stand beside her. "I planted a xeriscape garden—native wildflowers, cactus, other stuff that can take the heat and dryness. On my property over by the mountains, I found some great rocks. Big ol' things. The water runs over them, and makes a calming sound. It's good for nights when you can't sleep."

Mara looked up, wondering what could ever disturb Brock Barnett's sleep. Highlighted by the setting sun, his stony profile belied the softness in his brown eyes. Odd. All she had ever noticed about him in the past were those severely carved angles of jaw, cheekbone and brow. She'd seen the swagger and the cocky grin, heard the curt sentences, tasted the bitterness the man could leave in his wake.

Who was this person with gardens, art, waterfalls in his soul? Why had he built a beehive fireplace in every room? And what kept him awake at night?

"The baby's room is next door," he said. "Come on."

Mara accompanied him into the adjoining room. Everything he had mentioned sat in perfect showroom newness—crib, high chair, swing, bathtub.

"A rocker!" she exclaimed, delighted at the sight of the large, smooth wood chair with its high arms and comfortably curved back. "This will be perfect for nursing Abby."

She went straight to the rocker and eased her sore body into its cradling cushions. The chair glided evenly back and forth on the floor without a creak or a bump. Immediately, Abby turned her face inward, and her mouth puckered into an expression of hunger. Mara lifted her eyes to Brock.

He stood in the gathering shadows, hands in his pockets and hat pulled low. "You like the chair?"

"This is perfect." She let out a breath. "I love it."

As Abby began to whimper, Brock turned away. "I'll go see what's for supper."

Mara watched the door shut behind him, then she unbuttoned her blouse. She could get used to this, she realized.

"Knock, knock?"

Mara looked up from the crib where Abby lay sleeping peacefully. Rosa Maria Hernandez beckoned from the door.

"Pierre sent me to tell you it's almost time for supper," the housekeeper said as Mara crossed the room to her. "He wants to know, will you eat in the main dining room or in the lounge?"

"There's a lounge?"

"Sure. It's right down the hall there."

Mara gave Abby a last check, content that her daughter would be secure without her for a few minutes. As she stepped into her bedroom, she tried to envision this lounge Rosa Maria was talking about. It made the house sound like a hotel.

"You haven't seen it?" The older woman followed Mara into the room and began turning down the bed. "It's a big area with tables and chairs, bar, movie screen, pool tables, everything. Mr. Barnett has parties there, you know?"

"No, I didn't know."

"Sure! He has a big crowd of friends from Las Cruces. They come up to visit. Sometimes they stay all night."

I'll bet they do, Mara thought. Just when she was trying to accommodate the image of an art-loving Brock, the old party boy stepped back in. Maybe he simply liked to play with his money, spending it on expensive historical artifacts to impress his friends.

She unzipped her suitcase and wondered how long she could endure living right down the hall from Brock Barnett's Bar and Grill. How long before the Las Cruces crowd decided it was time to party? Would there be strange men sleeping in the empty rooms up and down the corridor? Women lolling around the pool? Going into Brock's bedroom? Her husband…

The whole idea made her nauseous—especially the fact that she had actually married such a man. So different from Todd. So opposite to her ideal.

Mara felt lonely enough without family to help her celebrate Abby's birth, without a mother to help her tend the newborn and with her few friends miles down the highway. To have Brock's pack of revelers around would be too much. Jerking a pair of jeans from the top of her suitcase, Mara frowned at the picture her mind had conjured.

"I don't think a lounge is the right place to bring up a baby," she said firmly.

"Oh, everyone will love Abby. Mr. B.'s friends are…well, they're…" Rosa Maria's voice trailed off, and Mara glanced at her.

"They're what?"

"I was just thinking about some of those who come. I don't know if he has told anyone."

"About me?"

"About the wedding."

"I would doubt if he had, Rosa Maria. This marriage is on paper only. Brock and I have been very honest with each other about that, and everyone else should be aware of it, too. The only purpose of the marriage is to provide for Abby."

"Mr. B told us—the ones who work here—that he doesn't know you very well." The housekeeper plumped Mara's pillows. "You're his best friend's wife?"

"Todd Rosemond was my husband."

"I'm very sorry about what happened."

Mara tried to think of a response as she placed her jeans, shirts and socks in the drawers of the large oak bureau near her bed. "I'm sorry, too."

"None of us could believe it when we heard the news. Mr. Rosemond was a good man."

Mara turned quickly. "You knew my husband?"

"Sure. He always stopped by the house when he and Mr. B. were going on trips. I remember he came by once when they were hot-air ballooning, and another time when they had explored a cave near Carlsbad. He was here a lot before he got married. But after that, we didn't see him as much. We all liked your husband. Mr. B. came back happier when they had been out on trips together. He seemed...lighter, you know?"

Mara shrugged. "Todd was like that. He made life fun."

Uncomfortable at the turn of the conversation, she realized she didn't like to be reminded of Todd's friendship with Brock. If the two had never known each other, Todd would be alive today. He would hold his newborn daughter and kiss his wife. The world would be normal, instead of a mess. It was hard enough to lose a husband without the reminder that his presence had been valued by someone else. Valued by the man who ultimately failed him.

"Mr. B. is lonely these days," Rosa Maria said. "Even though you would never hear him say it, he misses his friend a lot. Mr. B. is hard and tough on the outside, you know? He's closed off like a *torreón* with thick walls built high for protection. He doesn't open up for people."

"What about all those Las Cruces party friends?" Mara asked under her breath.

"Them?" Rosa Maria chuckled as she set a crystal water carafe and glass on the bedside table. "Oh, no. They don't talk together, those people. They dance, drink, swim, have fun. Nothing serious."

"Sounds like Brock is pretty lighthearted to me."

"Maybe for a while. Then he goes back to the same way. Quiet, working too hard, a little bit angry, you know? But after spending time with Mr. Rosemond on one of their adventures, he always relaxed. He whistled at his work. He made jokes and teased Pierre…like this morning. I'll tell you, when Mr. B. came back from a trip with your husband, we could always know. Can you guess how we knew?"

Mara shook her head, but she figured she was going to get an answer anyway.

"He put his feet on the dining-room table, that's how."

"What?" she said with a sudden laugh. "His feet?"

"Boots and all. You see, usually Mr. B. sits there in the morning very stiff and brooding with his laptop and cell phone and all his pencils and pens. While he eats breakfast, he plans out everything he wants to do that day. He talks into his little phone, taps messages on his machines, scowls at everybody. He makes us nervous."

"I can see why."

"But for a few days after he got back from spending time with his friend, he would be happy. Relaxed. He would leave the laptop in his car or his study. And he would lean back in his chair and put his feet on the table."

Mara couldn't hold in her smile. It wasn't only the image of Brock with his boots on the table that warmed her. It was Todd. Her husband had touched everyone he knew with his special brand of affection.

"Mr. B., he hasn't been the same since your husband died," Rosa Maria went on. "For months now, he doesn't talk to anyone. He's very difficult. Like he's on edge. Everything has to be done the right way."

"I know about that. When I was in labor with the baby, he told me I hadn't done things logically."

Rosa Maria laughed out loud. "Yes, logic. That's Mr. B. Always in control of everything. Logic, order, organization, perfection—that's what matters to him. 'Do it right, Rosa Maria,' he tells me. Everything must meet his standards."

Mara shook her head. "I don't know how you put up with him."

"Oh, Mr. B. has a big heart, great tenderness. But his heart is buried deep inside. Locked away. I don't know anybody who ever got in there but his best friend."

"Y'all, Pierre's pitching a fit!" Ermaline Criddle called from the door. "He's banging pots and flinging flour everywhere. He says he sent Rosa Maria down here half an hour ago to find out where the madame wants to eat her dinner."

Rosa Maria set her hands on her hips. "Ermaline, you tell that cook I said—"

"Hey, now!" Ermaline cut in. "He needs to know. Mrs. B., where would you like your supper?"

"It's Mara, and I'll…" She debated for a moment. The lounge would be closer to the baby, but she didn't like the idea of eating in a pool hall. On the other hand, she didn't want to encounter Brock more often than necessary. At the same time, she couldn't deny she was curious about this man with the hidden heart.

"Oh, eat in the dining room," Rosa Maria said. "You can hear the baby on the intercom. Look, I'll turn it on for you."

"Intercom?" Mara asked.

"Go on, Ermaline. Tell the old buzzard to set his precious supper in the main dining room."

"But I'm not sure I—"

It was too late. Ermaline had fled, and Rosa Maria was right behind her.

"Just pray Pierre hasn't cooked those snails," she sang out as she vanished down the hall.

Mara stared at the empty doorway. All of a sudden she felt tired. Todd was gone, and she was married to a man who had built himself a house with a bar. A man who rarely smiled, who constantly drove himself toward perfection, and who made even his closest companions nervous. She could hardly wait for dinner.

* * *

Brock was checking his watch when Mara walked into the dining-room, her doughnut cushion in hand.

"Supper's at seven," he informed her. "Unless we have an emergency, that's when we eat."

He liked to keep things running like clockwork on the ranch. That way he knew what to expect, and when. After arriving from the hospital, he had spent time with his foreman and household staff making sure all was well. As expected, the place was shipshape.

Brock had sent Rosa Maria down to the west wing to explain the dining routine to Mara. Neither woman had returned in time for dinner. Finally—with Pierre getting distraught—Brock had sent Ermaline to check on them.

"Newborn babies don't have schedules," Mara reminded him as she set the cushion in the chair and eased onto it as if every part of her had been in pain. "I was feeding Abby."

"You nurse her whenever she cries?"

"It's called feeding on demand." As she picked up her napkin, Mara's face revealed such discomfort and exhaustion that Brock's irritation faded immediately. But hers seemed to be in full swing.

"You might recall I don't have Todd or a mother of my own to help out," she said in a flinty voice. "Babies aren't into efficiency, Brock. They follow their instincts."

Brock studied his bowl as Ermaline poured a ladleful of soup into it. He hadn't thought about Mara being lonely or needing help. Nor had he considered how often a baby might need to eat. In the hospital, the nurses had brought Abby into Mara's room, but he had tried not to pay too much attention to the details. In fact, the process usually made him so uncomfortable he left.

"Suppose she gets hungry in the middle of the night?" he asked.

"I hear they usually do." Mara unfolded her napkin into her lap as Ermaline approached with the soup. "Let me do that, Ermaline. You don't need to wait on me."

"Oh, Mrs. B—"

"It's Mara."

"But we always serve—"

"No, let me—"

"It's okay, Ermaline," Brock said. "Set the tureen on the table."

With an anxious glance at Mara, the maid placed the soup dish beside the arrangement of fresh flowers. As Ermaline hurried toward the kitchen, Mara let out a breath.

"I'm sorry," she said to Brock. "I shouldn't have snapped at her. I'm just not used to this."

"Is something wrong?"

"It's all so grand. So formal." She said the words as though they were distasteful to her.

"It is?" Brock glanced around, trying to see the house through her eyes. To him, the large dining room looked pretty good. He had placed a few expensive pueblo pots here and there. A bright fire burned in the huge hearth. He and Mara sat facing each other at one end of a long, sleek table rimmed with twelve chairs. Candlelight from a pair of white tapers in silver holders gave Mara's face a soft glow. He had bought the white china in Paris.

Brock tried to think how it might be different, but his mind was a blank slate. Grand? Formal? What did Mara even mean by that?

"It's all so fancy." She filled the ladle with vegetable soup and poured it into her bowl. "Rosa Maria even turned down my sheets."

"What's wrong with that? She's turned down the sheets every night of my life practically."

"I can turn down my own sheets, Brock." Mara lifted her head and met his eyes. "I want my life to go the way I say."

"All right." He wasn't sure he liked the sound of that. So far, life on the ranch had always gone the way he'd said.

"I don't want to be called Mrs. Barnett," she told him.

"It's your name."

"I'm Mara. I don't want people fawning over me or waiting on me hand and foot. And I don't want parties in my part of the house."

"Parties?" He tried without success to read the message in her tired green eyes.

"The lounge," she said. "That bar down the hall from Abby's room. No wild parties in there."

"Wild parties in the den?" He dunked his spoon in the soup. "Mara, what are you talking about?"

"Rosa Maria called it a lounge. She said you have parties with your friends from Las Cruces. And don't you say grace at the dinner table?"

Brock stared at her. Tears perched just on the edge of her lower eyelashes, threatening to spill over. If those tears slid down her cheeks, he'd be lost. He was already lost. What was she upset about? Was it this business about wild parties? Or eating before saying grace? Or what?

"I pray before I eat," she enunciated, as if speaking to someone a little slow on the uptake. "To thank God for the food, you know?"

"Sure." Brock set his spoon back in the bowl. "Go ahead."

Mara let out a breath. "Todd and I," she said softly, "we held hands."

Brock looked at the wedding band still on her finger, then lifted his eyes to hers, finally understanding. "I guess you miss him a lot."

She nodded, unable to speak.

"Mara…you can hold my hands." He reached across the table, his palms spread open. Slowly she placed her hands in his. As his fingers closed around hers, he wondered what she thought of his sun-toughened skin and the hard ridges of calluses on his palms.

He bowed his head. "Go ahead."

"You," she whispered. "I don't think I can."

Brock swallowed and glanced up to find himself staring at the top of Mara's blond head. He had been to church in Las Cruces a few times as a boy, but he didn't have the first clue about praying out loud. Any other time, he'd have refused to try. Then he thought about those tears on her eyelashes.

"Dear God," he began, "here we are at the table. Well…I guess You already knew that. Anyway, we're thinking about Todd, and we both miss him a lot."

Brock cleared his throat and peered at Mara. Had he messed up the prayer? She sat in silence, head low and eyes closed.

"We wish Todd was here with us," he continued. "Wish he could see Abby. We thank You for the baby, for giving her to us…to Mara. And for the food, too. Thanks for that. Uh…in Jesus' name we pray. Amen."

When he opened his eyes, he realized he had blown it. Mara was crying into her napkin. He ducked his head and went for the soup. Blast it all anyhow! He didn't know what to do with her. Didn't know what to say or how to act. Mara was his wife, but he had no idea how to be a husband to her.

Besides, he knew that no matter how hard he tried, he would never live up to Todd's example. Todd had been a real Christian—one who knew the rules and regulations of religion. More than that, Todd had been a man of faith. Todd had surrendered his life to Jesus Christ, and he didn't have any trouble regularly reminding his best friend about the positive changes that decision had brought.

Brock, on the other hand, kept a tight rein on his existence. Though he was a believer, he wasn't about to give up any of his hard-won control. He knew his stubborn self-reliance somehow made him a lesser man in Mara's eyes, but to him there was no other way to get through life.

"Thank you," Mara whispered, dabbing the corner of her eye. "For praying about Abby."

"You're welcome."

"I don't want anything to happen to her."

"It won't, Mara. She's safe here." He downed another spoonful of soup, but it was tasteless. So much for all his self-reliance and confidence. Mara didn't trust him with her baby, and why should she? Look what had happened when he'd gone off with her husband.

"Could you have your parties in the east wing?" she asked.

"What is all this about parties?"

"Rosa Maria told me you have a bunch of friends from Las Cruces who come out to the ranch for parties in your lounge.

You have a bar and a pool table, and they spend the night. Brock, I won't have drunk strangers around Abby."

"Drunk strangers?" He set his spoon beside his bowl. "My friends come out here a couple of times a year, and they don't get drunk."

Her voice went hostile again. "Well, I don't want them near my daughter."

"Mara, they are good people. They're old college friends, business associates, ranchers. All we're doing is having a little fun."

"I know about what you call fun! Todd told me the things you do." Her green eyes blazed as the tears vanished. "You just keep your friends away from my baby."

"What are you going to do—hide for the rest of your life?"

"Hide?"

"Lick your wounds?"

"Oh, what do you know about pain?" Mara stood and grabbed her doughnut pillow. "Abby's mine, and I'll raise her the way I want to. You have no say in it whatsoever. Abby's the one I'm protecting, and if that means hiding her from bad influences, that's what I'll do. The wounds that need to be tended are Abby's—and the man who wounded her is you."

Tucking the pillow against her stomach, Mara stalked across the dining room and headed down the hall.

Brock clenched his jaw as her words reverberated through him. She was the one who was hurting, he thought bitterly. Mara was the one who had been wounded, and he wondered if anything could ever heal her.

Chapter Seven

✤

"Rosa Maria, where's my laptop?" Brock hollered the next morning as he strode into the dining room and tossed his Stetson onto the table. "I left it in the study next to the fax machine, and it's not there now."

He thunked his briefcase on the floor and dropped a handful of pencils beside his plate. Where could that laptop be? He stored all his records for the ranch in the small computer, and his backup files were in the safe.

"Leave things in someone else's hands for a week," he muttered as he dropped into his chair. "Chaos."

"Eggs Benedict," Ermaline announced. Breezing into the dining room, she balanced a silver tray on her upturned palm. "Hey, where's Mrs. B.?"

"Where's Rosa Maria?" Brock demanded to know. "I've called her three times."

"Isn't she in the living room? That's where she always starts dusting in the morning."

"She's not there now." Pushing back from the table, Brock

grimaced. He'd let everything get out of control. For most of the night he had sat on his porch or wandered the courtyard and tried to figure a way to put a stamp of order back on his life. Now he was dead-tired, he'd misplaced his computer, his housekeeper had vanished and he was supposed to be in the north section in fifteen minutes checking the cattle.

He walked to the intercom and flipped the master control switch. "Rosa Maria," he barked. "If you're anywhere in this house, get yourself to the dining room."

He waited a moment, then opened the intercom to every room in the house. A baby's loud wail blasted through the mesh screen and filled the dining room.

"Oh, no," Mara's voice groaned from her bedroom in the west wing. "Thanks a lot, Brock. It's okay, Abby. Mommy's coming."

Standing half a house away, Brock winced. It hadn't occurred to him that he might wake the baby. Well, that was the crux of the problem. With Mara and Abby in the house, nothing was functioning the way it should. Things didn't feel normal.

"Here she is, Mrs. B.," Rosa Maria's voice said softly through the intercom. "Here's your baby girl. You stay in bed there. You've been up all night, haven't you?"

"Most of the night. Well, hello there, precious girl. Are you hungry? Oh, Rosa Maria, I'm so tired and sore. It's really great to have your help. Thanks for bringing her to me."

"I'm glad to do it. I was here checking on Abby, anyway. Look at that, she doesn't want to nurse. She was just scared by that crazy Mr. B. yelling over the intercom. Tsk. He doesn't think sometimes, that man."

"I believe Brock wants you in the dining room, Rosa Maria."

"I heard him bellowing like one of his old bulls. He's forgotten he put his precious laptop in his car when he went to the hospital to visit you. He can't get through breakfast without his computer and all his pencils and papers."

Standing in the dining room, Brock scowled at the intercom. Half tempted to turn off the eavesdropping and half tempted to throw both women out of his house for their disrespect and ingratitude, he shoved his hands into his pockets.

Come to think of it, he *had* left the laptop in his car.

"Do you think Abby's all right, Rosa Maria?" Mara asked in a low voice. "I'm worried she's sick or something. Is it normal for her to be awake so much of the night?"

"She doesn't know it's night. All she knows is she's hungry or wet or lonely in that big new crib. Remember this was only the first night. She'll start to sleep better after a while. In the meantime, you're the one who needs some sleep."

"I feel like I've been run over by a truck."

Rosa Maria chuckled. "I know, I know. I remember how it was with all of mine. But you're doing good. It's hard by yourself. If you had a nice man to look after you—" She caught herself, then tried again. "I'm sure Mr. Rosemond would have stayed by your side… Oh, I'm sorry. I shouldn't talk about your husband—"

Brock snapped off the intercom. He was Mara's husband, not Todd. As much as everybody missed him, Todd was gone. Never coming back. But Todd—who'd never actually been a father—was doing a better job of it than Brock.

He studied the lumps of eggs Benedict in their cold white hollandaise sauce. Though he might be Mara's husband, he wasn't Abby's father. Mara had made that clear enough last night. Even if he wanted to go to Mara…comfort her…support her…she didn't want him. So, she could just cope with motherhood on her own.

Mara and Abby were nothing more than another of Brock's financial obligations. He had committed his resources to their care. He had offered a place to stay, food to eat, a car to get around in, money to spend. But he didn't owe them anything else.

Besides, he thought as he grabbed his hat from the table, he wouldn't know the first thing about helping Mara with her baby. He had never learned how to be a husband or a father, and he wasn't inclined in that direction anyway. Good enough.

Brock settled his hat on his brow and headed for the back door. So, there were two extra people in the house? He would put them into a file in his computer like a couple of head of cattle he might have bought at the state fair. He'd factor them into the ranch budget, calculate the cost of food and clothing, add their projected medical expenses and figure the outlay for wintering them. They wouldn't be economical, and there was no potential return on his money.

But those were the breaks.

Mara finished nursing Abby and adjusted her robe. For a moment she gazed down at the tiny face nestled in the crook of her elbow. Her daughter's eyes had dropped shut, their long, curling lashes brushing the round apples of her cheeks. Her miniature nose bore a blush from being pressed against Mara's soft skin. Like a pale pink rose, Abby's mouth formed a delicate bud, barely open with lips so soft and sweet, Mara thought her heart might overflow.

Four days had passed since Abby's birth, and already Mara loved this child more than she had ever known she could love anyone or anything. Long nights awake didn't matter. An aching body and a sore tailbone didn't matter. Nothing mattered but this precious weight in her arms.

Mara blinked back tears, wondering if she was ever going to be in control of her emotions again. Had she actually yelled at Brock last night? Had she really admonished the man for failing to pray before dinner? And what did she know about his Las Cruces friends anyway?

Shaking her head, Mara wrapped Abby in the warm white blanket she had crocheted during the summer. Brock had been nothing but kind and good to her since Todd's death, while she had chastised him and found fault with everything he did. She owed him an apology.

Easing herself up out of the rocking chair, Mara started toward the crib with its billowy white canopy. Halfway across the room, she stopped. Maybe she would just go and find Brock right now. It was almost noon, and he'd come in for lunch. With Abby sleeping in her arms, maybe they wouldn't be so tempted to argue. Maybe she could tell him how she felt.

For a moment, she hesitated again. She hadn't had a shower this morning, and she was still in her blue bathrobe. But she couldn't bear to put her maternity clothes back on, even though she had a sinking certainty they were all she could fit into.

Lifting her chin, she decided it hardly mattered how she looked to Brock Barnett. She walked out of the nursery and started down the hall. "Brock, I wanted to thank you for taking Abby and me in," she would say. "You've been so kind."

Kind? Brock Barnett? Mara had to smile. The word hardly fit her image of the man. Tucking Abby more closely into her embrace, she passed the lounge. Remembering her discussion with Brock the night before, she felt a sudden temptation to investigate his den of iniquity. She paused briefly, and then she pushed open the door.

"Oh, you scared the living daylights out of me!" Ermaline gasped as she lifted her head from behind the long wooden bar. Feather duster in one hand and spray wax in the other, she leaned her elbows on the sleek, aged wood. "Well, hey there, Mrs. B. What brings you in here?"

"Just looking around. What about you?"

"I clean this place every morning before I go to the kitchen to help Pierre with lunch. My job is the west wing and the meal serving. Rosa Maria takes care of Mr. B.'s rooms and the main living areas. Pierre's in charge of the kitchen, and Mr. Potter keeps up the gardens and courtyard. So, what do you think? Ever seen the likes of this little playroom?"

Mara surveyed the long room with its warm *saltillo* tile floor, comfortable seating area, entertainment center, pool table and neat kitchenette. "I thought…I thought it would be…different."

"This place hardly gets used anymore," Ermaline said. "Shame. Mr. B. used to have some dandy parties. Folks would come out from Las Cruces and make use of the pool, the barbecue pit, the whole shebang. There'd be lanterns strung across the courtyard and a band playing and everybody having a big ol' time. Christmas we'd have a bonfire. Frank and me got to come, too. Mr. B invited everybody, is what he did. New Year's we'd have a big time, too. Things are sure quiet now."

Mara studied the long linen drapes that covered the wall of windows, blocking the late-November light. "What happened?"

"Mr. B. told us he's just too busy for parties nowadays. Pierre was the one who finally faced him head-on about it. You know how Pierre likes to cook, and he gets tired of making meals for one. You should have seen the French stuff he used to turn out of that kitchen for Mr. B.'s shindigs."

"What keeps Brock so busy?"

"Running this ranch. I'm telling you, that's all he does day and night. He's either branding or roping or doing something to those crazy cows. He rounds them up and moves them here, moves them there. He goes to market, goes to shows, goes to the fair. He buys a prize bull, and we all have to take a gander at it. 'Come on, Ermaline,' he'll say. 'Don't you and Rosa Maria want to see my new Simmental?' As if I'd know one kind of cow from another."

"Why doesn't he take those friends of his to admire his cattle?"

"Well, he used to take your husband."

"Oh." Mara lowered her head and focused on the wedding band Todd had given her. Again, she had been brought face-to-face with the realization that he had not belonged to her alone.

"They'd go look the ranch over, your husband and Mr. B.," Ermaline went on. "There's some ruins over toward the mountains where the cliffs are, you know. Those two couldn't get enough of rooting around there and talking about the olden days. Once in a while Mr. B.'s friends from Las Cruces still come out here. The truth is, he's got nothing in common with them anymore, but he just doesn't like to admit it."

"Has Brock changed so much over the years?"

"Sure he has." Ermaline sprayed the top of the bar and began to rub it with a cloth she dug out of her apron pocket. "Used to be, Mr. B. was out all night and slept most of the day. That was in high school and college, when his daddy—we always called him Mr. Barnett, too—ran this place. The boy had lots of girlfriends, lots of fancy cars, big stereos, that kind of thing. Now, he just works all the time. His Las Cruces friends have become accountants and bankers and office types. They don't care much about Simmental bulls, and Mr. B. knows it. I suspect they want him back the way he was with his freewheeling life—easy money, fast cars and all that. But he wants this ranch to do good, and that can't happen if you're up all night having fun. You know how Mr. B. is. He doesn't do anything unless he wants to."

"I've learned that."

Ermaline laughed. "It's his way or no way."

Mara strolled down to the end of the room, admiring the bold paintings on the walls and the thick wool rugs on the floors. A huge fireplace dominated the end of the lounge, its grate loaded with heavy, unburned logs.

Beside the hearth sat an intricately crafted chair built from the sinuous branches of an alligator juniper. Mara touched the strange piece, its arms constructed from whole limbs twisted together and then jointed into the massive legs. A soft green cushion formed the seat, and she couldn't resist settling into it with Abby.

"Mr. B made that chair, you know," Ermaline called from the other end of the room where she was dusting lamps. "He likes to build stuff."

Mara glanced at the piece in surprise. "This?"

"Yep. He's got a big workshop over on the other side of the house with all his tools. When he can't sleep, that's where he'll be if he's not in the courtyard. Half this stuff I dust every day is furniture he made. That table there, the bench over yonder, that cabinet by the window. He made you that rocker."

"The one in the baby's room?"

"Sure. Every day last week after he got back from the hospital, he'd come into the house, change clothes and go straight to the shop. Sawdust just flew, I'm telling you. He was a man possessed. Now, Rosa Maria and me remember what he told us about this marriage being only to take care of you because you're his best friend's wife, and all. But we think he's got a heart for you anyway, Mrs. B. You, and for sure the baby. He made that rocking chair just for you, no doubt about it."

"Oh, Ermaline, I don't—"

"When he brought it into the house, he said, 'Put this in the nursery, Ermaline. It's for the baby's mama.' That's what he said."

Mara stared at Abby as she tried to absorb this news. Brock had made that beautiful rocker—for her? She could hardly believe it. She'd treated him so coldly even though he had come to the hospital every day. Because of what had happened to Todd, she had thought nothing but the worst of Brock. And all the while he'd been building her a rocking chair.

"I'm going to talk to him this minute," she announced, standing suddenly. "We need to clear up some things."

"Good luck finding him," Ermaline said as Mara carried Abby to the door. "He's usually gone from sunup to way past dark."

Mara paused in the hall. "He doesn't come home for lunch?"

"Not even for supper sometimes. I know, I know—if he's around, supper's at seven sharp. But Mr. B. likes to eat with the ranch hands when he can. Drives Pierre crazy, of course, but that's the boss for you. I reckon I've gone a whole week without laying eyes on the man."

"But this is his house."

Ermaline squirted the top of a table with the spray wax. "Sure it's his house, all fixed up and perfect. But what's a house if you don't have anything to come home to?"

She tossed her damp rag on the table and began to rub. "Let me know if you find him, Mrs. B. I've been needing a case of window cleaner in the worst way."

True to Ermaline's prediction, Brock was nowhere to be found. After lunch alone in her room and a deep afternoon nap, Mara showered and changed into a pink sweater-tunic. She told herself it didn't look as much like maternity wear as some of her other clothes. With a pair of knit pants, she felt almost presentable.

After checking the sleeping Abby, Mara brushed out her hair, then braided it into a full French plait and tied the end with a pink ribbon. For the first time since Abby's birth, she smoothed makeup onto her face, dusted her cheeks with blush and puffed a little powder over her skin. With a touch of liner, shadow and mascara for her eyes, she felt as though she were almost seeing the familiar face of Mara Rosemond in the mirror again.

But she wasn't that Mara anymore. Whether she liked it or not, she was Mrs. Barnett, rancher's wife. She was a mother, too. And she was jobless, penniless, almost homeless. The least she could do was offer her benefactor a polite thank-you.

Mara checked Abby again, made sure the intercom was on and then headed down the long hall toward the dining room. She still felt awkward and uncomfortable in the huge, empty house, but some things were looking up. She had discovered she could walk without wincing in pain. Even her midsection seemed to be shrinking.

"There you are!" Ermaline swung into the dining room from the kitchen just as Mara entered from the hall. "Pierre's fixed the best chicken you ever tasted. He's baked his famous hot rolls, too."

"Is Brock coming?"

"Doubt it. We haven't seen hide nor hair of him all day. You?"

"No. No Mr. B sightings today."

"Better get used to it." Ermaline grabbed a serving dish from the cupboard and hurried into the kitchen.

Mara pulled back the chair she had sat in the night before. This was her place at the table, she supposed. As she settled onto the chair, a memory suddenly surfaced. Growing up in a series of foster homes, she had never had her own place at a table. Then, after she married Todd, she had begun setting their plates anywhere on the little dinette, sometimes at one end, sometimes at the other. Sometimes they ate on the couch, sometimes the kitchen counter, and once or twice even standing up.

"From now on you sit here, Mara," Todd had told her one night, holding out a chair at the table. "This is your place."

For the next five years she had sat right there. Her place. How normal it had seemed to face her husband across their laminated table with their plastic plates and their chipped glasses in between. How comfortable.

"Pierre sends you his regards," Ermaline announced as she sashayed back into the dining room, her arms laden with a heavy silver salver and covered dishes. "Chicken marsala," she continued as she swept aside a silver dome. "That means he cooked it in wine—but don't worry, the alcohol's all gone. I made sure of that. And here's some veggies, some of those rolls, a little salad with tee-tiny onions in it, and I'll bring in the dessert when you're done. It's cheesecake. I peeked."

She started to spoon the chicken onto Mara's plate, then she caught herself. "Oops, I forgot."

Mara gave her a nod. "It's okay, Ermaline. Do it the way you always have."

With a sigh of relief, the maid loaded Mara's plate with food. "I've been working here a long time, first for old Mr. Barnett and now for young Mr. B. You learn to do things a certain way, you know?"

Mara nodded. "I was used to things a certain way, too."

"I reckon so. You live with someone a while and things kind of fall into a pattern. You get familiar with each other's habits, and you get real cozy with those ordinary little day-to-day things. I tell you, I don't know what I'd do if I lost Frank. Me and him go back a long ways. We've kind of got ourselves a routine after all these years being married. But, I guess you can't keep looking back at what you had. You've got Abby now, and Mr. B. You've got a lot right there."

"I don't think I do have Mr. B."

"Well, nobody really has him. He doesn't think he wants to be had, but that could be remedied." She clanged the domed lids onto their dishes and swept the tray into her arms. "Want some music? I can turn on the stereo in the living room and pipe it in here."

Mara stared down at her meal, then looked at the long empty table. "The intercom is on in the dining room, right? I want to hear Abby."

"I'll double-check it." Ermaline marched across the room and flipped a few switches. "Yep, you'll hear the slightest peep.

This is the eeriest machine. Never know if someone's listening in. Okay, well, just ring that little bell if you need anything."

"Thank you." Mara watched as Ermaline vanished into the kitchen.

She had eaten alone before. Ever since Todd's death, she had sat alone in her apartment, cooked alone, dined alone, slept alone. Why did this meal feel so strange and uncomfortable?

Mara inserted a fork and knife into the chicken and cut a few bites. The flavor was delicious, and at the same time the food tasted completely bland. Maybe she still had the baby blues. She should call Sherry and invite her over for the weekend. Mara could show off the baby to her best friend. Sherry could fill her in on things at church, people they both knew, events at the boutique where Sherry worked and the historical museum where Mara used to spend so much time.

She shouldn't need Sherry to keep her company. She shouldn't feel lonely at all. The three members of the household staff were in the kitchen. Abby was just down the hall. And Mara hardly even liked the man whose absence made the house seem empty.

Chewing on another bite of chicken, she tried to recall what she had hated so much about Brock. He had caused Todd's death, of course. Well, she had never learned the whole truth about that experience, and she didn't want to. But there was no doubt Brock was responsible for luring Todd on another reckless adventure, and he had been responsible as Todd's anchor on the cliffs. She had lost her husband forever because of Brock's foolhardiness. Abby would never know a father. Mara would never truly be loved again.

So, why couldn't she summon up the proper anger toward Brock? Mara stabbed a bite of salad. Because Brock had come to the hospital? Because he'd helped her give birth? Because he'd built a rocking chair? Those things didn't erase his part in Todd's death.

But she couldn't hate him, either. Maybe she just hadn't seen enough of the man lately to remember how to despise him. It had been so easy before.

"Dessert?" Ermaline's head popped around the door. "Chocolate cheesecake? Pierre puts cherries on top and drizzles chocolate syrup all around."

"Sounds good."

"It's delicious. We tasted it already, me and Rosa Maria."

"All right."

"She wants the cheesecake!" the older woman hollered over her shoulder into the kitchen. "You liked the chicken? Pierre wants to know."

"Very good."

"She liked it!" Ermaline called back again. "She said it was *très bon.*"

Mara watched the maid giggle, her oversize teeth suddenly seeming twice as large. She had to smile in return. *"Très bon?"*

"Pierre loves it when people talk French about his food." Ermaline cleared the dishes. "So what do you think, Mrs. B.? You think you'll like it here? You think you'll stay?"

Mara smoothed her napkin across her lap. "For a while."

"Me and the other staff hope you'll stay. We think you and Mr. B. will get used to each other after a while."

"Pretty hard to get used to someone you never see."

"Oh, he just drove in. Didn't I tell you? He'll probably want some cheesecake."

Ermaline sailed out of the room before Mara could call out. Suddenly her mouth felt like the bottom of an old shoe. Her heart skittered into a crazy dance, and she couldn't catch her breath. Grabbing the napkin, she debated bolting. She really didn't want to see Brock after all. She certainly couldn't bring herself to thank this man she'd always disliked.

No, she did want to see him. She wanted to understand why her palms had gone damp at the prospect of his appearance in the room. She wanted to know why he wouldn't be owned by anyone and why he'd locked his heart away. She wanted to feel that strange tingle in the base of her spine when he looked at her. She wanted to hear his voice.

No, she didn't! She jumped up and pushed her chair back from the table.

"Hey, Mara." Brock walked into the room and took off his hat.

She stared. He was tall. He was tan. He was black-haired and brown-eyed and handsome. Too handsome. Like a bashful schoolgirl in the presence of the high-school hero, she felt her heart flutter and her cheeks go pink. This happened every time she saw Brock, she reminded herself. It always had, even from the beginning. But when he talked and swaggered and tried to control everything and everybody, she despised him. She really did.

"You already ate?" he asked.

"Supper's at seven, remember?"

He gave an apologetic smile. "When I'm here, it's at seven. I ate at the bunkhouse."

"You missed the chicken marsala."

"I hear it was *très bon*."

"It was." Mara swallowed. He was holding her with those brown eyes of his. She couldn't move. Surely she could summon up her familiar dislike of him, couldn't she? He had let Todd fall. He had destroyed her life. Why on earth was she shaking? It had to be a hormone imbalance. Childbirth did that to a woman.

"I guess I'll have some cheesecake," he said, walking toward her. "Pierre's is the best."

"The *pièce de résistance* of this meal."

His mouth curved into a grin. "You learn fast. Speak French to Pierre, and he'll love you forever."

Mara grabbed the back of the chair to keep herself from asking the question that rolled to the tip of her tongue. *What would make you love a woman forever, Brock?*

Ridiculous! She didn't care how he felt or what went on inside his frigid heart. It was time to sit down. No, it was time to get out of this room and away from this man who was coming closer and closer.

"How was your day, Mara?"

"Fine."

"Get any rest?"

"A little."

"The baby okay?"

"Sleeping."

"That's good."

"Yeah." She tried to give a nonchalant smile. "Someone woke her up awfully early this morning."

"Sorry about that." He set his hat on the table. "You look different tonight."

She flushed and hated herself for it. "I took a shower."

"You have on regular clothes." He looked her up and down, and she felt every new lump and bulge with which childbearing had endowed her.

"At least I can see my feet again," she managed.

It was meant to be a joke, a reminder of their adventure in the tiny apartment bathroom, but he didn't laugh. He lifted his head, and his deep-brown eyes searched her face.

"I have a long way to go before I feel normal." She heard herself talking again, blabbering just to fill the silence, and he watched as her lips formed the words. "I need to start exercising. Right now, I feel like I'm doing well just to walk down the hall without it hurting too much."

"Hurting?" He reached out and touched her hand. "I'm sorry, Mara. I didn't realize… I know you went through a lot the other day. You want to use the hot tub? It's in my wing."

"Oh…a hot tub…" She should pull her hand away. The man was so close she could smell his scent, wild and somehow earthy after his day in the dust and wind and chilly, late-autumn sunshine. It cast a spell, like a fragile net, over her shoulders. She knew she must escape the spell, but she couldn't make herself want to.

"Feels good after a hard day," he said. "Warm water swirling around. Bubbles. Steam."

"Not tonight. Thank you." She instructed her knees to bend, and she managed to sit on her chair. "I'm too tired."

"Whatever feels right."

"Cheesecake!" Ermaline sang out as she swept into the dining room. "Have a seat, Mr. B. You want a dessert wine with this?"

Brock stepped away from Mara and walked around the table. "No, thanks," he said. "I think I'm a little off center tonight already."

"You boys ought to lay off that beer down at the bunkhouse, Mr. B. Especially on a work night."

Ermaline bustled out of the dining room, and Brock picked up his fork. "I haven't had a thing to drink," he said.

Chapter Eight

❧

For the first time in his life, Brock felt indifferent about Pierre's cheesecake. He stared down at the creamy confection dripping in chocolate and cherries, and all he could think about was Mara. She sat an arm's length away, the scent of her perfume mingling with the fragrance of burning wax from the candles between them. He shouldn't have looked at her again. Only the day before, he'd made himself a promise to steer clear of the woman. But the minute he had heard she was in the dining room, he'd headed right on in just as if he belonged across the table from her.

He jiggled his fork back and forth, then stuck it into the cheesecake and sliced off a bite. As he chewed, he realized the stuff felt like quick-drying carpenter's glue in his mouth. His attempt to swallow lodged the dessert right at Adam's-apple level, where it stuck firm and made any chance at conversation impossible. Just as well.

Brock knew he had no business daydreaming up a bunch of romantic nonsense about a woman who had nearly ruined his peaceful life. Despite his best intentions, he had thought about Mara all day long. While loading a steer or checking his barns or driving down a dusty dirt road, he would catch himself in the realization that her face had appeared right in front of him. He might picture her straining to give birth to little Abby, or smiling with that half-shy, secret smile, or lashing out at him like a snapping bullwhip.

From any angle and in any circumstance Mara looked beautiful to him. Her blond hair draped around her shoulders like a silk sheet. Her eyes glowed with an inner light of determination and intelligence that had always fascinated him. Her mouth…oh, Mara's mouth…

"I dropped by the lounge this morning," she said. "The one in my wing."

He worked at swallowing the gluey lump of cheesecake. "Oh, yeah?"

"It's nice."

"Mmm-hmm." He couldn't lift his head or he'd have to see her face again. But he couldn't take another bite or he'd be so gummed up he'd choke. Instead, he intently mashed the cheesecake into a pattern of crosshatched fork marks.

"I feel like I misjudged you, Brock," she said in a low voice. "It's just that I'm a quiet person, and I don't enjoy parties all that much. Especially with a baby around."

"Mmm."

"I was worried there might be too much going on in my wing."

He glanced up, but focused on the window behind her. "No, it's uh…quiet around here."

"It is very quiet." Mara poked at the crust of her dessert. "You're gone a lot, aren't you?"

He nodded. "Lots to be done."

"Cows."

"Yeah."

"I'm glad you're here tonight though," she began. "I wanted to talk to you. There are some things I think I should tell you."

Again he lifted his eyes, but this time he couldn't resist looking at her. Mara was concentrating on her cheesecake as intently as he'd studied his. A soft flush had spread across her cheeks to light her skin with a pink glow. He couldn't remember when he'd seen a woman look so gentle, so tender. In her pink sweater and golden hair, she was almost a vision. He had to get out of the dining room. Fast.

"Don't worry about parties," he said quickly as he pushed back from the table and stood up. "I keep things pretty dull around here. So anyhow, I reckon I'll just—"

"Thank you," she said softly. "For everything."

He stopped. "Pardon?"

"Thank you for all this. The house, the food. I'm grateful to you for paying my hospital and doctor bills, Brock. And the nursery...thank you for all the furniture. For my rocking chair."

Rubbing his palm around the back of his neck beneath his collar, Brock let out a breath.

"Ermaline told me you built it."

"Figures." He debated how to handle this inevitable situation. While Mara had been in the hospital, he could think of nothing but finding ways to please her. He had been almost obsessed with crafting the rocker for her. More than with any other piece of furniture, he had poured the sum of his carpentry expertise into that chair. While telling himself it was for the baby's comfort, he had known all along he was building it for Mara. When the piece sat finished, he had felt certain it was perfect. Only then had he begun to wonder what had possessed him to work so hard for a woman who couldn't stand him, and to worry how she might interpret his gesture.

"I do a lot of carpentry," he said, his voice carefully nonchalant. "Takes my mind off things."

"Well, I appreciate it." Mara stood and rounded the table toward him. "Brock, you've done more than—"

"I'd do just about anything for Todd," he said quickly. She was suddenly too close. He could smell the scent of her freshly washed hair, like flowers after a rainstorm. Frantic that he might touch her, he threw out the only barrier he could think of to push her away.

"Todd was my best friend, remember?" he said, his voice harsher than he intended. He went on, speaking too quickly. "I can't do anything to bring him back, but I know how to manage the business end of things. You and the baby are already figured into my operating costs. It's like you're part of the household staff, same as Pierre, the housekeepers, the gardener. You've just been absorbed right into the equation. Don't worry about what stuff is costing me. I know what my obligations are, and I intend to meet them."

Mara watched him with a bemused expression. "I'm not accustomed to thinking of myself as a line item in somebody's budget."

Brock looked at her, and the realization that she was easily within his grasp sent a solid weight to the pit of his stomach. He swallowed hard and shifted from one foot to the other. Her gray-green eyes were fastened to him as she waited for some response, but it was all he could do to keep himself from taking her in his arms and kissing her lips.

"I realize you're trying to do right by Todd," she continued. "But I prefer to be treated as a human being."

"Is anyone here treating you badly, Mara?"

Her shoulders drooped. "I'm being treated very well. It's just…"

"Has the staff said anything unkind about our arrangement or the baby or anything?"

"Oh, no. They've all been polite."

"Do you need anything?" Something was wrong, but Brock couldn't figure out what it was. Had he pushed her too far away—and hurt her in the process? "New clothes? Shoes? A different room?"

"No, I have all I need. More than enough."

"Then what's the problem?"

She ran a finger along the back of the chair. "I'm a person, Brock. I have feelings. I have needs that have nothing to do with clothes and shoes. It's hard to live with the realization that you're resented."

"No one resents you."

"I'm trying to tell you that I want to be treated like a woman, not a budget item. Can't you see that?"

"I see that." Unable to hold back, he took her shoulders firmly. "Mara, don't ask anything more of me. I'm doing all I can to…to manage this situation."

"You don't have to manage me, Brock. And I'm not a situation, I'm a human being. I'd like someone to talk to once in a while. I could use a little company at the dinner table."

Struggling for control, he forced out the words. "I told you I can't bring Todd back. I can't fix that."

"I know you can't bring him back."

"I can't take his place, either. I'm not Todd. I never will be."

"Am I asking you to be Todd?"

He shook his head slowly. Beneath his fingers, her sweater was warm and soft. Her shoulders felt so small and fragile. With one tilt of his thumbs he could pull her against him. "You're asking too much, Mara."

"Why?" The word was a breath against his skin.

He searched her face, hoping to find the contempt and disgust he had seen so often in her eyes. Instead he saw vulnerability. Loneliness. Sorrow. But he had built a wall of resolve to keep her and everyone else out of his life, and he couldn't tear it down. This woman, more than any other, was forbidden. She wore another man's wedding band, and she belonged to him.

"You're Todd's wife," he said, determined to restore the barrier she had threatened to topple. If he let this thing get out of control, he could never forgive himself. He might hurt Mara, hurt Abby. And then he would be guilty all over again.

Brock dropped his hands and stepped back from her. "Look, if I'm going to take care of Todd's business—and I am—then I have to work hard. You may have feelings and needs, but you're going to have to handle them without me around. I don't have time to eat here at the house every meal and then sit around visiting with you. I have to pay my bills, which are bigger now than they were before I took you two in, and that means I need to be out working as much as I can."

Unwilling to look at her again, he leaned over the table to grab his hat. As he settled it on his head, he started for the door.

"Todd never walked away from me in the middle of a conversation," she snapped.

He halted. "I told you—I'm not Todd."

"My husband never thought of me as a bill to pay."

"I'm not your husband." He squared his shoulders. "Not really."

"Yes, you are, Brock." Mara glared at him. "You know, after walking through your home and meeting your employees and seeing the rocker you built, I thought I had caught a glimpse of a man I might be able to forgive. I thought there might be room for a measure of cordiality between us. In fact, I almost forgot why I originally refused to marry you that day in my apartment. Thank you for reminding me."

"You're welcome."

As fast as he had come into the room, Brock bolted out again. And he made absolutely sure he didn't turn to look at her. Not until he was in the driveway and could see her through the window. Mara was crying.

"So, how's Brock these days?" Sherry asked over the telephone. "Is he doing anything to help out with the baby?"

In the first weeks after Abby's birth, Mara and her best friend had talked by phone nearly every day. But the calls became less frequent as the holidays approached and the boutique where Sherry worked grew busier. Now her voice sounded almost foreign—as though she were from another time and place.

Mara frowned at the pile of white cotton infant T-shirts she had been folding as she sat on the bed with the phone in the crook of her neck. "I haven't seen Brock for more than a week, Sher. I doubt the man's been home long enough to read his mail, let alone help with Abby."

"How could you not see him for a week? Aren't you living in the same house?"

"You should take a look at this place sometime. We could live here forever and not run into each other."

"What about meals and evenings?"

"He's never here. Works all the time." Mara dropped a T-shirt onto the stack. "Brock pointed out he has a lot more bills to pay these days, thanks to Abby and me."

"Ooh, what a rat. You don't suppose he's trying to turn the tables, do you? Maybe he wants to make you feel like you owe him, instead of the other way around."

"Who knows? I never think about the man."

"Ha. Are you lying just to me—or to yourself, too?"

Mara shook her head. "I'm sorry. That wasn't the truth, Sherry. I don't know why it popped out. Maybe because I don't want to think about Brock. And when I do, I sure don't know what to do about him."

Running her hand over the baby clothes, Mara admitted to herself that she thought about Brock Barnett way too much during her long, empty days. As she had studied each painting up and down every hall in his house, she wondered what about the artistry had touched him. As she had examined every stick of furniture, she imagined his hands smoothing over the hard wood, planing it and polishing it to a high, silken sheen. She'd looked through his living-room library, reading the notations he had penned in the margins and noting the titles of the books he'd obviously read more than once.

Every morning, she dressed for breakfast and wondered if she would run into him on his way to the day's labors. Every evening, she listened for the sound of his pickup pulling up to the house. At night, after nursing Abby, she wandered onto her porch and sat on the long wooden swing, where she tried to figure out why this man had possessed her thoughts.

It had to be a hormone imbalance.

"Well, just try to put Brock out of your thoughts as much as you can," Sherry said. "Abby must keep you awfully busy."

"Actually, she sleeps a lot."

"Just being around to nurse her all the time is such a responsibility, though. Don't you feel tied down?"

"That's not really the way I would describe it." Mara looked around at the huge, empty room. "I love Abby so much, and I'm thankful I can have this time with her. I feel as though I've been given a chance to rest and recover from the birth."

"But? Come on, Mara, I know you too well. What's the problem?"

"It's awfully quiet here. When Abby's sleeping, there are long spaces of time when it's just me."

"You're missing Todd, aren't you?"

Mara shut her eyes. Yes, she missed Todd, but she couldn't deny that much of that pain had eased. She didn't think about him all the time anymore. She didn't experience his loss as sharply as she once had. Should she feel guilty about that? Sometimes she did.

"I do miss Todd," she acknowledged. "I miss people."

"Why don't you come into town for church this Sunday? Everyone's been asking about you, Mara. They'd love to see the baby."

"I couldn't leave Abby in the church nursery yet. She still gets hungry too often. Besides, I don't have anything to wear that doesn't make me look like I'm still pregnant."

"Oh, Mara, I bet you look like you always have—Ms. Tooth-pick Perfection. How about if I drive out to visit you? I'd love to take a gander at that mansion of Brock's."

"It's not a mansion, Sherry. It's just a big house. A very big house." Mara let out a breath, realizing she couldn't even work up much enthusiasm to see her best friend.

"I've got some Christmas presents for Abby," Sherry said. "I could drop them off."

"Christmas? Oh great, I've hardly given that a thought. I don't suppose much will change around here. I'm married to the original Grinch, you know."

Sherry chuckled. "Maybe you should give Brock a chance. Didn't the Grinch's heart grow two sizes after he felt all that love and affection? You never can tell what might happen to Brock with you and Abby around. Be nice to him, and he might turn into Prince Charming one of these days."

"Dream on." Mara shook her head. "Why don't you come out for a visit in a week or two? Maybe by that time I'll even be able to put on a pair of jeans."

"How about Sunday afternoon? I'll give you a rundown on the sermon."

Mara laughed. It was a standing joke with Sherry that their beloved pastor—so good-hearted and genuine—was the most boring preacher in the world.

"It's a deal. See you then. Bye, Sher."

"Bye, Mar."

Mara hung up the receiver and stretched out on the bed among the piles of miniature dresses and nightgowns. She wasn't the least bit tired, and she knew Abby wouldn't wake up for a while. Of course, she couldn't leave the house, just in case Abby surprised her, but what could she do with all the empty time until dinner?

She had already walked every inch of this place. The art might be beautiful and the architecture noteworthy, but the house was a prison nonetheless. Mara felt trapped, and she could see no way out. In the midst of winter there could be no gardening, no wading in the pool, few warm days for picnics or walks with the stroller.

Indoors, things were only worse. With effort, Mara had convinced Rosa Maria to let her take on some of the laundry duties. But Pierre wouldn't dream of allowing her in the kitchen, and Ermaline refused to give up her dust rags. They had brought in a stack of jigsaw puzzles.

Mara hauled herself to her feet and crossed to the window. Brock certainly had enough to do. Once or twice she had caught sight of him from a distance. Mostly she had seen his pickup pulling in or out of the drive. If he came home in time for dinner, he ordered the meal sent to his study. If the weather was too bad to work outside, he spent the day in his workshop. Several nights while Mara was up feeding the baby, she realized his light was on. His room was directly across the courtyard from hers, but it might have been a thousand miles.

She had to find something to do or she'd go stark, raving mad. Mara thought about the old days when she had rushed here and there—teaching school all day at the academy, racing to the grocery store, throwing a meal in the oven, wolfing down dinner with her husband, poring over her students' homework or helping Todd with his research for the fort project before finally falling into bed too tired to move. What she wouldn't give for one hectic day.

How could God have given her all that and then snatched it away? Had she done something wrong to deserve this strange, quiet, empty life? On the other hand, Mara couldn't deny that God had blessed her beyond measure in the past few months. She had a healthy, contented baby. A comfortable place to live. Plenty to eat. Not a care in the world.

Wandering down the hall, she trailed her fingers along the smooth adobe wall. Was this some sort of lesson that God wanted to teach her before He let her back into real life? And if it was, why was she too dense to figure out the message?

Mara reflected on her few blissful years of marriage. She and Todd had naively believed things would go on the same way forever—the two of them together, building a future, a family and a faith that both could rely on to bolster them during the hard times. God had been so real, so ever-present. Where was He now?

Lately when Mara had tried to pray, she felt as if something was stuck in her throat. She just couldn't make herself really communicate with the Father. How could it be right to feel angry with God when He had given her this perfect child and this great place to live? Yet, she was. Mad at God. Mad at Brock. Even mad at Todd. Why had they all let her down? She had everything she needed, and the whole world felt empty and meaningless.

The fort restoration had been a task Mara and Todd had loved working on together. Though he was in charge of the project, Mara had done much of the research. Her files now lay abandoned in a box in the bedroom closet, awaiting the decision of some bureaucrats.

If Mara were forced to sell her husband's company, the buyers would be able to claim the research. Brock had assured her he was going to manage Todd's business. She realized she hadn't even asked him about the status of the company. Was it possible the project might continue?

The first tingle of enthusiasm she had felt in days ran through Mara's veins. If Brock could find a way to keep the restoration company going, find someone to take Todd's place renovating the old buildings, then Mara's work was still relevant. Instantly, she recalled a section in Brock's library devoted to the Civil War and the ensuing settlement of New Mexico. Might there be some mention of the old military forts? Of Fort Selden?

She almost ran down the hall and into the living room. The library formed one whole wall of bookshelves devoted primarily to history, archaeology and anthropology texts. Mara made straight for the section of titles she had glanced over previously.

In moments, she had loaded a stack of books in her arms, mounded a pile of sofa pillows against one wall and created a nook that would allow her hours of quiet reading before dinner. Fort Selden had been built in 1865 to protect settlers moving into the Mesilla Valley and those embarking on the Journey of the Dead into northern New Mexico. Indians had never been much of a threat in that area, so no wall surrounded the fort, but the buildings themselves were distinctive.

Mara flipped open a book and ran her finger down the index. After she dug her files and note cards out of the closet, she would use Brock's library to add to her research. Todd had always acknowledged that Mara knew more about the history of the fort than he did. His job was engineering and construction, while she provided the background details he needed to make sure the restoration was historically accurate.

"If you're going to go to the trouble of tracking me down in the middle of a cow pasture," Brock's deep voice boomed suddenly from the entry hall, "you might as well come on inside."

"It's Saturday afternoon, Brock," a woman responded lightly. "You're not supposed to be working. This is playtime, remember?"

Hidden in the shadows of her reading nook, Mara peered around the corner of the library shelving into the living area. A group of young adults—two men and three women—were following Brock into the room. Cheeks bright pink from the cold, they began shrugging out of heavy coats and tugging off leather gloves, rubbing their hands together, stamping their feet.

"It's freezing out there. Stoke up that fire, Brock." The woman who spoke was a tall, willowy redhead with copper lipstick and matching nails. She gave Brock a wink. "Do it for Sandy, won't you?"

"Anything for Sandy," he said.

Mara gripped the book as he leaned over and gave the redhead a peck on the cheek. Of all the nerve! Brock had just kissed some woman! A flash of outrage surged through Mara…but just as swiftly a drenching reality doused the flame of her anger. She had no claim on Brock. He could do whatever he wanted in his own house with his own friends.

Oh, Lord, please help me, she lifted up in silent prayer, her head against the wall and her eyes closed. This was exactly what she had dreaded. The marriage was real…but it was nothing. A slip of paper. An arrangement. A deal.

She had known Brock would want to end the marriage—and against all she believed was right and holy, she had married him anyway. What a fool she was! Mara could repent until she was blue in the face, but the deed was done. The Lord had promised to make all things work together for the good of those who loved Him…but this? This flat-out selfish thing she had done just to spare herself a hard life? How would she ever explain the marriage to her daughter? And how could she make herself let go of a relationship that didn't even exist? Why was it so hard to give Brock to these women and their friends when he didn't belong to Mara in the first place?

The worst thing possible would be to make Brock sneak around. They needed to be up front with their friends, and with each other. Let him go, Mara, she told herself. Just let him go.

Cringing in embarrassment, Mara knew she should emerge from her niche and introduce herself to these people. Though she felt foolish tucked away with her pillows and books, she debated staying put. That morning she had dressed in a pair of black stretch pants and a turquoise T-shirt that hung almost to her knees. She had bought the oversized men's shirt at the start of her pregnancy to cover the growing bulge in her stomach. The last thing she wanted was for these suave men and their svelte girlfriends to see that the bulge was still there—even though the baby wasn't.

"So are you coming with us to the party or not, Brock?" Sandy asked. "Stephanie and I have a bet riding on this. She says you won't come, and I say you will. You're not going to disappoint me, are you?"

Brock had thrown a couple of logs on the stack of kindling in the fireplace. He dusted off his hands, set them on his hips and studied the woman without answering.

Mara wondered what he would decide. Brock looked so good in the late-afternoon light, his denim shirt a little dusty and his jeans scuffed at the knees. He had taken off his hat, and she could see the glint of sun that softened his thick black hair. No wonder these women wanted him.

"Come on, Brock," Sandy said. "Don't be a party pooper." She balanced her weight on one leg, which threw her slender hip in Brock's direction. Clad in a black leather skirt, boots and a purple turtleneck, she might have stepped out of a magazine ad. She certainly hadn't had a baby two weeks ago.

"Looks to me like you've already been doing some partying tonight," Brock said, turning his attention from the redhead to her statuesque blond companion. "Stephanie, what possessed you to drive all the way out here?"

"We haven't seen your hide in six months, honey. You've become a regular hermit. When Joe and Travis cooked up the idea of dragging you away from here, I told them you wouldn't leave."

Brock shrugged. "I've been busy."

"Busy." One of the two men picked up a box of long matches and knelt by the fire. "Bunch of cows."

"Bovines," the other one hooted. "Brock, what's going on? You haven't gone this long without female company since you were five years old."

"Yeah, Brock," Sandy cooed, "you used to call me once in a while. What's up? You found someone you like better?"

Mara held her breath. Did these people have any idea what Brock had been through this past year? What kind of friends wouldn't know about the rock-climbing incident? Hadn't it occurred to them that their good buddy might have withdrawn because he was dealing with some personal difficulties? If they did know about the accident, they certainly didn't know about *her*. Mara knew she had to emerge. Shoving the books off her lap, she stood.

"Well, I have been on the go a lot," Brock was saying. "There are a few things you might not have heard about, but—"

"Excuse me, Brock," Mara spoke up. Everyone in the room turned to stare at her. She attempted to smooth the T-shirt over her stomach as she stepped into the light. "I was reading in the corner. Would you introduce me to your friends?"

Five pairs of eyes swiveled to Brock. He jammed his hands in his pockets. "Uh…this is Stephanie, Sandy and Justine's over there. This is Joe, and that's Travis." He straightened and looked at the guests. "This is Mara. My wife."

A stunned silence followed as the five pairs of eyes darted back to Mara.

"Brock!" Sandy said with a gasp. "You didn't! You got married?"

"The other day. But it's a different kind of deal than—"

"Brock married me to help take care of my baby," Mara explained.

"Baby!" Sandy's voice lifted into a near-shriek. "You have a baby?"

"Not Brock's baby," Mara said quickly. "My husband died. Brock was his best friend, and he wanted to help out. I was having some difficulties, and he offered to take care of us financially for the time being."

"You *married* this woman? Is she the wife of the guy who…" Sandy's blue eyes grew wider. "Brock, you married your best friend's wife?"

"It's a long story. Just take it at face value, Sandy. I'm a married man, so I've mostly been spending my time here. Seemed the appropriate thing to do under the circumstances."

"You don't need to stay here on my account," Mara said, crossing her arms. "I'm fine. Go and be with your friends, Brock."

"I don't believe this!" Sandy plopped onto one of Brock's long leather couches. She threw her arm over her eyes and laughed without humor. "The man is married. I can't believe it. Tell me I'm dreaming."

"Or tipsy," Brock suggested.

"It's an arrangement. It's legal, but it's not…real." Mara glanced expectantly at Brock. Instead of clarifying, he turned his back on the group and began prodding the fire with a poker.

"Brock felt responsible for me," Mara went on. "He knew I was pregnant, and I was facing some business debts my husband had incurred. The marriage is a way to provide insurance coverage and build some long-term security for Abby."

"Abby?" Sandy peered out from under her arm.

"My daughter."

"He's got a daughter."

"Abby is my daughter. Brock is her…her financial benefactor. Sort of a guardian or a godfather. Right, Brock?"

"That's what you keep telling me," he said to the fire.

She glared at his back. These people were *his* friends, not hers. Why did she feel compelled to explain his behavior?

"He likes to remind me I'm a line item on his budget," Mara said, forcing a laugh. "That ought to give you some idea of where this marriage thing stands. It's certainly fine with me if he goes out for a night on the town."

"Ooh, tension," Sandy said, sitting up. "This is sounding better. Your husband must have been that archaeology friend of Brock's. The guy who fell off the cliff."

"That 'guy' was like a brother, Sandy." Brock swung around, red-hot poker in his hand. He narrowed his eyes at the woman, then he fixed Mara with a cutting stare. "Nobody forced this on me. I offered to take care of you and the baby."

"And I thank you for that. Brock, you don't owe me anything. Especially not some misguided sense of spousal loyalty. If you want to go out with your friends, go ahead."

Mara watched his face harden as his hand knotted into a fist around the iron poker. He was angry, she knew. She had provoked him and backed him into a corner. He hated that. But what else could she have done? If he stopped spending time with his friends because of his marriage, he would resent her even more.

Though her heart begged him not to go, her mouth formed words of separation. "Go on," she said softly. "They're waiting."

Chapter Nine

✤

Jaw clenched, Brock fought the emotion that had welled up inside him the moment Mara stepped out of the shadows. Golden-haired, she stood with her arms locked protectively at her waist and her chin lifted in a gesture of defiance. She wore blue—a soft turquoise blue that made her gray-green eyes shine. Her long legs were sheathed in black. No wonder Sandy was acting so catty, he thought. Mara looked terrific.

There she stood, the sum of everything he had come to desire most, pushing him away. She didn't want him.

Mara would take his money, sure. She would live in his house and raise her baby there. But Abby was her daughter, she reminded him again and again. Both of them belonged to another man, even though he had been gone for many months. Brock wondered if those sparkling eyes would ever look at him with anything but rejection and distaste.

On the other hand, this group of men and women did want him. They wanted to laugh at his jokes. They wanted his social status to enhance their own at parties and gatherings. They enjoyed his tales of adventure, his daredevil stunts, his free-wheeling joyride through life.

And the women. They made no effort to conceal their interest in him. He could have Sandy on his arm whenever he chose. Same with Stephanie. And quiet Justine was biding her time, giving him little hints that she, too, would appreciate his attention.

Joe and Travis didn't mind. They were used to Brock and his women. Theirs was a sort of trade-around group—young professionals searching for the right person to marry eventually, and trying out everyone else in the meantime.

It had been fun.

Sort of.

Brock tossed the poker onto the hearth. Metal clanged against stone, an echoing sound magnified in the awkward silence. He looked at Mara. Then he looked at his friends. For some odd reason, the choice was simple.

"I believe I'll stick around here," he said in a low voice. "Keep the home fires burning."

Joe chuckled as the others headed for the foyer. "Well, Mrs. Barnett—sorry, I forgot your first name—you take care of ol' Brock for us."

Slapping Brock on the back as he passed through the doorway, Joe shook his head. "I've got to admit, Brock, you've pulled off some strange stunts in your time. But marrying your best friend's pregnant widow? This has got to take the cake."

"Later, Joe." Brock leaned against the door frame as the visitors strolled to their cars.

"I thought bungee-jumping off that bridge was pretty wild," said Travis, the last one out. He leaned toward Brock. "Your new bride's a looker, though. You might as well get some mileage out of your marriage license, pal."

"Get out of here, Travis," Brock said, giving his friend a shove.

Travis laughed and waved. "See ya later, Daddy Barnett."

Brock shut the door and stared at the beveled wood for a moment. Had he really liked those people? He knew he had. Once, there had been little better than a roomful of good-looking women, tough-talking men, liquor and loud music. Beer bashes, cocktail parties. Nightclubs, dance halls, bars. Sandy, Stephanie, Suzy, Sheila. He'd been caught up in that life. Now, he couldn't even remember why.

As he turned back to the living room, Brock had the sensation that he'd been a hollow man. He had grown up with an absent mother, a father who was always distant, and nothing to fill in the emptiness. So he had spent his time and money on thrill sports, taunting fate as he tested the limits of his own strength. And he had used those people who were driving away from his house. He had plugged up the hole in his heart with everything they could offer.

Brock had run them off tonight, but the truth was he still felt hollow. Instead of partying, he was filling his emptiness with work. Branding, roping, breeding, rounding up. Cows. Bovines.

Shaking his head, he recalled how Todd had tried to talk sense into his best friend. During childhood, the schoolmates had spent their time dreaming up adventures and exploring the New Mexico countryside. But when they were teenagers, Todd had pulled away from Brock's fascination with powerful cars, fast girls and alcohol. Warning his boyhood companion about the emptiness of such pursuits, Todd had advocated seeking fulfillment in a purer, more godly way.

His lifestyle had reflected that. He worked as a grocery stocker, went to church and eventually began dating Mara. Brock stayed up all night, slept during the day and partied hard. Whenever the two got together, they quickly resumed their familiar, easygoing friendship. But Todd was disappointed in Brock's choices, and he let Brock know it.

Brock didn't listen, of course. He assured Todd he was having too much fun. Three different times—each of which Brock clearly recalled—Todd had sat Brock down and talked about the important place Christianity ought to hold in a man's life. Brock remembered his friend's warnings and the hammered refrain, "You've got to make a choice, Brock. You have to make a decision to get off the road you're on and turn to Christ. Give him your life. Surrender."

Brock had laughed at the idea of ever giving up control of his destiny. Surrender? You're kidding! Give up parties in favor of church? No way.

But Todd had been right, as he usually was. Brock's pursuits had left him empty. And his current efforts to fill the hole in his life weren't turning out much better. He wondered if things would ever change.

As he entered the living room, he spotted Mara standing next to the blazing fire, her arms still crossed and her mouth set in a rigid line.

"Why didn't you go with them?" she asked without looking at him.

"I didn't want to."

"Why not?"

"Work."

She let out a sigh of exasperation. "You could take one evening off to go to their party."

"Look, no way am I going to drive to some shindig in Las Cruces. First, I have a sick cow to take care of. She's down in the barn, and I have to check on her every hour or so tonight. And second, I'm your husband, and people are beginning to find that out. If I go to a party with Sandy or someone draped around my neck, that's not going to look too great, is it?"

Mara swallowed. "I don't want your misguided chivalry, Brock," she told him, her voice hard. "You may be my husband, but I know better than to expect loyalty or celibacy from you."

"You don't know a thing about me."

"I heard the way your friends talked. You're not exactly known for long-term relationships."

"Yeah, but I've never been married till now."

"Oh, come on, Brock!" Mara twisted the wedding band Todd had given her. "We're not really married, and you know it."

"Are you trying to tell me you want out of this thing?"

"I'm telling you I don't want you to feel trapped."

"If I'm trapped, you're trapped, too. We're in it together, Mara, and it's a lot more tangled than I thought it'd be."

"Whose fault is that? Are you implying I tricked you into this marriage?"

"I said we're both caught. We chose it."

Mara stared into his eyes. "You offered me a way out of one deep hole. Sometimes I feel like I fell right into another one."

"What kind of a hole are you in, Mara?"

"This crazy marriage." She swung her arms out. "We obviously don't love each other."

"Don't we?"

"Well, no." Staring at him, her breath went shallow. "Of course not."

"So, I'm trapped in this crazy, loveless marriage, which keeps me from going out to parties with Sandy and her pals. Big loss. What's it keeping you from?"

Brock walked toward her, his hands at his sides and his eyes fastened on hers. He had felt this way before. Consuming. He wanted to devour Mara, and against all reason he suddenly believed she wanted him to.

He saw the wariness in her eyes. And the desire. If he tore down her walls, he could destroy her. And she could destroy him, too.

"This marriage is keeping me a prisoner," she said, taking a step backward.

"How?"

"This house."

"You can walk out of here any time. Take your baby and go. You've told me I'm useless to you. I'll never be Abby's father."

"Todd is her father."

He stopped a foot away and leaned toward her. "Todd is your prison, not this marriage. Look at the ring on your hand. You're still married to him, aren't you?"

"Yes," Mara whispered.

"You made a lifetime commitment to a man who died a long time ago."

"It's only been six months."

"Seven."

"So what? It doesn't matter how many months have gone by. He's still my husband."

"Todd isn't coming back, Mara."

"I know!" Her eyes filled with tears.

"Mara." He reached out a hand to her. "I'm sorry." He hadn't meant to hurt her. His words were the message he had told himself again and again. Todd wasn't coming back. Todd was gone. And it was Brock's fault. Now he had thrown those words at Mara and hurt her all over again.

"You're as committed to Todd as I am," she retorted. "You're just as bound and imprisoned by his memory. You married me out of some misguided sense of obligation."

"And I'll never break that vow."

"What do you mean?"

Brock turned aside and walked past her to the fire. As he knelt on the hearth and stared into the licking flames, he wondered what was happening to him. Had he turned his back on his friends to spend a lifetime with a woman he could never touch? Had he given up a life of freedom and pleasure for this? The anger, the resentment, the constant guilt… Yes, Brock concluded. Because it was the only way to pay for what he had done.

"Todd," he said to the fire, and he realized the word had somehow changed in meaning for him. "I'm loyal to Todd. It's because of him that I'll never break my vow to you."

"Todd is gone," Mara whispered behind him. "You keep telling me that."

"I know."

"How long can you honor a promise to a dead man?"

Brock slammed his hands on his thighs as he swung around and stood to face her. "How long, Mara? You tell me."

"I don't know!"

"I don't know, either."

They stared at each other, neither daring to move. Brock could hear the blood hammering in his temples. How could this have happened? How could he be standing a breath away, willing her to be the first to break the barrier between them?

If she said one word. If she reached out to him. If she touched him. Everything would collapse, and he would take her straight into his arms.

"Abby's probably hungry," she said in a low voice. "I'm going now. I don't want to talk to you anymore."

He caught her arm. "Mara, believe one thing. I didn't let Todd fall off that cliff. It was an accident."

"Don't!" She tried to break away, but his fingers closed tighter around her wrist. He couldn't release her. Not yet.

"If you won't hear me out, you'll never let it go, Mara. You'll never be able to forgive me."

"I'm not sure I want to forgive you."

"Because you would have to admit I'm not all bad? You'd have to see some of what Todd saw in me. If you forgave me, you would know me."

"Do those buddies of yours know you?" She shook her head. "I don't think anyone really knows you, Brock. I'm not sure you know yourself."

He dropped her arm. "Todd knew me."

"Maybe." Mara faced him, her eyes narrowing. "But I don't want to know you."

He nodded, bitterness in his mouth. "You want to nurture your pain like that little baby you keep hidden away in the back room. You know I loved Todd. You know I'd never hurt him. He fell off that cliff, and I did everything I could to save him, but he—"

"Stop talking about it!"

"You're going to hold on to your bitterness and nurse it every day of your life until it grows big enough to eat you alive."

"Why do you care what I do?" she exploded. "What difference does it make? What do you want from me?"

He grabbed her and jerked her against him. "I want…I want…" With every ounce of strength he could summon, he fought the need to embrace her.

"Brock," she gasped.

"Go feed your baby." He set her aside and turned his back. "I've got a sick cow."

He strode across the living room and through the foyer. He flung the front door open so hard it banged against the wall before slamming behind him. In a moment, his pickup roared to life and gravel crunched beneath its wheels as it blasted down the driveway.

Brock glanced at the old grandfather clock on his way down the hall to his bedroom. A little past one in the morning. He felt dead on his feet, but he was hungry enough to eat his own horse. Tending the ailing cow all evening, he'd missed supper, drunk nothing but black coffee and shot his nerves to shreds.

At least the animal had pulled through. She must have eaten some kind of noxious weed. With the onset of winter, the good grass had died back, and the cattle sometimes poked their noses where they shouldn't. This cow had been a good breeder, often giving birth to twins, and Brock sure didn't want to lose her. He had hauled her down from the pasture and tended her until she'd passed the poison.

Though he was no veterinarian, he had learned how to handle most livestock ailments, and he kept a good supply of medicines on hand. Now the animal was in the foreman's care, and she should be back on her feet by morning. Pedro Chavez cared as much about the ranch as Brock did, and Pedro never balked at being roused from his sleep after midnight.

After tossing his hat on his bed, Brock raked his fingers through his hair and gave a long stretch. His back ached from bending over for hours without a break. His muscles felt as though they'd been tied in knots. At least he hadn't had time to think much about Mara.

Unwilling to permit even her name to slip into his mind, he stripped off his shirt, tugged the tail of his thermal undershirt out of his jeans' waistband and rubbed a hand across his flat belly. Empty. But he'd better take a shower before he ate. He started to unbuckle his belt, and his stomach gave a loud rumble.

On second thought, the shower could wait another fifteen minutes, while his appetite couldn't. Still in his boots and jeans,

Brock walked silently down the darkened hall to the kitchen. He flipped on a low light over the stove and opened the refrigerator as he wondered if he would find anything besides Pierre's sauces, marinades and fresh vegetables. A thick roast beef sandwich and a couple of dill pickles would sure hit the spot.

Opening a few plastic-lidded boxes, he located some cheese, chicken breasts and carrots. He set them on the counter and pondered the usual absence of mayonnaise in the house. Pierre disliked store-bought mayonnaise even though Brock had complained that it was hard to make a decent sandwich without the stuff.

As usual, butter would have to do. There was never any sliced white bread, either, but Pierre's famous rolls usually could be found in the pantry.

Brock was crossing the kitchen toward the smaller room when he spotted a shadow moving slowly across the courtyard outside. He stopped in his tracks and studied the ephemeral shape.

Blinking, he wondered if he had imagined the movement. Two strides took him to the window. He leaned across the sink and peered into the darkness. In the moonless night, a shrouded, bulky figure vanished behind a thicket of shrubbery.

Brock frowned. In all his years on the ranch, he'd never had a thief. But everyone who worked for him knew payday was getting close, and Christmas bonuses already were stashed in the house's safe. Any familiarity with Brock's habits would tell a potential burglar that the master of the house was often away and inner doors were never locked. The courtyard wall was an easy climb. Too easy.

Brock slipped down the length of the counter and opened a cabinet door. Sliding across the top shelf, his fingers found the cool, slick steel of a pistol. He brought the weapon to chest level and checked the chamber. Loaded.

His heart thudding in his chest, he snagged a sheepskin coat from the hook by the door and pulled it on. Gun in one hand, he turned the doorknob with the other. The hinges barely creaked as he eased the door open. Hugging the wall, Brock edged out into the darkness.

"Hush little baby, don't say a word," Mara's voice sang softly, "Mama's gonna buy you a mockingbird."

Great, Brock thought. His thief was a tired mother with a fussy baby. He let out his breath as Mara emerged along the starlit path, her hair hanging loose around her shoulders and a whimpering Abby nestled in her arms.

"And if that mockingbird won't sing," she went on, her voice a little quivery, "Mama's gonna buy you a diamond ring."

She strolled past Brock, unaware that he stood a few steps away in the shadows, his gun now in his coat pocket and his eyes following her. He could see the round, pale curve of Abby's head tucked in the crook of her mother's elbow. How long had it been since he'd laid eyes on the baby? Mara had kept her daughter away from him ever since they'd come out to the ranch. Brock tried to swallow the ache that tightened in his throat as he recalled the moment the doctor had placed the tiny bundle in his arms.

Two weeks ago, he'd have done anything for Abby. Now he could hardly remember how she looked. In the hospital, he had watched the baby being carried in and out through Mara's door. Half the time, he had wheeled her bassinet down the hall himself. As she lay in the small plastic cart, he had studied Abby's petal-pink skin and wispy eyelashes. He had brushed a fingertip over her rosebud mouth. But once inside his own home, Abby had been kept from him. She was Mara's daughter. Todd's baby.

As Mara hummed her way around the courtyard, Brock gritted his teeth. In spite of his good intentions, had he made a terrible mistake bringing the two of them into his house? Had he given up what little pleasure he had in life for a woman who was bitter and unforgiving? If it weren't for Todd, he never would have married someone like Mara. He never would have married at all. Period.

Did he resent Todd? Maybe. But how could he be angry at a man for dying?

Once again, the memory of that afternoon on the cliffs at Hueco Tanks clicked on in Brock's mind. Though he knew he had done all he could to save his friend's life, he blamed himself as much as Mara did. Todd had never been the natural athlete Brock was, and he had neither studied as much about rock-climbing nor practiced as often as his friend. Todd had trusted Brock to keep him safe on the cliffs—and, as always, Brock had trusted himself. But Brock had failed. Todd was dead…and the angry Mara would make him pay any way she could.

"And if that billy goat won't…" she sang tiredly, pausing to search for the words to the lullaby. "And if that billy goat won't…eat, Mama's gonna buy you a…piece of meat."

She was making up the song. The edges of her nubby pink robe drifted around her slippered feet as she padded back and forth, back and forth, swaying Abby to the rhythm of her foot-steps. Her breath made little puffs of steam in the crisp night air.

"And if that piece of meat won't…cook," she went on in a low, almost tuneless voice, "Mama's gonna buy you a crochet hook. And if that crochet hook…gets bent, Mama's gonna buy you a canvas tent."

At the inane words to her song, Brock fought the grin that tickled the corners of his mouth. He definitely resented Mara and her self-righteous intolerance, but at the same time he was drawn to her. He knew he needed her forgiveness; he sensed that he needed more than that from this woman who somehow had become his wife.

"And if that canvas tent falls down, Mama's gonna buy you a wedding gown." She was over by the swimming pool now, walking past the empty, covered hole. Rocking Abby, she gazed into her baby's face as she sang.

What did Brock truly want from Mara? Acceptance? Peace? At this point he would gladly accept the barest smile.

"And if that wedding gown…" Mara stopped singing, stopped walking, stopped rocking. Her voice trembled as she went on. "If that wedding gown falls apart, Mama's gonna mend your bro-ken heart. And if your broken heart won't…stop hurting…"

Brock watched her from a distance. She stood like a statue at the edge of the pool. The baby had calmed down, and Mara let out a deep, lingering breath.

"Oh, Abby," she said softly.

Brock recognized the tone in her voice. She had said the same thing to him. *Oh, Brock.* But what did Mara want? What could he give her? Never in his life had he felt such a tangle of emotions.

"Let's go back inside," she said softly.

She started toward her room, and Brock stepped out from the wall. In less than a minute, Mara would be gone. He wouldn't see Abby again for days, maybe weeks. Hard telling when he would even catch a glimpse of Mara. But he had to let her go. He had no right to her.

Just as Mara pushed open her door, Abby let out a loud wail.

"Oh, no." Mara stopped and leaned her head against the door frame. "Not again, Abby. Please, I'm so…so tired."

She clutched the sobbing baby to her breast and lifted her eyes to the sky. Clearly frustrated and teetering at the edge of exhaustion, she swallowed back tears. Brock studied her, his own impulse to help manacled and impotent. With Abby howling at the top of her tiny lungs, Mara turned into the darkness of her suite and shut the door behind her.

Brock leaned back against the chilly wall and listened to the sounds of a baby crying and a mother attempting to sing once again. In the darkness, his stomach grumbled loudly, and he recalled the makings of his chicken dinner spread out on the kitchen table. He had been on his way to fetch a roll. Definitely, he was hungry. Too hungry to be walking across the courtyard toward Mara's door. He should head for the kitchen, eat his sandwich, take his shower. He sure shouldn't knock on her door.

"Brock?" Still holding Abby, Mara peered through the slit between the open door and the frame. "Is that you?"

Chapter Ten

❧

"I heard the baby," Brock said. He couldn't believe what he had just done. Two minutes ago, he had been hungry and tired. Two minutes ago, he had been determined to stay as far from Mara as possible. Now he was struggling to keep from lifting her into his arms and comforting her.

"Is Abby okay?" he asked.

"I don't know," Mara said over Abby's wails. Brock could barely hear her. "I can't get her to sleep."

"Maybe she's hungry."

"No, it's not that. I just nursed her. I've changed her diaper, burped her, checked her temperature, everything I can think of. I can't understand why she won't sleep."

They both looked down at the subject herself. The baby's tiny fists pumped the air, now and then batting her mother. Her little feet churned inside the white crocheted blanket. Cheeks bright red, her head was thrown back against Mara's arm as though she desperately wanted to escape but couldn't.

"She's raising quite a ruckus," Brock said.

"What?" Mara asked above the cries.

"She's loud."

The gray-green eyes lifted to his face, and Brock could see they were awash in tears. "I'm sorry she bothered you. I'd better try rocking her again."

Mara turned to go, but Brock touched her arm. "Let me."

Before he had thought through a plan of action and its consequences, he found himself ushering Mara back into the sitting room that was a part of her suite, switching on a low lamp and guiding her onto a nearby recliner. Then he took the squalling bundle from her arms and gave her a valiant grin.

"You get some rest."

"Are you sure?"

"Yes. You need it."

Spotting the rocker, Brock headed for it. Mara must have moved the chair from the nursery into this small living area so she could enjoy the sunny view as she rocked Abby. The two of them spent so many hours together, while he saw little or nothing of either one.

Brock could hardly believe he was actually holding this baby who had changed his life so dramatically. In his arms, Abby was almost weightless, her small, rounded body nestling easily against the soft contours of his sheepskin coat. Weightless, maybe, but noisy as all get-out. The kid could raise the rafters.

Brock glanced at Mara, who had collapsed onto the recliner in a heap, then he shrugged out of his jacket and kicked off his dusty boots. Gathering the baby closer to him, he eased his large frame down into the chair. Abby was a mess of rumpled blankets and twisted nightgown, so he peeled her out of everything that would come off. Then he laid her against his chest, pressed her little round head against the warmth of his body, and began to rock gently.

"Now then, no need to cry," he murmured. As he rocked, Brock leaned his head back against the chair and shut his eyes. Abby's wails gradually mellowed into whimpers. Her tiny fingers clutched the fabric of his thermal undershirt, and her nose nestled against his chest. She sure was little. He figured he could easily hold her in one hand.

Lowering his head, he drank in the scent of her downy hair. Baby shampoo and talcum powder. Something tugged at his heart, and he swallowed against the tide of emotion. He brushed the baby's forehead with his lips and let out a deep breath.

"You planning to sleep sometime tonight, girl?" he whispered. "Don't you know you've about worn your mama plumb out? I was on my way for a sandwich and a warm shower, myself. But you decide to set up a holler and everybody comes running, don't they?"

He studied the diminutive face. Abby was perfect. From her soft eyes to her small nose to her bowed lips, she was the image of her beautiful mother. Even her ears fit against her head like tiny seashells. Again, he kissed her, and this time her fussy cries wound down into a sigh. "This is what we call nighttime, Abby," he murmured against her shoulder. "It's dark outside the window, see? The stars are hanging in the sky. The moon's tucked away. Even the coyotes have gone to bed. Sleep now, baby. That's my girl."

As Abby fell silent, Brock lifted his feet onto the footrest of Mara's recliner and stretched out his long, tired legs. The creak of the rocker was replaced by the whisper of winter wind against the window pane. In the quiet, Brock let his eyes drift shut and his cheek settle against the top of the baby's head.

"And if your broken heart's too deep," Mara's soft voice filtered through the cobwebs of sleep gathering in his brain, "Papa's gonna come and rock you to sleep."

Brock opened his eyes. From the recliner, Mara was watching him. She lifted her bare foot and touched the tip of her toe to the end of his sock.

"And if my baby girl goes to sleep," she murmured, "I think she might have found her a man to keep."

She broke into a smile that lit the room like sunrise on a summer morning. Brock stared back at her and puzzled over the words she had sung.

"Mara," he whispered. "What do you—"

"Shh." She held one finger to her lips and glanced at Abby. "Good night, Brock."

When Mara opened her eyes the next morning, she realized it was the first time since they'd left the hospital that she had not awakened to the sound of a baby. In fact, there was no sound at all in the room, nothing but the chatter of birds and the rustle of bare branches in the courtyard outside. Sunshine lay like a pool of melted butter on the tile floor. A slice of cloudless blue sky peeped through the open curtains. An old, beat-up sheepskin jacket hung over the arm of the empty rocker.

Empty! Mara sat up on the recliner where she had spent the night. Where was Abby? Where was Brock? She swung her legs to the floor and sat for a minute, breathing hard. Oh, no—Abby hadn't nursed since midnight!

Mara retied the belt of her chenille robe as she padded across the floor. She jerked open the door to the nursery and hurried to the crib. Empty. Brushing a hand over her forehead, she tried to think. It had been a difficult night—Abby restless and whiny, Mara tired and sore—until Brock had showed up at their door.

The last thing Mara had seen before falling into an exhausted sleep was her daughter snuggled in Brock's arms. Brock must have her now. Mara walked down the hall, her throat tightening with worry. Brock had witnessed Abby's birth, but he knew nothing about babies. He'd held Abby only once or twice. What if he dropped her? What if he spilled something on her? What if he laid her down on a couch or a kitchen counter and she rolled off? If she landed on the hard tile floor—

"Once you get your teeth," Brock's distinctively deep voice said from the kitchen, "you'll be eating eggs and bacon for breakfast."

Mara came to a sudden stop in the doorway. With Abby neatly tucked like a football in one arm, Brock was stirring a batch of scrambled eggs with his free hand.

"Now, don't frown at me, girl," he said to the baby. Oblivious to the observing woman, he poured the egg mixture into a hot skillet on the stove and returned his attention to Abby. "You can have some milk, too, when you get bigger. But you'll drink it out of a cup, and it'll be cow's milk. Cows are what we do here on the ranch, so you'll have to learn to drink big glasses of milk and chow down on prime rib. Mmm-mmm. Good stuff. That is, if we can get Pierre to leave us alone in the kitchen for a few hours so we can cook together."

Mara stared at the broad expanse of Brock's chest and Abby's pink cheek snuggled comfortably against his thermal undershirt. As he tended to his breakfast, the man looked as though he'd spent his whole life with a baby wedged in the crook of his arm. One-handed, he salted and peppered his steaming eggs. He stepped to the refrigerator and took out two jars of jelly. Next he opened the oven door and set a couple of croissants onto the rack.

"You'll have to get used to French grub," he said to the baby. "But when you get really hungry, we'll sneak out to the bunkhouse and chow down with the men."

"Wuh," Abby said.

"I know just what you mean," Brock concurred. "Let me tell you about my foreman, Pedro Chavez. Now, he can cook enchiladas like nobody's business. Brings tortillas from home that his wife makes on weekends. And Nick Jefferson is our steak man. Loads us down with T-bones, baked beans and biscuits."

From the open doorway, Mara watched as Brock set a plate, silverware and napkin on the kitchen work table. Humming softly, he got a mug from the shelf.

"You know, for such a pretty little girl, you're smelling mighty whiffy," he told Abby as he walked toward the coffeemaker. "I reckon you may be due for a new diaper."

"Uh-behhh," Abby burbled.

"I'll tell you what. If you'll hang on till after breakfast, I'll do what I can to clean you up. Maybe between the two of us we can figure out what it is your mama does to keep you feeling bright-eyed and bushy-tailed."

He reached for the coffeepot and held it over the mug, which sat on the counter only an inch from Abby's tiny bare leg. As the steaming black liquid splashed into the cup, Mara gasped. Brock swung around.

"Whoa. You just about scared me and Abby out of our britches. 'Course, Abby needs to change her britches anyhow." He gave her a broad grin. "Coffee?"

"I was afraid you might spill it." Mara shoved her hands deep into the pockets of her robe as she walked toward Brock. "I'd love some. But let me pour."

"Don't trust me?"

"Not too much." She took down another mug and filled them both with hot black coffee. "But more today than I did yesterday."

"Keep that up and you might start to like me."

"I like what you've done for us." She set the mugs on the table and leaned toward him. "Brock, thank you for helping me last night. I haven't slept that many hours in a row since Abby was born."

"You were wrung out. I tell you what," he said, studying the baby in his arms, "I never knew someone who weighed less than ten pounds could wiggle like a rattler on a hot skillet, raise the roof with her hollering and odor up an entire kitchen."

Mara had to laugh. "I'd better change her."

"I thought I'd give it a shot, but I wasn't sure what kind of a surprise I'd find when I opened the package."

"Not a pretty one, I can promise you that."

He held Abby at arms' length and peered into her tiny face. "You leak, you drool, you squall, you mess your britches and you keep people awake half the night. What do you have to say for yourself, young lady?"

"Bah," Abby gurgled.

Brock laughed out loud. Hugging her close, he planted a kiss on top of her head. "Yeah, you'd steal my heart, wouldn't you? Go on, now, your mama's waiting."

He placed the damp little bundle in Mara's arms. "When you're done, come back and have some breakfast," he said. "Pierre's off on Sunday, so we're on our own."

Mara snuggled her daughter, aware of the tiny lips rooting against her neck. "Abby's hungry, too. You go ahead with your breakfast. I'll nurse her, and then I'll fix something later."

"No point in that." He grabbed a chair and pulled it back from the table. "Feed her in here. Might as well all eat together."

Mara stared at him as he sat down, leaned back in his chair and cocked his hands behind his head. His smile was as broad as all New Mexico. "I was there when they showed you how, remember?" he said. "Go on, now. I'll keep the eggs warm."

Carrying her fragrant little bundle, Mara strolled down the hall. Abby whimpered, as if dismayed at the feel of chenille robe against her cheek instead of a male chest. Mara frowned.

"You like him, don't you?" she whispered. "Scamp. I heard you cooing and gurgling over that man. You just wrapped him right around your little finger."

Mara carried Abby into the nursery and quickly changed her diaper. A strange sense of satisfaction came over her as she realized how easy the task had become. She could bathe, diaper, nurse, rock, burp and sing lullabies like a pro. In fact, in the last couple of weeks she had become a fairly competent mother.

"So, the cowboy wants to have breakfast with you, does he?" she said, hefting Abby in her arms. "All right then. Here we go."

As Mara walked toward the dining room, she thought of the man who waited there. She recalled Rosa Maria's statement about Brock. *After spending time with your husband,* she had told Mara, *Mr. Barnett always relaxed. He would be happy. He would lean back in his chair and put his feet on the table.*

Relaxed. Happy. This was a man she could tolerate a lot better than the driven perfectionist she had always known. What had calmed Brock? Was it Sunday, a quiet house and a sunny December morning? Was it Abby and her soothing, snuggling acceptance? Or did Mara herself have something to do with mellowing the man? For some odd reason, she hoped she had played a part.

As she stepped into the kitchen, Mara again knew a sense of betrayal. The picture was all wrong. It should be Todd, his wife and their baby gathering in the little apartment kitchen. They should sit around their dinette, talking and laughing in the comfortable way they had together. A family.

She walked toward Brock, suddenly overwhelmed with the guile in her heart. How could she actually look forward to spending time with this man? How could it be fair that he and not Todd held Abby and rocked her to sleep? Worst of all…how could Mara be feeling the wayward emotions she felt every time she was in Brock's presence?

All the hours she had invested in trying to pray away her guilt—repent of her reckless marriage and make atonement to God—and here she was actually enjoying Brock Barnett. She had begged for the Lord to show her His will and to make something good of the knotted mess she was laying at His feet. Everything in her brain pointed her away from Brock. But her heart…oh, it was willful…

"Hey there," Brock said, looking up at her. In worn and slightly wrinkled jeans, his long legs stretched across the expanse from chair to table. His feet were comfortably crossed at the ankles and propped on the table.

"You'll never guess what just skedaddled past the window there," he said.

Uncomfortable at being drawn into an easy banter with him, Mara settled on the edge of her chair. She tucked Abby close and fought the swirl of tingles that swept down her spine as she looked into Brock's brown eyes.

"A roadrunner," he said. "A chaparral bird. Ran right through the courtyard. Never seen one this close to the house."

Tearing her focus from his face, Mara searched the walled enclosure for the fabled bird, but it had vanished. "Maybe it was hungry."

"I don't know about the roadrunner, but I know about me." Brock set his feet on the floor, stood and headed for the stove. In moments, he had served up two plates of scrambled eggs, bacon, warm croissants, farm butter and jelly. He refilled Mara's coffee mug.

As he sat down and reached for the pepper grinder, Mara draped a cloth diaper over her shoulder to cover Abby's head. Beneath it, she pushed back her robe and Abby quickly began to nurse.

At the sound of the baby's loud, satisfied gulps, Mara flushed a bright pink as she lifted her eyes to Brock. He was grinning. "Reckon we can pray over that little barracuda?" he asked, holding out a hand toward Mara.

"Oh, Brock, really?"

"I decided you had a point about praying before meals, Mara. I wasn't brought up in the church, and I'm not too sure about my doctrines and theologies, but that doesn't mean I'm not grateful for what I've been given."

Mara shut her eyes for a moment, elated at the promise that somehow God was touching Brock's life…and stricken with guilt at her eagerness to take his hand. It wouldn't be right to feel euphoric about any man so soon after her husband's death. It was doubly wrong to be melting inside over Brock Barnett. He had been Todd's best friend. That made her attraction to him seem so wrong. And worse, Brock was the one who had led Todd up those cliffs.

She planted her hand firmly in her lap and twisted her wedding band around and around. "Brock, I don't think—"

"There's been an empty place inside me, Mara," he said, his hand still outstretched. "I got to thinking about it after the crowd from Las Cruces dropped by."

"Empty?"

"There's a hollowness that's built into everybody. It's uncomfortable, so you try to fill it up. I used to think I could fix things by partying, until I realized what a waste of time that is. Then I started trying to work it out of my system by putting in eighteen-hour days on the ranch. That's not going too well, either. Then you mentioned how you and Todd used to pray together, and I remembered that about him. After he became a Christian, Todd had a peace I sure envied."

Mara looked down at Abby and let out a breath. Maybe it wasn't as wrong as she thought to be friends with the same man her husband had loved so deeply. "Todd's faith filled in the hollowness in his life," she acknowledged. "He had a deep, personal relationship with Jesus."

Brock nodded. "And with you, Mara."

She searched his eyes, trying to read the message in their brown depths. Did he understand what she felt? Did he want the same things she was beginning to want? Slowly she unknotted her fist and stretched out her hand. Brock's warm fingers closed around hers, covering the gold band she wore. He cleared his throat, and she gave his hand a slight squeeze.

"Dear God," Mara said softly, "thank you for a good night's sleep. Please bless this food to the nourishment of our bodies… Thank you for Abby and…and for Brock…and teach me how to forgive. In Jesus' name I pray, amen."

"Amen." Brock glanced at her. Continuing to hold her hand, he picked up his fork. "Forgiveness. That's hard work."

Realizing she was immobilized—one arm wrapped around Abby and her free hand clasped firmly in Brock's—Mara watched him chew a bite of breakfast. At the sight, tenderness filled her heart, and she went completely helpless inside.

"I don't know how to forgive," he said. "Never have figured it out in all these years."

Mara studied their clasped hands, aware that his fingers were tanned and hard against her soft pale skin. She remembered how their fingers had been entwined during her labor, and how she had stared at them, loving them. She wanted his hand to touch more than her fingers. More than her arm. All he had done in the past two weeks was grab her, shake her, propel her here or there. But she craved those brown hands on her neck, rubbing her shoulders, massaging her back.

Oh, no. This was not good.

"My mom, for instance." Brock pointed his fork out the window, as though his mother were standing in the courtyard. "She left my dad when I was a little boy. Just up and headed East. It was like I'd never been born. I watch you and Abby, and I wonder how she could do that to me. How do you forgive that?"

Mara focused on the man who was speaking and realized how poorly she had been concentrating on his words. He had been baring his soul in a completely uncharacteristic flow of confession.

"I don't know," she said honestly. "I haven't had much to forgive in my life."

"Until recently."

She looked down at her plate. "It is hard to let go of things that are embedded so deeply inside. Things that have changed your life."

"If forgiving is the same thing as forgetting, I can't do it. My dad wasn't a whole lot better. He did stay in my life, but I might as well have been invisible around the house. For most of my life, I've treated people the way he treated me. I see most folks as pesky flies buzzing around my head. You tolerate them as long as you can, then swat them back if they get too close."

"You never treated Todd that way."

"Todd." Brock took a sip of coffee. "He was different."

Mara studied her plate, unwilling to remove her hand from Brock's grasp. "Todd would have wanted me to forgive you," she whispered.

His eyes darted to hers. "Do you think so?"

"I know so. But I don't know how."

"You could start by letting me tell you what happened on the cliffs."

She shrugged away from the offer, unable and unwilling to return to that place of pain. "It doesn't matter what happened up there," she told him. "What I can't seem to forgive is the fact that you asked him to go."

"And I was responsible for him."

Mara bit her lower lip. "Please, Brock, I don't want to talk about it."

"All right."

"Does it really matter if I never completely get past this?" She asked the question, knowing the answer but hoping he might somehow excuse her hardheartedness. And yet, why couldn't she let go of this thing that felt like a fishhook she had swallowed? Did she actually cherish her hurt? Was she even now nurturing her own pain?

"Sure it matters that you get past this." Brock set his mug on the table and leaned toward her. "If Todd would want you to forgive me, then it matters. You owe that to his memory. Plus, it matters to me."

"Why?"

"Because I don't want to see you turn bitter. Bitterness will eat you up, Mara. It'll make you hard and gruff and cold. It'll turn people away. It'll hurt Abby and everyone you let get close to you. Look at me. Hey, am I the kind of warm, loving guy a woman would want to spend the rest of her life with? Am I your basic family man—a wife, two kids and a dog? The truth is, you don't hold on to bitterness. It holds on to you."

Mara studied the cynical tilt to Brock's mouth and realized how deeply his parents' rejection had cut him. It was his own swallowed fishhook. Had he become too hard to give and receive love? She ran her eyes down his shoulders and gazed at his chest for a minute. Did it matter what kind of man he really was, when he could have anything he wanted? When he could have Mara herself...if she weren't careful.

Yes, it did matter.

"I watched you with Abby this morning," she said, absently rubbing her thumb against the side of his finger. "You may be hurt and you may be bitter, Brock, but you're not cold. You loved Todd. Your household staff adores you. And you cooked breakfast with my daughter in your arms. Maybe you are a family man by nature."

His fingers tightened on hers as he struggled to control an emotion she had never seen in his eyes. He swallowed hard. "You suppose?"

"Well, why not?"

He studied her plate for a minute. "You're not eating."

"I can't," she replied, nodding toward their clenched hands.

"Great." He pulled his hand away, swept up her plate and strode to the microwave oven. "I'll zap these eggs for you. They aren't half bad. Then I need to check on that cow. What would you say to a drive around the ranch?"

Mara glanced at him. He was studiously watching the plate revolve in the oven. She wasn't sure why he had opened up to her. But she was intrigued.

"Can I bring Abby?" she asked.

He turned, and the smile on his face warmed her soul. "You bet."

Chapter Eleven

✤

The ranch on the western plains beneath the San Andres Mountains welcomed Mara like the mother she had never known. As Brock's pickup sped down long, dusty roads, she felt warm arms enfold her. Dry grass, old mesquite and gnarled juniper decorated an arid landscape that felt more like home to her than any house she had lived in. The nip of crisp mountain breeze against her cheeks nurtured her as profoundly as did the up-and-down warble of meadowlarks and the coo of doves. Yuccas pointed toward the turquoise sky and the pale yellow sun.

Mara gazed at her own child, tucked safely in the car seat, eyes closed in peaceful slumber. No bigger than a pearl, Abby's nose drank in the clean New Mexico air as her tiny chest rose and fell. Layered beneath a pile of flannel blankets, quilts and crocheted afghans, her infant tummy was warmly filled with nourishing mother's milk. Little hands, curled like miniature sweet rolls, were nestled against her chin. A few wisps of hair as pale and soft as corn silk escaped her white knitted cap.

How could this child be so new, so small, and yet so essential? Mara could no longer remember life without Abby, nor could she imagine it. Her thoughts were consumed with images, plans and dreams for her baby. Her arms were rarely empty. Even her body was so connected with the child that their rhythms of sleeping and eating had meshed. Without Abby, what would Mara do?

Swallowing back tears of love mingled with fear, she stroked her daughter's round cheek. What would Abby do without her mother? If Mara were to die, as Todd had died—as Mara's own parents had died—what would become of this baby?

Would she be pushed into a government-run system as Mara had been? Would she be passed from foster home to foster home where it was so difficult to form personal bonds? Would she struggle the rest of her life with a fear of abandonment and a reluctance to entrust her heart to anyone?

Nearly overwhelmed with her own imaginings, Mara lifted her eyes to the man who sat beside her. The cause of her pain…and her rescuer. She disliked, resented and blamed Brock for the terrible turn her life had taken. She reminded herself that she belonged to Abby and to Todd. And she always would.

Yet how could she sever the ties that kept drawing her closer and closer to Brock? Black hair ruffling away from his forehead in the breeze from the open window, he stared evenly ahead at the dirt road. With one strong, sunbaked hand he worked the gearshift, with the other he steadied the jerky steering wheel. His deep-set brown eyes surveyed the landscape, back and forth, up and down. His domain.

"Glad we checked on that cow this morning," he said, unaware of Mara's turmoil. "She's looking as good as new. The trick will be to keep her out of the weeds." He drove on, speaking almost as if to himself. "I've got a new Simmental bull over here in this pasture. He ought to make a fine breeder come spring. The Simmental is a Swiss breed, you know. Big, sturdy animals. Good beef and milk. Usually they're either a buff color or a dull red and white. Whoa, there he is."

Brock swung the pickup off the road, eased it across the borrow ditch and pulled up alongside a fenced pasture. In the distance, a lone animal lifted its head to stare. For a moment, the bull studied the intruding vehicle, then it returned to the monotonous task of grazing the stubbly winter range. Brock cut the engine and stretched his arm along the back of the seat.

"You wouldn't think a bull would be much to look at," he commented, "but sometimes I drive out here and just stare at that young fellow. He's got the future of this place locked up inside him. Of course, he doesn't know that. Doesn't have a clue. It's up to me to see that he does his job."

It was the first note of genuine pride Mara had ever heard in Brock's voice, and it told her how much this land meant to him. He did care about something more than himself, she realized. It was a side of the man Mara had never seen, and she was intrigued in spite of herself. Throughout her marriage to Todd, Mara had disparaged Brock's reckless, foolhardy adventuring. Though she respected their deep friendship, she had never warmed to Brock. He was careless with money and people, she warned her husband. But Todd, as always, rose to his best friend's defense.

Now, Mara realized Brock's eyes—as soft as brown molasses—had moved from his bull to the woman beside him. When she glanced across at him, she felt herself melt inside like thick, creamy butter in the summer heat. Half afraid she might slide right into his gaze, she struggled to pull away. It was useless. Her heartbeat slowed to a dull, lopsided thudding, her breath hung in her throat.

"I guess you're not too interested in cows, are you?" he asked in a low voice.

She watched his mouth form the words, moving over every syllable in a mesmerizing dance. "I don't know much about cows," she whispered.

"I guess not." Brock ran his finger over the ribbed shoulder of her blue sweater.

She knew he could sense her misgivings. Perhaps he even felt how the touch of his hand disturbed her. Between them lay her baby and all the built-up anger, resentment and sorrow that could possibly separate two people. Brock had given up his friends, his fun and certainly his money for Abby, and Mara realized that his resentment was well-founded. As was hers.

So why did she read a sense of longing in those mysterious eyes of his? Were they reflecting her own desires? Was it possible he felt as confused and torn about her as she felt about him?

She wished Brock would start the car again. This was unbearable. Even as she struggled with her grief over the loss of her husband, Mara realized she was capable of dealing his memory the ultimate treachery. She wanted desperately to know the intimate touch of his betrayer.

Fighting human desire, she prayed for strength. This couldn't be God's will. Not this. She had jumped into the marriage out of fear. She had married a man of little faith and almost no Christian practice. It was all a huge error on her part. A sin. She had repented, given it to God, and asked Him to transform it into something that would glorify Him. How could sitting here feeling overwhelming carnal need for Brock Barnett be anything close to what God intended? She felt weak. Panicky. And so confused.

But she had to say something.

"I suppose I could be interested in cows," she managed to babble, "if I knew more about them."

"They're not as complicated as some animals. They're pretty basic. As long as their needs are met, they mostly do all right."

His focus trailed down her cheek to her neck. She gripped the edges of the seat. What was he looking at? Her hair? Soft and slightly out of control after her morning shower, it lay scattered across her shoulders—her normal barely-brushed style. He picked up a strand and fingered the wispy ends.

"Is it working out for you two to live here, Mara?" he asked. "Well enough to stay awhile?"

"For the most part," she said, incapable of lifting her eyes to meet his. "As for staying, that depends."

"On what?"

"Lots of things." She tried to keep breathing steadily as he wound her hair around his finger. The lock shortened and grew tighter. His finger touched the tip of her earlobe. She gave a silent start, then slowly let out her breath. "I have to do what's right for Abby."

"What about you, Mara? Seems to me if you're happy, she'll be happy, too."

"I'm not sure I can be happy here."

"Too boring?"

"I found your library. I'm not bored."

"Neither am I."

She glanced up, and he captured her eyes. In his own, she read what she feared the most. Desire. But surely he could see the uncertainty and dismay in her face. Surely he knew she couldn't respond. She wouldn't. Yet, she wasn't pushing him away either.

"It's difficult to think about Abby's future," she murmured, fighting to keep her voice even. "Or mine. I know I can't allow us to live on your goodwill forever."

"Why not?"

"I need something of my own. Something to do."

She sucked in a breath as his finger traced the outer edge of her ear. If she didn't cut him off soon, he would thaw what was left of the frozen core of her heart. And then what? Did she want to know what could happen between them? With great effort, she pushed up the barrier she knew would stop him.

"Todd has been on my mind," she said quickly. His hand froze. "I was thinking about his restoration business. You said you were going to keep Rosemond Restoration solvent. You wrote to the Bureau of Land Management, right? Have you heard from the administrator?"

"Dr. Long." His finger slid out of her hair. "I got a letter Thursday. The BLM concedes the contract is still in effect, but Long wants to know who's going to do the restoration. If we can't come up with someone pretty fast, he's going to terminate the contract. He claims they have grounds."

"What grounds?"

"Time. The contract contains a deadline for completing the restoration. Since Todd's death, nothing's been done at the fort. It would be next to impossible to finish the project on time."

Mara studied the bull wandering toward the pickup. "What are you going to do?"

"Legally, Rosemond Restoration is your company. What do you want to do?"

"I think I could pull the project together myself."

"Are you serious?"

"Why not? I did most of the research for Todd, so I know the historical period well and Fort Selden in particular. I have the plans in a box in my closet. Right before he died, Todd was gearing up to start the restoration. We had discussed it all so thoroughly that I know exactly what he was going to do. If I could find a competent builder and a crew that knew how to work with adobe brick, I could supervise the project."

With a last look at his bull, Brock turned the key in the ignition and steered the pickup back onto the road. Abby stirred as the vehicle bounced across the graded dirt, then she slipped back into slumber.

"Do you think the BLM would let you run the project?" he asked as he drove toward the mountains.

"I don't see why not. I have a degree in history. That's what Todd had."

"You're a teacher, Mara. You don't have any experience in reconstruction and restoration. They would say you're not qualified."

"Oh, really? Let's see, I went to Fort Selden umpteen times with Todd. I've studied all the structures inside and out. I've read and memorized every last detail of those plans. I have a concrete understanding of the historical period. Most important, I have an intuitive feel for that era and how to recreate it. That should be worth something."

"Intuition as a credential?" He shrugged. "That won't cut any ice with BLM. Todd had more than a history degree. He spent every summer during high school and college working with a construction crew—mostly building and remodeling adobe houses. He had more than head knowledge. He had real experience."

"Brock, I can manage a restoration project as efficiently and effectively as anyone else, including Todd. Maybe I can't operate heavy equipment myself, and maybe I don't have the training in engineering and construction he had. But I could hire out the specialized jobs. What really matters is the end result. The detail work is what lends authenticity to any restoration. And yes, intuition plays a part in that. If I employed a builder to follow Todd's plans, and then I monitored the historical accuracy, I believe the project would be a success. What makes you think it wouldn't?"

He gave her a sly grin. "Just testing you. Wondered if you'd have the gumption to fight for a dream."

Mara frowned. "Well, of all the—"

"Look, there are my horses." He slowed the pickup again. "Beautiful, aren't they? I ride every day if I can make the time. Around sunset is the best. Once you get to feeling better, I'll take you out."

Still a little off-kilter at the mental game Brock had played with her, Mara looked over his shoulder at the six fine-looking horses grazing in the open pasture. Sleek and healthy, they pawed at the grass and shook their manes in the chill air. Behind them, the mountain range loomed in shades of purple, brown and sage.

"I've got cattle spread out all over this range," he said as he pushed the gas pedal. "This is the dream I'm fighting for."

The pickup wheeled past miles of neat barbed-wire fencing, herds of grazing cattle, windmills creaking in the breeze, lonely yuccas and prickly pears, half-filled sinkholes and clumps of foxtails and catclaws. The vehicle's riders fell silent, Brock surveying his ranch, Mara focusing on the possibilities in her own life.

"Do you think I could do it, Brock?" she asked finally. "Run the restoration company?"

"Why not? Go ahead and give it a shot."

Mara stared unseeing at the passing landscape. "I'd need to contact builders in Las Cruces. I'd have to invite bids and work on getting the BLM's approval."

"Use the phone all you want. My house is your house."

She felt a smile tug at her lips. "You know, even though I enjoyed my students and I felt good about teaching, I liked doing research for the fort project more. I felt I was touching history—my real passion—more directly."

"Why didn't you quit teaching sooner?"

"Todd discouraged that."

"How come?"

"In the beginning, we needed my income. Later…I don't know. I guess the restoration company was his personal dream. Todd was never a selfish person, but I don't think he wanted to share that."

"Maybe not. Shame, though. A person ought to be able to do what she wants to do."

Mara leaned her head back and thought over this turn of their conversation. It felt oddly releasing to be angry with Todd—to use that resentment to help let go of him. A love of history had brought them together. So why had he held her back? More important, what could stop her now?

"If you want to touch history," Brock said, "you ought to see this place up the road. Todd and I came out here once in a while to explore. It's an old adobe house, just about gone. Worn from the elements. Walls look like velvet, don't they?"

Mara focused on the rippled mahogany-hued structure in the distance. Behind the old walls rose a line of steep cliffs dotted with rocky crags and overhanging mesquite shrubs. At the familiar anticipation of tackling the mystery contained within any historical site, Mara's heart sped up and she leaned forward for a better look.

"What was the building's function?" she asked. "Was it a homestead?"

"A trading post, I think. I've found bullets, broken glassware, tools, rusty nails, even a shoe sole."

"Can you put a date on the place?"

"Never have. You'd think a document somewhere would mention it. Believe me, I've looked. Searched every book in my library and the one downtown. *Nada*. Not a word."

Brock pulled the truck under a huge old cottonwood tree. In tandem, he and Mara leaned toward the baby and began to unbuckle her from the seat. For the first time since Todd's death, Mara knew a heady sense of hope. Within her grasp she had both a dream and a plan. More than that, she felt the promise of building a future—without anyone's charity.

At the recognition of that freedom, she looked up at Brock, the man who had somehow pointed her toward it. He was gathering Abby into his arms and settling her wobbly head against his chest. Holding the baby securely with one hand, he used the other to tuck blankets and quilts tightly around her little body. As he slid out of the pickup, he brushed a kiss across Abby's forehead.

At the simple gesture, Mara felt an unexpected ripple race down the backs of her legs. Brock's lips had touched Abby. His large hands held and comforted the baby. His chest supported her head. His muscled arms cradled her weight.

Mara stared, stunned at the realization rocketing through her. The moment Brock's mouth had left Abby's skin, Mara had wanted to take her baby and press her own lips to that spot. A sudden urge came over her to bury her nose in Abby's blankets just to smell Brock's scent. Just to know she was touching places he had touched.

Dear Lord, she prayed silently. *Help me! What is happening? This can't be right. I can't be feeling this!* Despite her prayer, Mara held onto the pickup door handle for support as she watched Brock amble toward the adobe ruin. His long legs moved in an easy stride, and his boots kicked up little spirals of dust. The tip of Abby's white-capped head appeared just over one broad shoulder, her cheek resting comfortably on his sheepskin jacket.

"I figure this was the entrance," Brock called, turning back toward Mara. "It's a wide opening, and there are a few old planks lying around that might have been the boardwalk."

She could only stare.

"You coming?" he asked. "There's nothing to be scared of. Rattlers are all hibernating this time of year."

Realizing how foolish she looked, Mara started toward him, willing common sense back into her head. But as she approached, Brock's eyes surveyed her up and down.

"You know, Mara, you look good for so soon after having a baby. I figured it would take you a long time to get over what you went through."

Mara tried to squelch the flush that had spread across her cheeks. He was standing just inside the ruin, one hand holding Abby and the other stretched out to her. How could she be having these unacceptable feelings and thoughts in broad daylight, in a baggy old sweater, in a body that had given birth only a few weeks before?

It just wasn't possible. But when she took his hand and felt his fingers weave through hers, she knew it was more than possible. Her breath trembled as she lifted her focus to his face.

"This must have been the front of the store," he said, speaking to her eyes. "When I was a kid, I found an old coffee grinder in this room. Rusted, but you could tell what it was."

Mara nodded, fighting the urge to move closer to him. "Did you find anything else? Signs? Scraps of fabric?"

As if sensing her unspoken turmoil, he pulled her toward him. It hardly mattered that they wore coats and sweaters against the December chill. As his arm grazed hers, Mara felt as warm as if it were midsummer.

"I carried everything back to the ranch house," he replied, looking at her mouth. "It's in my workshop. Labeled."

She swallowed. "Did you make diagrams?"

"Yeah."

"Done any digging?"

"No."

Neither spoke again. Neither looked at the ruin. Or the baby. Brock ran his eyes over Mara's face, across her lips, down her neck. Her fingers gripped his so tightly they throbbed.

"Mara…" he said in a husky voice. "Listen, I…"

"Brock," she said softly, "I'm…so…" Mara tried again to swallow down the lump in her throat. What was she? Afraid, uncertain, eager? "I'm very…"

"Mara, you and I—"

"I think it's—"

"Things are—" He paused. "I'm sorry. I keep interrupting you. What I'm trying to say is…if you…"

She shook her head as his words faded off, his attention riveted to her lips. "No, it's really…um…. Do you…do you suppose there might be a record of the trading post in the county courthouse?" She pulled her hand out of his, swung away from him and headed across the bumpy ground. He had almost kissed her. She knew it. But it would have been a mistake. A terrible mistake. They could never have gotten past it. What little goodwill they had built would come tumbling down. She couldn't let it happen.

"The deeds office?" she asked as she bent to examine an odd-looking stone. "Have you looked there?"

"No." Holding the baby, he walked in the opposite direction to study a fallen wall. "I guess there could be an old title in the record books."

"Or a survey." She hugged herself tightly, fighting the dizzy sensation that had swept over her. If she hadn't pulled away, he really would have kissed her. And she would have let him.

Dear God, where are You? You're supposed to help me! This is more than I can bear. It's too much!

"Next time I'm in Las Cruces," he said, "I'll check it out."

"Good idea." Trembling, she walked along the length of crumbled wall. How could this irrational, illogical thing be happening to her? She felt like a child—lost, uncertain, even afraid. And she felt like a woman for the first time in months. Her body tingled and her breath would hardly come. Had she ever felt this shaken with her husband…her comfortable, teddy-bear Todd?

Where was Todd at a time like this? She needed him! How dare he die and leave her in turmoil. How dare he bail out on his wife and daughter when his calming presence was required. Mara clenched her jaw and marched around the perimeter of the ruin without seeing anything.

Her parents had deserted her when she was six. How could they die in a car wreck just like that? She had needed them.

Then Todd did the same thing. Vanished from her life. Would everyone?

Is this the kind of life God had planned for her? One heartbreaking loss after another? Where was her Heavenly Father when she needed Him most? She felt as though she was careening down a mountain road in a car without brakes. Someone was supposed to help her—and that someone was God.

Mara had begged the Lord to help her forgive Brock. Evidently He had reshaped and softened her hard heart enough to allow this man the grace he didn't deserve. But this was far enough! God was supposed to stop at forgiveness—not let her go recklessly running into Brock's arms. What kind of a crazy plan was that?

It wasn't God's plan. That was certain. And if it wasn't God's plan, it had to be Satan's—and Mara wanted nothing to do with it. Brock was a temptation. He was wrong for her. Everything about him had to be resisted.

She could hear the man talking somewhere in the distance, explaining his theories about the old trading post. She ventured a glance at him, and instantly another chill ran through her. Oh, no. This was not good.

If Todd were around, he would laugh and tell a joke and everything would feel normal. But he had to go and die, didn't he? He had to leave his wife with a belly full of baby and a pile of debt. Now look. She was living with Brock! Brock Barnett— the man she had resented and hated through all those many months of terrible grief and loss. And she was gazing like a lost sheep into his brown eyes and aching for him to take her in his arms and kiss her.

Why God? Why, why, why?

"Back here it looks like there might have been a wood-burning stove at one time," Brock was saying. He had stepped through the doorway of the main room and into the quarters behind. "There's a hole in the wall where the pipe would have gone. Maybe somebody lived here. Do you reckon the trader's family made their home at the back of his store?"

Mara scowled at the ground. She didn't want to chat with Brock. She didn't want any of this. She couldn't want it. Couldn't want him.

"I guess they could have," she answered. "It wouldn't be unusual."

"Then there ought to be a trash pile somewhere. Todd told me those are the richest digging places. You can tell a lot from someone's garbage, can't you?"

"Depends."

"Do you suppose we could date the place if we found some old bottles or china plates or something?"

"Maybe." She stepped over the raised threshold between the front room and the back.

Brock was standing by the back wall, looking through a hole that had once been a window. A fragment of wood frame remained, nothing else. "I think this was the bedroom," he said.

Mara almost choked. She wanted him to hand over her daughter and then turn over his keys. She wanted to drive to Sherry's house, lay Abby in a crib and bury herself in bed where she wouldn't have to see Brock Barnett or hear him or smell him ever again.

"If this was your bedroom," he was saying, "you could lie in bed and look right out the window at those cliffs."

"Why on earth would I want to look at a blank wall?" She realized her voice sounded harsher than she had intended.

"The cliffs aren't blank. They're a canvas of shadow and light." He glanced at her. "Come here."

When she didn't move, he stepped over and took her hand. At his touch, a shower of sparks scattered down her spine. No! Not again! Moving as stiffly as a wooden puppet, she followed him to the window. There she removed her fingers from his and tucked her hand safely under her arm.

"See, Mara, the cliffs protected the trading post from the mountain winds." His voice was low, almost hypnotic. "At sunrise, these cliffs are a deep purple. Velvety purple-black like an overripe plum. At dusk when the setting sun shines on them, they change from bright pink to beet-red. At noon, they're stark white. In the summer sun, you touch a bare rock and your fingertips just about blister. You have to watch for scorpions and rattlers, too, when you go up."

"You've been up there?" Mara craned her neck, trying to see the top of the enormous bluff. "To the top?"

"It's where I train. I climb—"

"You climb these cliffs?" Todd's face flashed before her eyes. She could hear the animation in his voice. *Brock trains all the time. He's got cliffs on his ranch where he practices. He's good, Mara. Brock knows what he's doing.*

"Yeah, I climb here," Brock admitted. "At least I did. This is a good place to work on technique. It's a fifth-class rock face, which means you need ropes and special gear. Every year or two I've gone to a rock-climbing school. It can get to be an expensive hobby."

One that Todd should never have taken up, Mara thought. And he wouldn't have, if not for Brock. She studied him as she remembered her husband and ached to ask all the unanswered questions. How had Todd fallen? Why had he fallen? And why hadn't his best friend saved him? Brock could answer those questions if Mara would let him. But she would never ask. She had to shut it away—that final day of her husband's life. If she knew, if she felt Todd's pain, if she heard the story from this man's mouth, all the agony would return. She couldn't relive it. She had to move on.

"Do you plan to keep climbing, Brock?" she asked, turning to face him.

His hand stroked over the form of her daughter's sleeping body. "Does it matter to you, Mara?"

"You answer my question."

"Climbing helps me relax and release tension. When I'm up on those cliffs, I feel a peace I can't touch anyplace else." He looked down at Abby. "Yeah, I guess I can see myself climbing again."

Mara stared at him, a whirlwind of emotion tearing through her. Was it the death of her parents…or the loss of her husband…or the fear of abandonment…or the insecurity of her future? Or was it this man himself? Would losing Brock be too much to bear? Or would it serve both of them right?

Mara cut off the answer to her question before it had time to form. It was only Abby's future that mattered.

"Well," she said evenly, "if you're planning to continue climbing cliffs, I hope you've updated your will to include my daughter."

Chapter Twelve

❦

Brock lifted his head to study the hues of gray, gold and pink mingled in the rock face he had scaled countless times. He knew the easiest routes up the slab, where balance and friction were more essential than brute strength. And he knew the more challenging paths that followed the natural line of cracks. These required such techniques as smearing, edging, clinging and fist-jamming. He had often gone up the cliff alone; he had led skilled companions; he had guided groups of novice climbers. More than once, he had successfully free-soloed the cliff using neither rope nor equipment. He was never careless nor casual, but he understood the soaring wall of stone so well it seemed like a comfortable old friend.

Yet to Mara—standing beside him in the ruins of the adobe house—the precipice represented death. He understood that, too. And for the first time in his life, another person's feelings mattered more than his own.

"I have updated my will," he told her quietly. In his arms, he held Mara's baby, a soft, cuddled bundle who knew no better than to trust him instinctively. "Two weeks ago in Las Cruces I met with my lawyer to discuss the situation. A few days later I approved the revisions. When I die, my estate will belong to Abby...and to you, Mara."

At the simplicity of Brock's statement, Mara's expression softened. She closed her eyes for a moment. "It's not that I don't care what happens to you," she said softly. "I would never want...I mean, I'm hoping that nothing..."

"You just want to make sure your daughter has a future."

"That's right." She looked up again, her eyes searching. "Do you understand?

"If I'm going to keep spelunking and parasailing and white-water-rafting and rock-climbing," he said, laying his cheek on the baby's head, "you want to know you and Abby are secure."

"I'm not hoping something happens to you, Brock. But I just don't—"

"You don't trust a man who would let Abby's father fall off a cliff." He spat out the words, and there was nothing he could do to hide his own pain. "There are a lot of things you don't know, Mara. Did Todd tell you that he and I practiced on this slab until he could just about run up the thing?"

"No," she whispered.

"Did you know that I bought two of every piece of equipment so Todd and I both would be outfitted safely? Did you know he made up for any lack of dexterity with his uncanny sense of technique? Todd could climb just about anything."

She gave a mirthless laugh. "Obviously not the cliffs at Hueco Tanks."

"Oh, he scaled those, too. We were on our way down when he fell." The image of that terrifying moment flashed before Brock once again. "It was late in the afternoon. Since it was getting dark, we decided not to rappel down. Rappelling can take a lot of time, because you have to secure the ropes, anchors and slings. Todd was afraid we'd have to leave some of the equipment behind, and he never liked to do that. We checked to see that the route was free of loose, rotten rock, and we began down-climbing the crag without ropes. I led, since I'd been at the Tanks a few times before. So we started down from the top, face out with our backs to the wall—"

"That's enough," Mara broke in. "How many times do I have to tell you not to talk about it, Brock? I don't want to hear this. I can't. I know what happened, okay? Todd fell."

"Not there, at the top. It was later." Unwilling to buckle to her denial, he kept talking. "The angle got steeper, so we knew we had to turn around and face the cliff wall. I decided we should use a rope at that point, just to be safe. I tossed mine up to Todd." Brock could almost see the moment when his friend had caught the end of the rope. "We had it tightly stretched between us, and he was working to anchor it—"

"Stop it!" Mara cried.

"You need to know what happened."

"No, I don't. It won't change anything."

"Why won't you hear me, Mara?"

"Why should I? To learn how Todd suffered? To be able to picture his pain more clearly? Why do you insist on telling me?"

"So you'll know, so you won't just imagine what happened for the rest of your life."

Tears trickled down from the corners of her eyes. "You want to tell me for your own sake! You think you can get rid of the memory and pain and guilt by dumping it on me."

"You think you're not wallowing in it right now?" he barked back at her. "You'll never get over Todd's death. You're going to let it haunt you forever."

"Who's it haunting?" she burst out. "Me, or you?"

"Us!" He grabbed her arm and pulled her tightly against him. Pressed between them, Abby let out a muffled cry. "It's haunting us."

"There is no *us*."

"You're lying to yourself, and you know it. Until we talk about what happened, Todd is as alive between us as this baby."

"It's Abby, Brock," she choked out. "I'm so afraid for her. Todd's gone. What if something happens to me?"

"Mara, I'm here for her. For you."

As she swallowed a sob, he brushed a kiss on her lips. A quick touch of his mouth to hers, and then he drew back. He hadn't meant to do it, had intended to maintain some distance between them. With other women, Brock never prefaced a kiss with explanations, rationales or apologies. But for some reason, he felt he ought to have talked this over with Mara beforehand. She wasn't just any woman. She was different, a special treasure who had stepped into his life and might walk back out at any moment. During the past few days, he had begun to realize that he couldn't afford to startle or frighten her. He couldn't take the risk that she might bolt.

At the same time, how could he deny his own desire for her? They were two adults. Married to each other, for goodness' sake. What harm could one chaste kiss do?

But now she was looking into his eyes with an expression he couldn't begin to decipher, and he felt more tangled and confused than ever. In his arms, Abby squirmed, her tiny fists pummeling against the sheath of quilts, but the only sensation Brock absorbed was the scent of this beautiful woman's skin as his hand slid up the side of her damp cheek.

"Mara," he ground out, "I know you still love Abby's father. I know you're not over Todd."

"You don't know anything, Brock." She spoke as though she could barely breathe. "You don't know me at all."

He wove his fingers through her hair, reveling in the strands of silk. Her breath was warm and clean, and her mouth was so very close to his own. And he wanted to taste her lips again.

"I know you'll always love Todd," he murmured. "I know that. I understand it. I'm trying to honor that."

Brock tried to think about the baby, about Todd, about anything but his desire to stroke Mara's sweet skin. He imagined his lips moving down her neck, and he reached to touch her.

"Brock!" she gasped as she caught his arm with her hand. "I do love Todd. I'm sure I do. It wouldn't be right to feel any other way, would it?"

Every muscle in Brock's arms went rigid with tension. Was she asking? Did she really want to know what he thought? Her scent drifted around his head in an intoxicating perfume. The warmth of her hair spilled through his fingers, and her mouth beckoned. He gazed at her lips, aching to kiss her again in spite of a squirming baby and the threat of tears for a lost husband.

"It might be all right," he said slowly. "It might, Mara."

He saw her tremble as his eyes traveled to her mouth. Ragged breath escaped his chest. His hand slipped to cup the back of her neck, and he drew her close. He wanted her so badly, and every male instinct he possessed told him she was eager for his kiss. But he hesitated…so scared that he would frighten her away.

"Mara," he began, demanding order of the words that tumbled through his mind like falling blocks. "I don't understand everything that's happening between us—"

"Nothing's happening." She placed her hand on his chest, holding him back. "Between us there's just…we both loved Todd, and now…now there's Abby to take care of…"

"There's more than that, Mara." His mouth covered hers. With a gentle kiss, he tested the soft curves of her lips. His hand behind her head drew her closer, increasing the pressure of his kiss.

"Brock," she murmured, allowing the kiss as her hand slid up his arm and over the rigid mounds of his muscle.

For minutes he could never have counted, they were lost to the winter sun, the scent of dried grasses, the fidgeting of a baby. Brock memorized her mouth as his hand traced down the line of her back. And then she broke away from him, gasping for breath.

"Oh, no," she whispered. "What have I done? What have I done?"

"Mara—"

"No, Brock, we have to stop this right now." She stepped backward, breaking out of his arms. "I have to feed Abby. I have to take care of my daughter."

She reached for her child, but he placed his hand on her arm. "Mara, please don't go."

"Let me have my baby!" Lifting Abby, she turned and half ran from him, stumbling on the uneven ground as she fled. He had lost her.

Watching her go, he thought of the trail of debris he had left in the wake of his selfish pursuits. Used-up cars, broken-down boots, wrecked boats. Wounded friendships. Cast-off women. Todd. It had been Brock's idea to climb Hueco Tanks. And he had lost his best friend.

Now Mara. She ran from him, eager to escape. More than anyone, Mara knew. She understood his empty heart. She saw through his futile effort to pay off his guilt. To erase his sin. She saw, and she fled.

Good for you, Mara, he thought. Run from me. Run, before I hurt you, too.

At the entrance to the trading post, a huge cottonwood tree lifted denuded gray branches into the chill air. Desperate for refuge, Mara carried her now-howling bundle toward it. A fallen limb provided a sturdy seat, and she settled onto it, tucking her baby into the nest of her lap. With expertise born of practice, she tossed a blanket over her shoulder and lifted her sweater.

Abby's wails faded instantly, but Mara felt nothing close to the comfort and warmth she was able to provide for her child. She stared down at the wedding band on her free hand and focused on the shimmering gold.

What had she done? She had kissed Brock Barnett, that's what. She had more than kissed him. She had practically devoured him. Every ribbon of moral, God-fearing restraint and decency had unraveled and shredded and been blown to the wind. How exciting and wonderful! How shameful and terrible.

She had never acted this way with Todd. They had been compassionate and gentle and never, never impulsive. Todd had been Mara's first and only lover. Never for all the world would she have broken their bond of faithfulness.

But less than a year after his death, she had fallen into Brock Barnett's arms like some teenager crazed with hormones firing out of control. Even now, her breath came in tiny, hot gasps. Her lips were still damp, tingling from the pressure of his kiss. She ran her tongue over her lower lip, tasting him.

Dear Lord, where are You? She lifted her eyes to the bare limbs in a prayer for heavenly aid. She needed help. She needed a refuge. She needed a miracle.

Why had she done this awful thing? She hadn't meant to. She had prayed against it. And yet, she had given herself to Brock's kiss as though they were married.

They *were* married. But, no, they weren't. Not really. Not in God's eyes. Oh, this was bad.

Lord, please forgive me, Mara prayed as she stroked her hand over her daughter's velvety head. *I know I let Brock kiss me. I wanted him to kiss me. I still want it. But I shouldn't. It's not Your plan, and I know that. Forgiving him doesn't mean I should just let him into my life. I should love him, right, Lord? But as a friend. That's all. Right?*

Mara groaned. Why had this happened? How could she and Brock ever pretend it hadn't? How could they go on in their separate, uninvolved circles of life? But they had to.

Brock was wrong. There was no *us.* There was nothing between them. It was far too soon, and she didn't even like him.

But she did like him. He was kind to her baby, he loved his ranch and he cared about Mara's thoughts and feelings. He was everything a woman could want.

That was the whole problem! Women went wildly crazy for him, and he knew it. He took advantage of his masculine appeal with every available female—including Mara. She had fallen for his wiles like a silly schoolgirl. What a fool she was.

Abby continued nursing as Mara lifted back the blanket and studied her tiny daughter. Her face was still a bright mottled pink from her distress, and her miniature fingers gripped her mother's finger tightly. The knitted white cap had fallen away somewhere, leaving the baby's wispy tufts of pale hair to blow and drift in the chilly winter breeze.

A flood of guilt washed through Mara as she tucked blankets around the precious little face. In Brock's arms, she had

forgotten all about her own child. What evidence of his treach-
erous hypnotism could be more obvious than that? She gently
turned the baby on her lap and settled her on the other side.

When she lifted her head, Brock stood ten paces away.

"Mara, don't run away from me again," he said, his voice
deep and his tone angry.

Slipping her arms around Abby, Mara drew the baby closer.
"What happened back there was a mistake."

"I don't make mistakes."

"Everyone makes mistakes."

"Not that kind. Not with you."

"Go away, Brock."

"Don't try to stop this. It's right, and you know it."

"It's not right." She shook her head. "No, I will not play this
game with you."

"This is no game. You're my wife."

"Stop it! You know why we got married. It was for Abby, for
Todd. Not for us. Not for thoughtless…stupid…mistakes."

"I won't stop. I won't quit on you, Mara."

"What do you want?"

"The same thing you want."

She studied him as he observed her. Tall, confident, he
waited for her admission of desire. Shaded beneath the brim of
his Stetson, his brown eyes regarded her. He had settled his
hands in his pockets, waiting.

"What I want," she said evenly, forcing her wayward heart
and her impetuous body into silence, "is to be left alone."

"Why?"

"Because I need room to breathe, to grieve. I need to heal
and grow past everything that has happened to me. I need to
be Abby's mother. I need to be Todd's widow."

He took a deep breath, then released it slowly. "Maybe that
is what you need. What you want is another thing. I think you
know what you want, and it doesn't have a thing to do with
being a mother or a widow." Giving her a last glance, he turned
his back. "I'll take you and Abby to the ranch house when
you're ready."

Mara watched him walk away, his broad shoulders outlined
in morning sunlight.

* * *

Brock did give Mara room. He decided if she needed time to think things over, she could have it. He hadn't learned to bury himself in work for nothing.

It took him two weeks to put up new barbed-wire fencing on the north side of the ranch. Nights, he slept in the bunkhouse with the men he had rounded up to crew the project. They ate beans and steaks, played their guitars and sang ballads, and he told himself he wasn't thinking about Mara at all. Hardly at all, anyway.

The week before Christmas, Brock drove to Santa Fe to buy gifts for his staff. It was a tradition. He stayed at the La Fonda Hotel near the plaza and looked through the galleries for Indian paintings, pottery and jewelry. He bought Rosa Maria a turquoise-and-silver squash blossom necklace with rows of blue stones. He found a coral-encrusted silver hair clip for Ermaline and some games for her kids. At a gourmet boutique, he located the new grill attachment Pierre had been wanting for his stove. The chef would be in seventh heaven over that.

For his men, Brock bought heavy, waterproof canvas duster coats. Good protection against the howling winds and driving rains of New Mexico's vast plains. He picked up a few new lariats, a good saddle and a bundle of wool blankets woven by a Hispanic family who lived near Chimayo. He ate blue corn enchiladas at The Shed one afternoon and a big bowl of *posole* at The Pink Adobe another night.

Trying to push Mara out of his mind, he went down to the hotel bar and introduced himself to a pretty woman, an attorney for the state. She was smart, confident, aware of her good looks. When she asked him to dance, he considered it…for about two seconds. He begged off and spent the rest of the evening walking the cold, empty streets of Santa Fe.

He didn't want another woman. Couldn't imagine ever wanting anyone but Mara. He wasn't sure how such a thing had happened to him. Maybe it came about the day he watched her give birth, or maybe in those long hours at the hospital while she learned to be a mother. Maybe he had lost himself to her only that morning in the old adobe ruin when she had looked into his eyes and welcomed his kiss.

But he thought it had probably started a long time before. Images of Mara had floated through his life for years, beginning with the evening Todd had introduced them at an art gallery. She had talked about the Anasazi tribe and some research paper she was working on. They had all been in college then— he was tightly strung, wild and brazen; she was serious, high-minded and religious to a fault. They had nothing in common. But the moment he met her he saw something in her gray-green eyes…something that connected with him deep inside…and he'd never quite gotten over it. Not even during all the years when she was his best friend's wife.

Now Mara was his own wife. In spite of another man's ring on her finger, she wanted Brock as deeply as he wanted her. Their kiss had proved that. But she was scared and confused. She had built herself a wall of protection—nearly as insurmountable as his own. Out of respect for her, and for Todd, he knew he ought to let that barrier stand.

Maybe it had something to do with religion, too. Mara held a deep faith in God that Brock found hard to understand. Despite all she had been through—maybe because of it—she trusted God more than she would ever trust any human being. She and Todd had shared that. Todd called it their "faith foundation."

Brock had no foundation but himself. Until Todd's death, he had held up the walls of the fortress he had built around himself pretty well. But with his best friend's slip on a cliff face, Brock finally understood his frailty. He couldn't save Todd. He couldn't save himself.

Could Mara's God? Was God the answer to the empty hole inside him? The foundation was missing…the fortress was weak…and the walls were crumbling into a giant cave that had been there the whole time. Brock had tried to convince himself that Todd's death had carved out that gaping maw. But he knew it had been there long before that tragic evening at Hueco Tanks.

After checking out of the hotel, he drove back to his ranch, arriving at midafternoon on Christmas Eve. Every year his friends threw a party in Las Cruces, and he'd never missed it. This would be his first time to go alone. He dreaded the thought of unwinding Sandy's tentacles all evening. As he pulled his Jaguar into the garage, he again mulled over the option of asking Mara to go with him.

But to take her into that den of wildcats? She would never go. Besides, he hadn't seen her since the incident at the cliffs three weeks before. He wasn't even sure she still lived at his house. Maybe she had moved away and taken the whirlwind of emotion with her.

As he walked across the drive toward the kitchen door at the rear of the home, a light flurry of snowflakes sifted out of the gray sky. Loaded with packages, he elbowed the door open and backed into the room. At the sound of something hitting the countertop, he turned around.

"Brock," Mara said, her voice almost a whisper. "You came back."

"Hello, Mara." Looking at her, he felt like a starving man set before an unexpected feast. "You're still here."

She was standing by an open cupboard door, a can of mixed nuts in one hand and a string of Christmas-tree lights in the other. She had pulled her blond hair up into a high ponytail fastened with a garland of silver tinsel. A red sweater skimmed over her curves and ended at the waist of a pair of black slacks. Her shoeless feet wore bright crimson socks decorated with little white snowmen.

He pushed the door shut behind him with his boot and set his packages on the counter. She was beautiful. Too beautiful. He felt his control slipping. Make conversation.

"How's Abby?" he asked.

"Big."

"She's a month old now?"

"Five weeks."

He took off his hat and brushed the snowflakes from the brim. "You okay, Mara?"

"I'm fine. I've been busy. Calling builders, doing more fort research, talking to the BLM." She closed the cupboard door. "How are you?"

"Good." He held her eyes, unable to pull away. "You look great."

A pink flush blossomed on her cheeks. "Pierre and I have been working on meals to help me trim down. He's even cut back on the butter and cream sauces."

"Whoa. You must have won his heart."

She smiled. "We like to work together. I asked him how he made eclairs, so he invited me into the kitchen. Now I take lessons almost every day."

Brock drank in the sight of her mouth, her white teeth, her almond eyes. Every wall he had worked to erect came tumbling down the moment she smiled. He shoved his hands into his pockets to keep from taking her in his arms.

"Sounds like you're getting used to things around here," he said.

"Everyone's been wonderful. Rosa Maria's daughter helps me look after Abby."

"Ramona?"

"Yes, she's fabulous. I've even been able to leave Abby with her a couple of times to go into Las Cruces for meetings. I found out about your trading post, too, by the way. It was built in 1887. I have copies of the deed in my room. And Ermaline's teaching me how to quilt. We found a pieced quilt top up in a cupboard in the lounge, so we're finishing it. I really like her."

"You haven't been lonely."

"Well…" She hesitated as though unwilling to answer. Then she brightened suddenly. "Oh, Sherry drove out for a visit. She brought Abby some Christmas presents. Which reminds me…I invited the staff and their families over this evening. Sort of a thank you and tree-decorating party rolled into one. I didn't expect you…and I thought it might be fun to share Christmas with someone."

He nodded. "Sounds nice."

"I was getting the appetizers ready."

"I won't be in your way. I have to go to a party in Las Cruces tonight."

"I see." Her expression changed. "Sandy, Stephanie, Justine—that bunch?"

He shrugged. "Probably. Well, I have more stuff to bring in. Go ahead with your party fixings."

"Sure." She swung around and hurried out of the kitchen into the living room. He felt as though the light had just gone out of his whole life.

Abby lay tummy-down on a thick, pink blanket spread across the living-room floor, and Mara smiled to herself as the baby's small round head bobbled up and down. Moonlight gleamed through the window onto a towering pine tree that Ermaline's husband, Frank, had cut and brought in.

Bowls of popcorn and cranberries sat beside the fire. Boxes of old ornaments that had been in the Barnett family for generations were stacked against a wall. Rosa Maria had dug the decorations out of a storage closet while lamenting how rarely they had been used through the years. Christmas at the ranch had always been more of an off-again, on-again whim than a cherished tradition, the housekeeper told Mara.

Mara had been determined to change that. Now bayberry- and cinnamon-scented candles burned on the mantel. Christmas music drifted through the room. An evergreen wreath hung on the front door. Everything was ready, just perfect…

Swallowing the unexpected lump in her throat, she opened a carton of eggnog and poured the creamy liquid into a huge punch bowl. The aroma of nutmeg swirled upward to mingle with the fragrance of newly cut pine and fresh popcorn. The scents said Christmas … hope, peace, joy. They spoke of past years with a loving husband. They whispered of precious memories, laughter around a spindly tree, a first turkey cooked in a too-small oven, gifts wrapped in newsprint and tied with twine, two voices lifted in carols at a small church. They spoke of Todd.

Why had Brock come back?

Mara blinked at the sting of hurt. She didn't want Brock. It was his fault this Christmas had pain and aching loss at its core. She might paint a bright veneer of tradition and happiness, but beneath it all she had to face the truth. Her husband was dead.

Sherry had reminded Mara just what kind of man Brock was. Together the two friends had recalled the bullheaded, insensitive womanizer who had always annoyed Mara. Sherry had been right, of course. Brock was no different now.

So he had returned—the focus, the cause of her sorrow. He had been away so long, and she had prayed so hard to forget how he looked. She hadn't. Her heart had thudded against her ribs as his eyes took her in that afternoon. And all she could think of was how giddily happy she felt to see him…how much she had missed him…how desperately she had longed for his touch, his voice, his kiss.

"Oh, Abby." She knelt beside her baby and lifted the gurgling infant into her arms. "What am I going to do?"

But there was no time for reflection as the front door burst open. Rosa Maria and her husband, Fernando, brought in a swirl of snowflakes and laughter.

"Feliz navidad!" Fernando exclaimed. The longtime ranch hand always wore a smile. "Merry Christmas, Mrs. B. How's the little one?"

"Wonderful, Fernando." Mara greeted the couple as their youngest daughter, Ramona, followed her parents into the house.

In her love for little Abby, Ramona reflected the contentment of a happy upbringing. Just nineteen, she had graduated from high school the past spring, and she was hoping to become a kindergarten teacher. She had confessed a desire for a family of her own one day, but first she wanted to get a college education. After putting an armload of presents under the tree, she hurried to Mara's side and lifted Abby from her mother's arms.

Ermaline's cheerful clan was only moments behind the others. Frank carried in firewood, and the four children had each brought an empty stocking. Mara had promised to fill them to the brim. They swirled around the room, cooing over the baby, sampling the popcorn, chattering with excitement over the prospect of Christmas morning.

Into their midst stepped Pierre and his plump wife, Yvonne, who was as jolly and effusive as her husband was stiff. She hugged everyone in the room, her French accent bouncing off the vigas as she wished the gathering a *"Joyeux Noël!"* Pierre had brought boxes of pastries and a beautiful cake.

"And where is young Mr. Barnett?" he demanded loudly. "I have seen his car on the road this afternoon."

"Mr. B. is back?" Rosa Maria turned to Mara. "Ah, *que bueno!* I thought he would miss this Christmas with the baby."

"He won't be here tonight," Mara said. "He's going to a—"

"A party in Las Cruces," Brock finished as he walked into the room. He had changed into a black shirt and jeans, black leather coat and boots. In his somber colors and jet-black hat, he looked anything but merry. "You know the one I always go to. At Joe's house."

"Oh, that one." Again, Rosa Maria looked at Mara. Her eyes softened. "Well, then you must go, too, Mrs. B. We'll have our little fiesta here while you two go into town."

"I think it is best," Pierre intoned, nodding sagely. "The friends will expect it."

"A husband and wife together—*mais oui!*" Yvonne clapped her hands. "And when the cats are away, the mice shall play. We will have a lovely time here. Go on with you both!"

Mara shook her head. "Oh, no, really. I don't want—"

"I'd like for you to come." Brock held out his hand to her. "We'll be back before midnight."

"But Abby—"

"She'll be fine," Ramona said, hugging the baby against her cheek. "Go on with him, Mrs. B. There's enough milk in the freezer to feed the baby for one evening. I'll take care of her."

"But I've spent all day—"

"Come with me, Mara." Brock took a step toward her. "Please."

"Go on, go on!"

Mara stared at Brock's outstretched hand. It would be a terrible mistake. She knew it even as she placed her palm on his.

She was going away with him, leaving her baby, her home, her friends, her security. And she felt as happy as a child on Christmas morning.

Chapter Thirteen

❦

Mara stared in dismay at her ankles as Brock's Jaguar hummed down the highway toward Las Cruces. In the rush, she hadn't thought to change her socks as she stepped into a pair of loafers. She was stuck with the bright red ones decorated with white snowmen. Perfect for a party with loving friends…but a fashion *faux pas* for a gathering of the young elite. Sandy would probably laugh her right out of the room.

Groaning inwardly, Mara lifted her eyes to the man at the wheel. Dark, silent, Brock was absorbed in thoughts he obviously didn't care to share. Maybe he was regretting the impulse that had led him to invite Mara. He had no reason to be happy about going to a party with a woman wearing snowman socks.

As forbidding as he looked in his black clothes and hat, he had been a different man back at the house. Before they left, he had walked over to Ramona and had taken Abby from the young woman's arms. While Mara tugged on her coat and gave instructions about the party food, she had observed Brock stroking the baby's cheek. His brown eyes had gone soft, and the hard set to his jaw had relaxed. Abby had cooed and batted him on the nose, and his mouth curved into a gentle smile. Before he was bustled out of the house by Rosa Maria and Ermaline, Mara had caught sight of Brock returning the baby to Ramona. Bending over the cuddly bundle, he brushed a kiss on Abby's forehead. And as she gave her daughter a kiss of her own, Mara melted inside.

Did Brock truly care about Abby? Had the little girl really captured his heart? Mara couldn't help but want his affection to be genuine. Even as she felt her thoughts betray Abby's birth father, she admitted how deeply she longed for her daughter to know Brock's love.

"Did Abby look any bigger to you?" she asked into the silence.

Brock glanced at her as if surprised there was someone else in the car. But as their eyes met, his deepened. He shifted gears with a leather-gloved hand and returned his focus to the road.

"She's grown a lot," he replied. After a moment he spoke again. "I missed three weeks."

"I'm sure you've been busy. Rosa Maria told me you're usually gone from the house a lot."

"Yeah." He turned on the wiper as snowflakes began to brush the windshield. "This time I shouldn't have left."

When Mara decided he wasn't going to continue the conversation, she leaned back against the headrest and shut her eyes.

"My dad was always gone," Brock spoke up. "Building fences or checking on his oil wells."

Mara opened her eyes and observed him. The solemn line of his mouth and the tension in his jaw wrote a message of pain. For the first time, she knew exactly what the man was thinking.

"Your father missed out on more than three weeks. He missed your whole life," she said. "Your mother did, too."

"So did yours."

"Not by choice."

"No. You're not missing Abby's life, are you, Mara?" His eyes skimmed her face. "You're right there all the time. Todd would be, too. He'd be at her side. He wouldn't go off for three weeks to build a fence."

Mara took a deep breath. Brock was speaking honestly. Could she?

"I'm glad you came back, Brock," she said finally. "You're good with Abby."

"I missed her, even though she doesn't belong to me. And I missed you, Mara."

"Even though I don't belong to you, either," she reminded him.

"You belong *with* me."

"Brock, please don't start."

"You've had three weeks to think over what happened between us out there at the trading post. Three weeks to get more used to motherhood. Three weeks to continue coming to terms with Todd's death. I want to know where you stand."

The perfectionist was back, Mara thought as she stared at the snowflakes blowing against the windshield. Brock couldn't simply let things happen. He always had to manage things, to put it all in order.

"Don't pressure me, Brock," she warned him. "I have to think about practical things like the Fort Selden project and Abby's next pediatrician appointment. I want to forget about the trading post, okay?"

"No, it's not okay. In the past three weeks, I've done my best to put what happened between us out of my mind. I tried to convince myself it didn't mean anything. But this afternoon when I walked into the kitchen and saw you standing there, I knew it hadn't worked."

He fell silent for a moment, and Mara's heart thudded as her blood puddled in her knees.

"I failed in a lot of things," he went on, his voice so low it was almost inaudible. "I failed Todd. I failed you. I failed Abby. I failed myself. I failed to understand what it was about you and Todd that made your marriage work, that made you both so different and good and clean and right. I failed God. I'm still failing everyone—every day. I know I'm not right for you, Mara. I see that. But as hard as I try to make myself believe there's no hope for us, I can't."

The car had rolled into the outskirts of Las Cruces where Christmas lights cast a multicolored glow on the gathering snow. Brock said nothing, obviously waiting for her response as he steered through a subdivision, past a park and up a gentle hill. Mara concentrated on her red snowman socks. It was impossible to believe he had said what she thought she had heard.

"Brock, I think what happened out at the trading post was just reaction to the situation." Choosing her words carefully, she tried to make sense of it even as she spoke. "We were alone, and we'd been through so much, and it was…well, it was an impulse, right? It happened on the spur of the moment. It didn't mean anything."

He pulled the car up to the curb in front of a stucco home with a sloping front lawn and perfectly trimmed evergreens. Cutting the engine, he leaned back against his seat and let out a breath. Mara could see the muscles in his thighs tighten as he tapped his fingers on them. Suddenly his big shoulders turned, and he pinned his focus on her.

"That kiss didn't mean anything to you?" he demanded. "Don't evade the question, and don't lie to me when you answer."

Mara shivered at the intensity in his brown eyes. If she was timid, he would devour her. She had no choice but to stand up to him. "Listen, Brock, I'm doing my best to work this out in my mind. The bottom line is, I'm a widow and a mother. I can't let a kiss mean anything. I shouldn't have let it happen."

"But you did. You wanted it."

She turned away. "Is this Joe's house?"

"You wanted to kiss me, Mara. I'm no fool. This has been brewing between us for a long time. You know it has."

"No," she whispered, and her breath formed a circle of mist on the window. "I'm cold. Let's go inside."

"But you loved Todd, and so did I. Neither of us would have betrayed him for the world, and neither of us wants to betray him now. So what do we do?"

"I'm going in."

"No, Mara!"

"Stop pushing me."

"Stop running away."

"I don't want to feel this!"

"But you do. Mara, look at me and tell me you wanted that kiss."

"Leave me alone, Brock." She grabbed the door handle and shoved with her shoulder. Stumbling into the snowy night, she heard him slam his door behind her. She ran up the hill, her heart hammering with every step.

This was not happening! She couldn't allow it. She couldn't let him say the things he was saying…and she couldn't feel what she knew she was feeling.

"Mara!" Opening the front door to Mara's ring, Stephanie hailed her. "This is a surprise. Where's Brock? We had just about given up on him."

Mara was engulfed by strangers, men who helped her out of her coat and placed a warm drink in her hands, women who stared appraisingly as they stepped aside to let her pass. She walked beside Stephanie on wooden legs.

"Brock's coming," Mara said. "He's locking the car."

"Well, come on into the living room. Did you bring the baby?"

Mara shook her head. She glanced behind her to see Brock entering the foyer, a sprinkle of snowflakes scattered across his shoulders and the brim of his hat. Turning her back on him, she trailed Stephanie into a cavernous great room. The home was modern with chrome-and-glass tables, sleek leather sofas, plush gray carpet, recessed lighting. It smelled of expensive perfume and men's cologne. A gas-log fire glowed between a pair of potted green neon cacti on the hearth.

Mara took an offered chair beside Stephanie, who seemed inclined to want to talk. Around them, fit-looking men and thin women clad in cashmere, silk and leather stood in laughing, talking clusters. The women sparkled with diamonds and gold. The men shone in silver and turquoise.

"So, how is your daughter?" Stephanie began.

"Oh, it's her!" Sandy in a tight red skirt minced across the floor, with three other women close behind. "I didn't know you were still with Brock. Ladies, this is Brock's sweetie. I'm sorry, I forgot your name, honey."

"Shut up, Sandy. And go easy on that punch." Stephanie rolled her eyes at the others. "This is Mara Barnett. She's Brock's new wife."

"Wife? Wait a minute, I thought Brock told us it was a monetary arrangement," Sandy complained loudly. "You know, she gets the dough, he gets the—"

"Excuse me." Mara stood and gave Stephanie a nod. "I think I'll take a look around the house."

"Hey, love the socks!" Sandy said in a stage whisper as Mara brushed past. "Snowmen! Wow, those are cute!"

Sandy solicited Stephanie to join her in giving the others an animated reenactment of their recent visit to the Barnett ranch. Mara wished she could shrink into her snowman socks and disappear completely.

Why had she come? At the ranch house, everyone would be enjoying the eggnog, sugar cookies and homemade *posole* she had worked so hard to prepare. They would be stringing popcorn and cranberries, hanging ornaments and singing the Christmas carols she had been looking forward to all day. Abby would be the focus of love as everyone reveled in the contentment and peace of the season. Instead, Mara was stuck at a party with a female Attila the Hun.

To her surprise, she realized that Stephanie had followed her across the great room to the ceiling-high Christmas tree. Decorated in silver and blue, the tree sported chromed icicles interspersed with tinsel. The artificially flocked branches looked as though they were choking in their muffler of goopy fuzz.

"So, how are things going at the ranch, Mara?" Stephanie asked. "Are you getting used to motherhood?"

Mara studied the woman for a moment and concluded she wouldn't bite. She let out a deep breath and tried to relax her shoulders.

"Motherhood is a slow process," she said. "I don't get much sleep at night. My nerves are a little frazzled."

"Are you, like, nursing your baby and all that?"

Mara smiled. "It's not hard once you get used to it. Do you plan to have children, Stephanie?"

"Who knows? At this rate, I'll hit menopause before I get married. That's Sandy's problem, you know. She's so bitter. A lot of us haven't found the right guy, but we'd really like to start families. So we date around. It's been a bust for Sandy and me. Most men just aren't into commitment. I think Sandy was hoping Brock would be it for her. Anybody could have told her differently. A lot of us tried to warn her, but she wouldn't listen."

Taking a sip of spiced cider, Mara studied the tree. "Brock's not the kind to settle down, is he?"

"You ought to know that by now. He's a smooth talker, and when he turns those big brown eyes on a woman, there's no holding back, you know? But the man doesn't have a heart. Or if he does, he's not about to give it away."

"Sounds like you've been burned."

"Who hasn't? Most of the women in this room have probably gone after him at one time or another. Just look at the man."

Mara glanced behind her at the group gathered in the foyer. Brock stood head and shoulders above the others, his hard, sun-tanned face contrasting with the paler complexions of his cit-ified companions. Holding his black Stetson, he chuckled at a joke someone had told. Two women giggled, and one of them leaned her head against his shoulder for just a moment. He seemed oblivious to the flirtatious ploy.

Mara turned away. "Has his moves down pat, does he?"

"Oh, yeah. Brock's got charisma in spades. If he fixes his sights on someone, she'd better look out. It's like he has this uncanny sense for knowing what will make a woman melt. Once he has her in the palm of his hand, he loses interest. He's broken a lot of hearts, I can tell you that."

"Yours included?"

"Sure. We dated a few years ago. I thought Brock was so in-telligent, so handsome, the whole bit. But he was always hold-ing back, you know? It was like his mind was somewhere else.

His heart was locked up tight, and I sure wasn't the woman with the key. I don't believe there is such a person."

Mara recalled Rosa Maria's use of the same image to describe Brock. These were women who had known him longer and more intimately than she had. If they believed he was impossible to reach, they must be right. Certainly Mara didn't hold the key to Brock's heart. And she wasn't about to become another notch on his six-gun.

"Anyway," Stephanie went on, "you're probably smarter than the rest of us have been. You're enjoying his money and his company without making a fool of yourself over the man. You've got your baby and your memories of a happy marriage. I wish I'd been wiser where Brock was concerned."

"I'm just doing what has to be done to survive." Mara spotted Brock across the room. Though surrounded by people, he was staring straight at her. When he left the group and started her way, she turned quickly and took out her cell phone. "Could you excuse me a minute, Stephanie? I need to check on Abby."

The rest of the evening became a cat-and-mouse game as Mara did her best to avoid Brock. Every time he appeared at her side, she invented an excuse to get away. She asked Joe for a tour of his house. She made two phone calls to the ranch. She went to the bathroom umpteen times. In fact, Joe's downstairs powder room became her ultimate refuge.

She perched on the closed lid of the toilet seat and stared at her snowman socks. The truth was dismaying. She was no better off than Stephanie and Sandy and all the rest of the women at this party. Brock had spoken just the right words to weaken her heart. Every time he came near, her pulse sped up to double time. When he spoke against her ear, she got woozy. If their hands brushed, she went weak in the knees. She was an absolute fool.

As she sat in the chrome-and-gold bathroom, Mara tried to pray through the situation. But she found that as usual lately, she could only mouth a desperate plea for God's help. Her prayers seemed to go as high as the marble-tiled ceiling and stop cold. What was wrong? She knew from experience and faith that God hadn't abandoned her. Had she done something to place a barrier between herself and her Lord? Was it the marriage to Brock? Was it her human desire for a man's touch? Or was there something else in her life that she needed to examine, confess and turn over to Christ?

Mara attempted to turn her thoughts to Todd. Instead she tasted her betrayal of her late husband in Brock's arms. When she made the effort to focus on Abby, she pictured her daughter gurgling happily as Brock cooked breakfast.

The only way out, Mara finally decided, was literal escape. She would insist on a job with the fort project. If she could earn even a small income, she could rent an apartment in Las Cruces. She could take Abby on-site at Fort Selden. Or—as much as she hated the thought—she could leave the baby at the church day-care center. Mara would give herself a month to work out the details.

During that time, she would do her best to ignore Brock. She could have her meals brought to her room. She could spend her days in Las Cruces attending to details of the restoration project. Brock would be out on the ranch somewhere, anyway. It could be done. She had no choice.

Stepping out of the bathroom, she drew a deep breath. Brock stepped from the shadows and slipped his arm around her shoulders.

"You feeling okay, Mara?" he asked. "You've been in there for quite a while."

Startled by his unexpected presence, she shrugged out of his arm and stepped to one side. Had he been waiting for her all this time? She felt like a wary rabbit around a hungry wolf.

"It's getting late," she said. "Can we go home?"

Brock looked her up and down, a concerned expression on his face. "You look too thin, too pale. Have you been sick?"

"No, I'm fine."

"Are you worried about the baby? Or did Sandy say something to you?"

"Really, Brock, it's all right." She hugged herself, unable to meet his gaze.

"Let's get your coat," he said, taking her elbow. Again, she edged away as he walked beside her toward the foyer. "How's Abby?"

"Ramona put her to bed a couple of hours ago."

"Everyone still at the house?"

"They've all gone home but Ramona. She said she'd be happy to stay until we got back."

In the foyer, Brock tried to help Mara into her coat, but she took it from him and put it on herself. She avoided his eyes and kept her mouth shut tight. She would not say anything to Brock, she decided. Nothing. Then she would be safe.

As she thanked Joe for the party, she buttoned her coat clear up to her chin.

"You seemed to hit it off with Stephanie," Brock said on the way to the car. Before she could get to it, he grabbed the handle and pulled open the door. "She's a nice lady."

"She's a real estate agent, you know." Mara glanced at him as she slid into her seat. "She thinks she can find me an apartment."

Pulling the door shut on him, she turned her attention to the swirling snow. It was important to re-establish the barrier, she reminded herself as she watched him stride around to his side. If he had any thoughts of resuming their previous conversation in the car, she intended to squelch them. In fact, she probably should tell him exactly what she intended to do with her future. If that made him want to sever his financial commitments to Abby, so be it.

Brock climbed into the car and started the engine. As he pulled out onto the street, he spoke. "You're moving out of the ranch house?"

"I'm going to start looking for a place of my own."

"Did Sandy put something in your head? She can be pretty hostile."

Mara shook her head. "It was no big deal. She implied that I'm a kept woman."

Brock bit off an expletive.

"Stephanie set her straight," Mara said. "Sandy was tipsy, and everyone knew it. I'm not worried."

"I'd have set her straight if you hadn't kept dancing away from me all night."

"I wasn't dancing. You were stalking."

"I was under the impression we had come to this shindig as a duo. It seemed appropriate to at least get within your range of vision once in a while. You are my wife."

"Please, Brock, don't—"

"How soon do you expect to move out?"

"It's time now. I'm back on my feet physically. I can get a job either with the fort project or somewhere else."

"What's the point? You've got a place to stay. You've got food, money, transportation. Why move?"

"You know why."

"Are you planning to run from the truth the rest of your life, Mara?"

"I'm not running from anything."

"You ran from me all night. You hid in the bathroom so you wouldn't have to face me."

"I needed to be alone. I had to pray. And think. I decided it's time to move away from the ranch."

"God told you that?"

"No. I can hardly focus on Him anymore. Things are so confusing. I can't even seem to pray right these days."

"It's that big old lump of bitterness stuck in your throat. It's got you all stopped up."

"I'm not bitter!"

"Oh, really? Then how come you won't forgive me? Why are you running from me?"

"I'm not running from you, Brock. I'm stepping into my own future."

"You're running from me and everything in your past. You lost your parents. You lost Todd. You're not about to let anyone else into your life, just in case you might lose him, too. Am I right?"

Mara clenched her fists inside the pockets of her coat. She felt trapped by this man. Trapped by his words. Trapped by her own desire for him. Again, she tried to turn her thoughts to something else, something less upsetting. Abby was probably awake and needing to nurse. Ramona would need to go home and rest for her family's Christmas celebrations. Ermaline...Rosa Maria...Todd...

No, she couldn't make anything stay in her mind. Not even Todd. For the first time since his death, she wanted her husband's memory to release her. She wanted freedom from the turmoil. She wanted to stop hurting, to enjoy life, to feel her own feelings again without guilt and bitterness weighing her down.

Brock was right. He was the man she wanted ... even though she felt certain his words were hollow and his desire for her had no depth.

"Am I right?" Brock repeated. "You're running from the past. You're running from the future. You're even running from the present. From God. From me. You don't have the guts to find out what's going on between us."

Mara glared at him. "I'm no coward, Brock Barnett. If I'm running from you, it's because I have every reason to keep my distance. You want to know how I felt about you in the beginning? From the first time I met you—at that gallery—I didn't trust you. I still don't."

The muscle in his jaw worked as he steered the car through the driving snow that had begun to make the dark highway slick. She had pulled out her ammunition, and she knew it was going to hurt. But she didn't care. He deserved it.

"If I had to hide in the bathroom tonight," she snapped, "it's because you're a predator. You always have been. I don't want to be tracked down. I don't want to be devoured like Stephanie and Sandy and every other woman you've worn on your arm."

"What makes you so sure I'd devour you? Have I taken advantage of you? Have I gone back on my word?"

"No, but you have a lousy track record. Stephanie told me you've gone out with nearly every woman at that party, and you've left a trail of broken hearts. When Todd was alive, you had a different woman every time we saw you. You're not a long-term—"

"No, I'm not Todd. I didn't grow up in a solid home, or on the first day of college meet the woman I knew I wanted to marry. My world was a split-up family and a father who couldn't commit to anyone. Except for Todd, my circle of friends played the dating game endlessly. And don't believe Stephanie and Sandy aren't using their wiles to play along just like Joe and Travis and every other single person at that party tonight. It's a game, and I won't deny I played it, Mara."

"Well, I don't want to play."

"Maybe I don't want to play anymore, either."

"Maybe, or maybe not. Like I said—I don't trust you."

"What do I have to do?" He pulled the car over to the shoulder of the highway, stuck the gearshift in neutral, and jerked up on the emergency brake. Turning to her, he took her shoulders. "Mara, your mouth is saying one thing and your eyes are telling me something else. Forget the past and the future. I want the truth right now."

She stared at him, terrified she would blurt out everything that had built up inside her. If he came any closer…if he leaned toward her…

"I'm going for a walk," she whispered.

She threw open the car door, letting in a rush of frigid air and snowflakes. Gasping with the cold, she stepped out into the darkness and slammed the door shut behind her. She shivered and buried her hands in her pockets. Her body told her she needed to nurse Abby. Her heart told her she was a fool. If only she were home.

Home? Did she even have a home? Mara shook her head. Brock had given her his home. Why had she been so harsh with him? Maybe it was because she couldn't deny the truth in his words. She was bitter. She had been running from the past. More important, she was running from him.

Even as she felt chagrined for hurling words of doubt at him, she heard Stephanie's voice. *If he fixes his sights on someone, she'd better look out. It's like he has this uncanny sense for knowing what will make a woman melt. Once he has her in the palm of his hand, he loses interest.* Had Brock fixed his sights on her? Would he use her up and then discard her?

Why not? He had admitted he wasn't like Todd. He had played with women's hearts his whole adulthood. Why would it be different with Mara?

Huge flakes of snow drifted out of the black sky as though a feather pillow had burst. The highway was completely dark. No trucks blasted past. No cars traveled this late on Christmas Eve. Everyone was tucked away in warm houses, wrapping presents and happily anticipating the next morning.

Behind her on the sloping shoulder of the road, Mara made out the black form of the silent Jaguar. Inside it she could see Brock's dark silhouette. He seemed to be staring off into the night, his gaze fixed on the falling snow. Her feet damp in the ankle-deep snow, Mara shifted uncomfortably. She shouldn't have shouted. She shouldn't have cut him with her words.

She was angry. Bitter. Unforgiving.

Was that the barrier she had erected between herself and God? Was that why her prayers went nowhere?

With a sinking sense of truth, Mara realized she had been lying not only to herself and Brock, but to God. What was right? What was wrong? How could she face her own feelings when they seemed so unacceptable?

If she were honest, she would have to admit that she had felt a connection between Brock and herself from the day they first met. She had thought him handsome, as most women did. But it was more than that. The interest in Southwest history, architecture and Native Americans that united Todd and Brock drew Mara as well. But it was more than that, too.

Mara couldn't define the connection she felt with Brock. She had never wanted to and had never tried. But somehow, in all they had gone through with Todd and then Abby, that connection had turned to attraction. Yes, she had wanted his kiss that morning at the trading post. She wanted it now, which was why she couldn't go back to the car.

Again, she glanced at the shiny contours of the Jaguar. Brock was sitting in the utter stillness of the night as snow collected on the hood and roof. If only the man would evaporate. But Brock wouldn't go away any more than her desire for him would. He would always be there waiting for her, tall, volatile…and very warm beneath his black leather coat.

Her heart hammering in her ears, Mara squeezed her eyes shut for a moment. *Lord, what am I supposed to do? Why won't You answer me?*

She waited, fighting tears, trying to swallow the lump in her throat. Bitterness. *Okay, Lord,* she prayed. *I forgive Brock Barnett for taking Todd up that cliff to his death. Will You please forgive me for holding that against him? And will You forgive me for marrying him when I should have been more trusting in You? And will You please, please help me!*

Mara stood in the silence, and she knew her first sense of peace in many months. God was with her. Jesus had already taken her sin to the cross. The Holy Spirit dwelled inside her. He would be her comforter, her counselor, her guide.

And yes, she would go back to the car. She would go back because, in spite of everything, she wanted to be with Brock.

She moved her feet through the deep snow. Dampness seeped over her shoes and into the soft cotton of her red socks as she walked toward the car. Her coat hem drifted at her knees. Her teeth chattered.

"Mara."

At his voice, she lifted her head. Startled to find him so close, she realized he had left the car and come to meet her.

"Mara, I'm sorry," he said, his voice ragged. "I'm pushing, I know that."

"No, it's me," she replied. "You were right. I've been running from everything."

"Whether you can believe this or not, I have tried to hold back. I've tried hard."

"I know."

"Please don't run from me anymore, Mara."

She trembled inside her wet shoes as he lifted his hand to a strand of hair that had escaped her ponytail. At his slight touch, her heart began to gallop, and her breath grew shallow. In the darkness, she could just make out the outline of his mouth, and she could feel his eyes on her face.

"Brock, I have to get away from you," she said, as tears welled. "I have to."

His fingers closed on her shoulder. "Don't run, Mara."

"Please, don't try to keep me."

"Don't run from us, Mara."

She shook her head as his hands slipped around her and pulled her against him. "Brock, I can't trust—"

"Don't run."

"But you might hurt—"

"I won't. I promise."

At his words, Mara began to sob against his chest. The harder she cried, the tighter he held her. Time stood still as she poured out the unforgiveness and fear and doubt she had held on to so tightly. Finally, when nothing more would come, her shoulders stopped heaving, and she raised her head.

The snow had stopped falling, and the boundless sky above the desert glowed with the light of stars beyond number.

Chapter Fourteen

❧

As Brock held her on the roadside, Mara allowed her hands to move up the arms of his sheepskin coat and over his broad shoulders. How long since she had touched another human besides her baby? How long since anyone had embraced her? How long since she had felt anything beyond motherhood and grief and loneliness?

*Oh, Lord, Lord…*her heart cried out. Beneath the blurred veil of tears clinging to her eyelashes she saw the tiny, dark point of each whisker on Brock's jaw. With her fingertips, she feathered the coarse black strands of his hair and touched the sides of his face with her thumbs.

Her prayer wrenched through her chest. *This must be wrong, Lord… or not wrong… he's my husband… not my husband… help me, help me, Lord…*

"Mara," he murmured, "It's all right—us together. I know it."

She drank in the scent of his hair as he lowered his head and brushed a kiss on her cheek. At the touch of his lips, she shivered. "I missed you those three weeks, Brock. But all of this scares me so much."

"Please don't be afraid of me. I won't do anything to drive you away."

"I'm here now," she said softly. "Just hold me."

As his strong arms enfolded her and drew her closer, she remembered she was not just a mother, not just a widow. She was a woman. Todd had died, but Brock's engulfing presence reminded Mara how very much alive she was. Everything that had gone before vanished like snowflakes on warm asphalt, leaving only this man whose touch lit a fire inside her heart.

As the scent of leather and aftershave drifted around her head, images filtered through Mara's mind. Wrapped in the warmth of Brock's embrace and bathed in the soft glow of starlight, she pictured them together...as husband and wife...as God intended....

The picture seemed so real she could hardly believe they were standing on a roadside in the middle of a snowfall. And then she thought of her body's limitations so soon after childbirth. She remembered stitches and torn muscle and stretch marks. He wouldn't like that. Wouldn't think her beautiful. Wouldn't want her.

She pulled back, but this time he found her lips. "Mara," he murmured. "Mara, this is right. This is the way it's supposed to be."

"Is it, Brock?" Blossoming inside at the touch of his mouth against hers, she stood on tiptoe and sought him again. This time the kiss lingered, entranced, fulfilled her. "Oh, I feel out of control," she said as she let out a breath. "I can't tell right from wrong."

"Mara, we're married. You're my wife. How can it be wrong for me to kiss you?"

His words made such sense, and she was so lost in him...lost to him...aware only of his arms so tight around her...and his mouth so near...and a flashing red light...

"Excuse me," the voice came out of nowhere. "You folks all right here?"

Mara let out a muffled squeak. Brock stiffened and pulled her into the protection of his chest. "Who's there?" he barked.

A bright white light shone into his eyes, nearly blocking the blinking red beam behind it. "Dona Ana County Sheriff's Department," the voice said. "I noticed your car on the shoulder."

Blinded by the glare of the flashlight, Mara barely made out the face and uniform of a deputy.

"We're fine," Brock said. "Just...uh...enjoying the evening."

"You all right, ma'am?"

Flushing, Mara peered around Brock's shoulder. "I'm fine. Thank you, Officer."

"And the car's okay?"

"Car's fine," Brock said. "Running great."

The deputy nodded. "Well, I guess you know, we really prefer that people don't stop so close to the roadway. Could be dangerous to park on the shoulder, especially at night. Sir, would you mind if I took a look at your driver's license?"

Brock groaned. Tucking Mara against him, he pulled his wallet from his back pocket and handed the license to the patrolman. "I guess you'll want to see the car's registration?"

"Yessir. Proof of insurance, too."

Brock and Mara asked for and received permission to wait in their car while the deputy ran a check on Brock's documents. Everything was in order.

"Merry Christmas, now," the officer called as Brock finally started the Jaguar. "You folks go on home. Santy Claus will be here before you know it."

"Merry Christmas," Brock and Mara said in unison. Brock glanced at the clock on the dashboard. "It's Christmas morning."

Mara snuggled into the depths of her coat as the Jaguar's heater blew warm air on her wet feet. She felt confused and worried and unbearably happy. Most of all, she felt alive. When Brock reached over to take her hand, she wove her fingers through his.

He drove along in silence, his eyes focused on the snowflakes that were falling once again. Mara studied him through half-open lids and realized that at this moment, she didn't care what their future held. All she knew was the pleasure of his kiss. *We're married,* he had said. That made it all right. She had forgiven him, and God had brought them together, and everything was going to be fine. Perching on the tip of her newfound confidence, she held her breath. Hoping. Praying.

When a smile tilted the corner of his mouth, she savored it, tucking it away in her mind to think about when he was away. "You're grinning like the cat that ate the canary. What are you thinking about, Brock?"

He chuckled. "'Twas the night before Christmas, Mara. I'm having visions of sugarplums."

Ramona insisted she didn't mind the late hour. She seemed especially pleased when Brock handed her a fifty-dollar bill. After giving Mara a rundown of Abby's feedings over the course of the evening, Ramona slipped on her coat and headed out to her car. With calls of "Merry Christmas," she drove away, leaving Mara and Brock in the silence of the big house.

"Looks like everyone had a good time," Brock said as he surveyed the great room with satisfaction. The tall tree glowed in the firelight, its myriad ornaments hanging between long garlands of red cranberries and white popcorn. The scented candles flickered on the mantel, logs popped and crackled on the grate.

"They left everything so tidy," Mara observed. She had taken off her coat, but she stood in the foyer, as if suddenly uncomfortable at being alone with Brock. "I guess that's what you get when you invite the housekeeping staff to a party."

He chuckled. "I've never known Rosa Maria to leave a room anything but spotless. I wonder if she and Pierre got through the evening without one of their squabbles."

"They haven't been bad these past few weeks. Maybe they just like to argue around you."

Brock slung his leather jacket over his shoulder and gave the fire a stir with the poker. Orange sparks shot up the black wall of the chimney. Out of the corner of his eye, he could see Mara moving hesitantly into the great room. Her tightly clasped hands and pale face told him exactly how she felt. Nervous.

As much as he hated to risk breaking the truce between them, Brock knew he couldn't keep up this elusive dance with her. The attraction between them was real and powerful. He had never been the kind of man to sidestep an issue. If he wanted something, he went after it until he got it.

Brock set the poker in its stand and straightened from the fire. What he wanted was Mara. She was so different from any other woman he had known. Mara was complicated—intelligent, passionate and, most significant, moral. She was a Christian, and that meant things Brock couldn't quite understand. Todd had told him they had waited until their wedding night to consummate their union. The notion had baffled Brock. Intrigued him. And made him feel somehow dirty.

He certainly was not Todd. The first tinges of guilt he had felt with women were quickly squelched. He'd hardened his heart and put a heavy blanket over his conscience. He was in charge of his own life, after all. At least, that's what he had believed for so many years. Now he knew it had been a lie. He had deceived himself.

His roving ways had not given him as much pleasure as he had told himself. In fact, he realized, spreading himself so thin had diminished him. Left him emptier than ever. Made him look into that hollow pit he now knew so well.

Brock studied the fire. As much as both of them might want to consummate their marriage, Mara wouldn't just climb into Brock's bed. He knew that. She would think about the impact. She would dwell on consequences and ponder implications for the future. Her deliberateness and morality frustrated him, but it was one reason he had come to desire her as he had never desired anyone.

"I'd better check on Abby," Mara said as she skirted the leather sofa a safe distance from him. "It's been hours since I nursed. She's bound to be hungry."

He reached up to a panel on the wall and flipped a switch. "She's quiet," he said in a low voice. "Intercoms never lie."

"Then I guess I'll head for my room." She eyed him from her position across the open space. "Thank you for taking me to the party, Brock. Stephanie seems nice. Maybe she and some of the others could come out to the house one of these days. I doubt it would be a—"

"Mara, come here." Brock held out a hand.

She glanced down the darkened hall as if making certain of her escape route. When she looked at him again, her eyes were luminous. She let out a deep breath. "I'm not ready for this, Brock. It's not right."

"I want to hold you."

"I'm sorry…but I can't—"

"You don't trust yourself."

"Maybe not. Back there on the road, I…I got carried away and didn't think. It was…wonderful… and I still feel so… I did want what happened between us, Brock. I can't deny that anymore. There's no point in trying to lie to you or to myself. But I need time to pray about this. I have to think it all through. You ought to think it over, too."

"I know how I feel. I know what I want. And God knows I'm willing to wait for it."

"God? How can you be sure what He knows?"

He stepped toward her. "I'm not religious like you and Todd. But I do think about God. There are times… Well, I wish I understood God better. I might not have done things the way I have. Maybe I would have been a better man."

"It's not too late."

"It's too late for Todd. Too late for Abby. I blew it. I urged Todd into my life and all my craziness, and look what it got him. He died." Overwhelmed with the loss, the guilt, Brock lowered his head and rubbed his eyes. He couldn't cry. Not in front of Mara. He had shed so many tears, felt such remorse. And he didn't know what to do with it but stuff it away and try to rebuild. Build the fortress with no foundation. The fortress over the big pit in his heart.

"Look, Mara," he said. "About this thing between us… I'll wait until you get it all figured out, if you want to try. And I'll try, too. But in the meantime, I'd like to sit by the fire and hold you."

She wrapped her arms around her stomach and shook her head. "Stephanie was right. You have all the words."

"This is no memorized speech, Mara." He walked toward her, frustration bubbling inside him again. "You make me out to be something I'm not. I'm just a man. I speak my mind."

"Brock, stop right there."

He kept walking. "Don't run again, Mara."

"This is Christmas. I should be thinking about Todd. I am thinking about him."

"I'm thinking about him, too." Pausing a pace away, he ran his hand up her arm. "I'm remembering the time I bought him a collection of baseball cards for Christmas. We were eleven years old, and we went to summer camp together. When Todd opened the box of cards, he was so happy he cried. He told me it was okay to cry, because it was the best present he'd ever gotten."

"Oh, Brock…"

"And I'm remembering when he gave me a decorated chest he'd made out of Popsicle sticks and glued-on shells. I kept my rock collection in it. I still have that box in my bedroom. Todd was my best friend, Mara. I'll never live through a Christmas without thinking about him."

Her lower lip trembled as he pulled her closer. She unknotted her hands and allowed him to draw her into his arms. "I miss Todd," she whispered.

"I miss him, too." He fought the lump that formed in his throat. "But it isn't helping anyone if that keeps us apart."

She laid her cheek on his shoulder, and once again he felt a tumult of emotion tear through him like a tornado. He wanted this woman in every way. He wanted her smile in the morning over coffee, her conversation, her spiritual depths and her intellectual pursuits. He wanted her in his bed at night, a wife with a husband.

And yet he couldn't deny the ache inside at the memory of her true husband. She had married Todd, and in her heart, she was still married to him. Brock couldn't release his own need to be forgiven for ripping Todd out of her life. He didn't want to push

Mara, didn't want to betray his friend, but how could he make himself hold back from something he'd never wanted more?

"Todd won't ever see Abby open presents on Christmas morning," Mara said in a choked voice. "Sometimes it hurts so much."

He kissed the tear that slid down her cheek. He'd made her cry. No wonder she had hated him. She blamed him for the loss of Todd, her husband and Abby's father, and she had to deal with that grief every day of her life.

Brock pondered the guilty joy he felt when Mara came willingly into his arms. Standing on the roadside, she had wanted him as honestly as if there had been no barriers between them. Yet Brock knew that if Todd had not died, his best friend would never have known the taste of Mara's lips. How could he allow himself to take pleasure in that?

"It seems wrong to be anything but sad." Mara's voice broke into his thoughts. "When I let you hold me, it's so good…and then I hate myself for liking it."

"I feel that, too." Brock cupped her face in his hands and tilted it toward the soft light of the candles. "But I can't help what I feel, Mara."

"I'm afraid to let myself even think what I feel."

"You want to be whole, just like I do. You don't want to be a half-empty widow anymore. There's more to you than being a mommy, too. You've got a mind and a body that are waking up after months of numbness. You're churning with new thoughts. You're ready to get on with your life."

"Getting back to work on the fort project has done me good," she acknowledged. "And I know Todd would be glad I'm trying to finish it."

"You're ready to be complete again in other ways, too, Mara. You lost your husband, but you didn't lose your own needs."

Her gray-green eyes searched his. "Come with me, Brock." She took his hand and walked ahead of him toward the fire. "I have something to say to you." She knelt on the woven rug, took off her damp shoes and set them on the hearth. As he sat down beside her, she gazed at the gold ring on her finger.

"You know a lot about me," she said in a low voice. "Sometimes you seem to understand things I'm only beginning to figure out. But there's one thing about me you don't know."

Mesmerized by her closeness, he slipped the silver tinsel from her ponytail and watched the heavy mass of hair fall to her shoulders. "I'm listening, Mara."

"What you don't understand is that I'm a forever kind of person. You're right that I have a mind and a body. But please don't forget I also have a heart. I never fool around with my heart."

She looked at him for affirmation. When he said nothing, she continued. "When I was a young girl—after my parents had been killed in a car wreck—I once lived with a foster family who took me to church every Sunday. They were amazing. Real. Flawed. But filled with a kind of joy and peace I had never seen. I was young, but I understood what I needed and wanted. I turned over my heart, my body, my mind, my whole life to Christ. I gave up trying to control my little world, because I knew I would be so much better in His hands."

"And were you?" he asked. "Look how things turned out."

"My life hasn't been easy. God didn't give any promise that it would be. In fact, just the opposite. Christians can anticipate a lot of hardship. We're to expect persecution, trials, temptations."

Her eyes softened as she continued. "I've struggled every step of the way, Brock. Even now, with a home and financial security, I feel a lot of confusion. I'm not sure which path to take. I don't know what to do about you. But I'm not alone. My faith in Christ has never wavered. He's always available to me. He's my guide. I'm impatient and weak. But Christ is strong, and His Holy Spirit knows when and where to lead me. He's a fortress I can run to. I can hide in the holiness of His name and find safety there. I wouldn't give that up for anything."

"A fortress." Brock thought of the crumbling edifice he had built for himself.

"There's a song that asks, 'Where can I go but to the Lord?' It's the only way, Brock."

"It was Todd's way."

"Yes, and that made all the difference in our marriage. Nine years ago, I gave my heart to Todd Rosemond. I wanted to give him my body, but I waited four years to sleep with that man. That wasn't easy, either." She gave a low laugh. "There were times I was sure I was the last virgin in America."

Though she glanced at Brock, he didn't speak. Rubbing his hands on his thighs, he waited for her to continue.

"On our wedding night, I loved Todd for the first time." She slowly turned the ring on her finger. "I never betrayed that bond. Maybe I never will. Not long ago, I gave my heart to a newborn baby. My body nurtured her for nine months. It still does. It doesn't matter what happens in the years to come. No matter how Abby may hurt me, no matter what paths she chooses in life, no matter how hard things get, I'll never stop loving my daughter."

Mara shut her eyes for a moment. When Brock remained silent, she let out a breath. "What I'm trying to tell you is…I don't give myself lightly to anyone."

"It's all or nothing, is it?" he asked. "Mara, I think I did know that about you."

She studied the fire. He sat silent in the stillness of the great room and tried to read the message behind her words. He had never doubted Mara would be loyal and faithful in whatever she did. For years Brock had observed the passion that drove this woman even now. Her zest for life had appealed to him from the moment he met her.

He knew what Mara was telling him. She hadn't given herself to God, to her husband, even to her child without fully understanding what she was doing. When Mara committed herself to someone, she counted on that person to commit in return.

Now she was asking herself whether she could give her heart to Brock. And she was asking how ready Brock was to give up his own heart. Not only to Mara, but to God.

As he studied the fire, he considered the question. He had married Mara. That showed a certain level of commitment, didn't it? But they had based their marriage on financial terms, nothing more. Another crumbling foundation. Any fortress built on it would crack and topple in time.

Was he willing to turn over his whole life, his dreams, his future to God? Mind, body, heart. Mara talked with such certainty about the seriousness of giving her heart away. He wasn't even sure he knew what had become of his heart in the years he'd spent wandering, lost. Did he even have one to give?

Could he commit the rest of his life to Mara? To one woman? To a life so different from the one he had tried to create for himself? It meant letting go of everything. And grabbing on to something else. To faith. To hope. To love.

Even if he wanted to, he wasn't sure how. Mara said she had turned over her life to Christ. She had given Him control of her world. Todd had urged Brock to do the same thing. Make a decision. Give up. Surrender. What did those words even mean?

"I guess we won't have to worry about you hitting the singles bars," he teased.

She looked up at him and smiled. "Not a chance. I'm not single."

"Whew." He brushed at his forehead in a mock gesture of relief.

"Brock, don't joke about this. I'm serious."

"Always serious." He laid one hand on her damp sock. "I like these snowmen, by the way."

"Thank you. Sandy thoughtfully brought them to everyone's attention. I momentarily had the fashion spotlight at the party."

He winced. "There's nothing more prickly than a jealous woman. I guess Sandy figured out where I stand with you."

Mara's eyebrows rose. "Where do you stand with me, Brock?"

"As close as I can get." He looked into her face. "Something occurs to me, Mara. You tell me you gave your heart to God and to Todd and to Abby. Have you considered what each of them might think about you and me?"

"Constantly. Every time I imagine how Todd would feel if he knew I had kissed you, I get a terribly guilty sensation. It's like I'm being unfaithful to him."

"I know. This evening after I saw you in the kitchen, I went into my room and turned his picture around to face the wall."

"Are we wrong to feel attracted to each other?"

"Attracted? I'd call it a little stronger than that." He picked up her foot, set it on his knee, and began to rub. "I don't know whether it's wrong or right. I just know that even though I would never betray my friend, Todd isn't around anymore. He's gone, Mara. At some point, we both have to get used to that. And when you think about it, Todd had the most generous heart the good Lord ever created. Would he expect you to live the rest of your life grieving him?"

"I don't know."

"I think you do." He studied her. "Who would Todd rather see come together than the two people he loved the most in this world?"

"Maybe…"

"Then there's God. Now, I don't claim to know a lot about religious matters, but it doesn't take a preacher to figure out that life moves according to a plan that's bigger than any of us."

"You believe that?"

"Sure. You told me you've given your life to God, Mara. You reckon He would leave you high and dry? I mean, you lost your husband—do you think God would want you to be unhappy forever?"

"God doesn't want me miserable. But I'm not sure you qualify as the right person to—"

"And what about Abby?" he inserted. "Do you want your daughter to grow up without a man in her life? Don't you want her to have someone to look up to and count on?"

Mara caught her breath. "What are you saying?"

He slid his hand around the back of her neck and pulled her toward him. Their lips met in a soft, tender kiss. As he held her, she clutched his shoulders.

"Brock," she whispered. "Oh, Brock."

"I'm trying to wait for you, woman." His voice was raspy. "I'll hold you all night and every night for the next ten years without touching you if that's what you want. But it's killing me."

"Don't talk, Brock. Don't make me think."

"Then come here and kiss me."

She did, and with her kiss she slid her fingers through his hair and let her lips explore his whole face, his neck, his hands.

"I want to know you as my wife, Mara," he murmured against her ear. "Every day and night for the past three weeks, I thought about you. I told myself I had put you away in a safe place, but I was wrong. You were right there, pervading all my dreams."

"I've tried so hard to remember that I hate you. To resent you. To hold on to my bitterness."

"Please don't hate me, Mara," he whispered, fighting to keep from losing control. "Do you know how difficult this is?"

"Yes," she answered. "Oh, Brock, I want you so much."

At her confession, his heart slammed against his ribs. She did want him. He could see it in the heavy-lidded look in her eyes. As he kissed her, Brock knew if he pushed hard enough, he could have her.

But he had begun to want more. He wanted something beautiful and right. Something holy.

If she gave in to temptation tonight, would she hate him tomorrow? After she'd had time to think…and pray? Would she feel conned? Would she believe he had manipulated her, used her?

"Mara," he said her name again as he set her away and locked his hands together in his lap. "I don't want you to wonder tomorrow if I qualify in God's book of approved men, because I know I don't. Not yet. And I don't want you to wake up and think you betrayed Todd. Don't you see? I want your heart, too."

She touched the side of his face as wonder filled her eyes. As if struggling to find words, she shook her head. "You've always amazed me, Brock."

"And anyway," he said gently, "I think I hear a little girl who's hungry for her midnight snack."

Mara turned her attention toward the intercom. The soft snuffling of a waking baby filtered through the room. The little whimpers quickly grew in volume.

"I'd better go," she said.

Unwilling to release her, he caught her hand. "Mind if I come along?"

"Might as well. Someone once told me Abby needs a man in her life."

He grinned. "So does her mom."

Mara slipped out of his arms and started toward the hall. "I know," she said softly.

Chapter Fifteen

❧

After leaving Mara and Abby snoozing in the nursery, Brock returned to his room and discovered a stack of mail Rosa Maria had placed on his desk while he was gone. Letters, magazines and bills lay in a neat pile. Nothing of interest caught his eye until he spotted the address of the United States Bureau of Land Management.

He opened the envelope and scanned the single sheet of paper inside. The Bureau had decided to terminate Todd's contract. A terse message from the regional director, a Dr. Stephen Long, stated the services of Rosemond Restoration were no longer required at Fort Selden or the other historic forts in southern New Mexico.

Frowning, Brock read the rest of the letter. He knew it had been addressed to him because of his contact with Long around the time of his marriage to Mara. Under financial stress and concerned about her pregnancy, she had accepted his offer to negotiate with the BLM on behalf of Todd's company.

But the contents of this letter told him Mara must have written the agency about her plans to run the business herself. Dr.

Long responded that he could not accept her request to resume work on the reconstruction project, and he warned that her doing so would invalidate the contract that had been made with her late husband.

Frustrated by what he saw as a lack of vision, Brock sat at his desk and turned the contents of the letter over in his mind. Finally he made the decision to keep the news to himself until he could work out a solution. Instinct told him Mara would be angry if he didn't discuss the situation with her right away, but he didn't want to risk throwing anything in the path of their growing relationship.

Besides, Mara might have received the same letter. Maybe she was processing the news even now. If Brock brought it up, she might start feeling cornered—trapped by the circumstances in her life. He couldn't let her withdraw. Not now.

Brock awoke on Christmas morning to a blanket of snow thicker and whiter than a newly washed wool fleece. He lay alone in his huge bed and stared out the window for a long time, thinking about the previous evening—the party, the trip home, the letter from the BLM. He grimaced at the last thought.

Was he being unfair to Mara by not talking to her about the letter? He had always been the kind of man who fixed things himself. Alone. He repaired broken chairs and wobbly tables. He mended fences and nailed shingles on barns. Once already he had stepped into Mara's life to fix a bad situation. He could do it again…as his gift to her.

Brock settled back on his pillow, arms behind his head. Right after the new year began, he would call the BLM and deal with the matter. He would see to it that the Bureau honored the contract, and he would preserve and build on the goodwill growing between Mara and himself. He would force himself to hold his physical desire for her in check. Like a teenager on his first date, he would be careful only to slip his arm around her shoulders or take her hand or give her an occasional peck on the cheek. It wouldn't be easy, but he could do it.

Recalling their conversation from the night before, Brock realized how easily he had slipped into his familiar pattern of thinking this morning. He would take the BLM situation in hand. He would control his emotions. He would do it all.

Mara had told him she gave her whole little world to Christ—mind, body, heart. If that was true, then how could she ever belong to anyone but God? Could Brock possibly hope to have a part in Mara's life?

Slinging back the covers, he stepped out of bed and threw on his robe. Christmas morning—a celebration of the birth of Jesus Christ. For Brock, it had always been a day for giving and receiving gifts. But he knew it meant more than that to Mara. She would be thinking about the holiness of the day and the One who held her life in His hands.

Brock stepped to the window, leaned his arms on the sill and watched the falling snow. He had always believed in God. In Jesus, too. But he recalled how Todd had urged him to relinquish control of his whole life. It was an issue that demanded a decision, his friend had insisted, and Brock needed to choose surrender.

Could he do that? Did he want to? Did God want him to? The last question cinched the matter.

Straightening, Brock clamped his teeth together and nodded. There. He would just do it. Not for Mara. Not for Todd or Abby. He would give up control, because he knew God was his only hope for filling the emptiness inside.

Things might not go better, as Mara had warned him. But he wouldn't be alone. He wouldn't be trying to manage everything and everybody and making a mess of it. Just as important, his priorities would change, and it was past time for that to happen. No more trying to fill the empty pit with business deals, women, adventure, thrills. The Spirit of God would be inside him, and that would be the best foundation a man could have.

Hands against the window frame, he bowed his head. "I give up," he said. "I've botched the whole thing, and I'm sorry. Please forgive me. Take it all, God. Take me. Take my life. Make me more like Jesus and less like Brock Barnett. Erase who

I was and change me into the man You want me to be." He nodded. "I ask this in the name of Jesus Christ. Amen."

Lifting his head, he realized he was looking through a mist. Odd that tears should come when suddenly everything seemed so much clearer.

"Brock?" Cradling Abby, Mara stepped into the kitchen, surprised to find him there already. It was early, and they had stayed up so late the night before.

"Hey there," he said, his voice gentle. "How are my two Christmas angels this morning?"

She smiled. "I just nursed Abby, and she's so drowsy I almost took her back to bed. But I'd put her in the velvet dress you gave her when she was born, and I couldn't wait to take her to the tree. Can you come?"

"Sure."

Mara swallowed as Brock stood and picked up his coffee mug. He wore a pair of faded jeans and a T-shirt, and as he stretched, she thought of the pumas that prowled southern New Mexico.

"I wonder what Santa Claus brought me," he said as they walked down the long hall to the great room.

"What did you ask him for?"

"Dangerous question, Mrs. Barnett."

Mara tried to control her blush by concentrating on settling herself in front of the tree and situating Abby in her arms. She knew what Brock wanted. It was the same thing she wanted. But every time she had stirred during a restless night, she had prayed to be delivered from this agony. She could not accept that they were truly married. Not in the eyes of God. Brock wasn't God's plan for her. He couldn't be. He was too rough, too wild, too materialistic. He didn't love the Lord the way Todd had—the way Mara knew her husband must. And that meant she had to get out of his house. Fast.

"Here you are," she said, placing a gift on his lap. "I made this while you were away."

As she held Abby, he unwrapped the afghan she had crocheted for him in shades of New Mexico—the purple of a mountain sunset, the sage green of the prickly pear cactus, the dusty brown of the high desert. Brock ran his hand over the careful stitches that undulated across the coverlet like rolling hills.

"It's beautiful," he said with a breathtaking smile that made her heart sing. "Thank you, Mara. And here's something for you."

Opening her gift, she saw a small box carefully crafted and polished. It had a hinged lid and a small, brass clasp. "Did you make this, Brock? It's lovely!"

"I used woods from the ranch—mesquite, cedar and pine— sandwiched to show their different shades of brown. I thought you might like to keep jewelry in it. I'm afraid it's not big enough to hold much."

Mara gazed at the box, too overwhelmed to speak. He had made this just for her? Like the rocker, it revealed something about him she had tried too hard to ignore. Brock was more than a reckless man on a joyride through life. He was an artist. A craftsman. He cared about his ranch, the gifts of nature, beauty. He cared about *her.*

And he had made this for her jewelry. She looked down at the hand that held the box. Her left hand.

"Is the box too small?" he asked. "I had a little trouble with that hinge right there. Maybe I should have bought you something in Santa Fe. Mara?"

A tear slid down her cheek as she placed the gift in her lap and turned her hand first one way and then the other, front and back. Unable to explain the emotion filling her heart, she slipped off the wedding ring Todd had given her. She put it inside the box, closed the lid and fastened the clasp.

She had worn the ring every minute of every day since she had been married to Brock. She had worn it through labor and delivery. She had worn it washing dishes and playing in the snow. Now it was time to put it in a special place, in a box crafted by Todd's best friend. It was time to let it go.

Unable to look at Brock, Mara began opening his second gift. This one was for Abby. Brock shifted uncomfortably as she tore away the wrapping paper to find the little Popsicle-stick chest

Todd had given to him so many years before. Stuck on with white school glue, fragile shells clung to the bare wood.

"I thought Abby might like to have something from her father, even though she's too young to understand," Brock explained. "And I left my rock collection inside, too."

"Her father," Mara choked out. Suddenly the word meant more than she had ever realized. Todd was the man who had given Abby life—her father in the traditional sense. But Brock…whose boyhood rock collection included bits of obsidian and a chunk of quartz…he was the man who could give Abby a future. He was the man who could teach Abby the names of the stones, how to ride a horse, how to build a fence. He could coach her soccer team, take her out for ice cream, teach her to drive a car, buy her velvet Christmas dresses, give her away at her wedding. Brock might be Abby's father, too, if Mara could let him.

"Brock, the box is…it's…" Tears rolling down her face, she shook her head and hugged Abby tightly.

"Mara, I'm here." Brock went to her and wrapped his arms around her.

"I know," she whispered. "I know."

When she looked into his eyes, she saw a man she longed to call husband. His lips were warm as his mouth tenderly claimed hers. She slipped her arms around his neck, and with the baby nestled between them, she gave herself to his words of promise.

But when Abby began to whimper, Brock straightened and turned away from Mara. "I can do this," she heard him mutter. "Not on my own."

He grabbed the nearest present. "Here's something from Pierre. I guarantee this'll be for the kitchen. He always gives me something like a pastry crimper or a noodle maker."

Mara brushed her damp cheek and tried to concentrate. "I didn't know you liked to make noodles."

"I don't," he said. "Pierre likes to make noodles."

But when he unwrapped the large square box, it wasn't a kitchen tool at all. It was a heavy, leather-bound family Bible.

Brock opened the cover and turned to the first gold-edged page. The family tree had been inscribed in beautiful black calligraphy.

"Abigail Rosemond Barnett." He read aloud the central inscription complete with Abby's birthdate. Then he read the words beneath the baby's name. "Mara Rosemond Barnett...Mother."

When he fell silent, Mara leaned against his shoulder. "Brock Davis Barnett," she said softly. "Father."

Brock had never known the kind of peace and comfort the following days held. Kept away from his work by the snowstorm that had covered the plains, Brock spent hours with Mara and Abby. Together Mara and he bathed and diapered, rocked and cuddled the growing baby girl. Abby blossomed in the attention.

She wasn't the only one who felt nurtured and secure. Brock reveled in the knowledge that he was a changed man. He felt new and different inside. For the first time in his life, he understood what had made Todd so special. Step by step, he tested himself, letting go of one thing after another. Praying silently before he made decisions. Reading the big Bible Pierre had given him. Putting Mara and Abby ahead of himself. Thinking about their needs before his own.

This new life felt strange and awkward at times. But Brock had no doubt he had done the right thing. He wanted to be different, whole, complete. And he was.

Unwilling to tell Mara until he felt sure he could follow through on his decision, he basked in the beauty of quiet time spent with this woman God somehow had seen fit to allow into his life. Their hours of cooking in the kitchen or watching the snow fall outside the window were a tonic to him. If the years of his lonely childhood had caused Brock to build a wall around himself, Mara's presence gently removed brick after brick.

On impulse, they decided to host a New Year's Eve gathering to introduce some of their friends to each other. Mara phoned Sherry and two of the teachers she had worked with at the academy. Brock invited Joe, Travis, Stephanie and a couple of others from the Las Cruces crowd. Everyone was encouraged to stay the night at the ranch house rather than drive back to the city on the dark, snowy highway. Brock dismissed Pierre and the housekeepers to spend the holiday with their families.

While preparing hors d'oeuvres the afternoon of the party, Brock couldn't keep his eyes off Mara. Dressed in jeans, a blue T-shirt and a pair of white sneakers, she again was the young girl he had met with Todd years before. She laughed and teased him, her eyes sparkling in fun as she hurried around the kitchen clinking pots and stirring saucepans.

"We should have asked Pierre to do all this, you know," she said, her fingers deep in a bowl of mushroom stuffing. "I'll bet he knows how to use shoestring carrots to tie asparagus in neat little bundles."

Brock gave a mock scowl at the sight of his own large fingers working to remove the tiny, soft mushroom stems. "I still don't see what was wrong with my idea. Red string licorice and green peas—it even goes with the holiday season."

Mara laughed. "I suppose you'd have us put this stuffing into chocolate cupcakes?"

"Easier than pulling the stems off these little mushrooms."

She giggled. "Those caps are starting to look more like pancakes, Brock."

"Oh, yeah?" He held up a small brown mushroom, its delicate edges hopelessly split. "Wait'll I put the stuffing in."

"You'd better do it right, or else," she said, starting across the room.

He caught her around the waist and swung her toward him. "Says who?"

"Says me."

"Woman, I'd do just about anything you asked me to," he said, his voice dropping. Her lips tilted toward his, and he brushed a kiss across her mouth. Before he knew it, he had pulled her into his arms.

If they hadn't been expecting company, Brock might have lost what slender control he had left. As it was, he remembered Sherry was due any minute to help them get ready. Lifting up an urgent prayer, he let Mara go almost as fast as he had grabbed her. She stood before him, flushed and breathless, and it was all he could do to keep from taking her in his arms again. As he hesitated, Mara whirled on her heel, announced she had to nurse Abby and change clothes for the party, and half ran out of the kitchen.

Busying himself with stuffing the mushrooms and arranging slices of cold meats on a silver tray, Brock spent the next half hour trying to push images of Mara out of his mind. Impossible. It was all fine and dandy to pray before he acted, to tread carefully, to avoid mistakes. But how long could this go on? He wanted Mara as his wife. He wanted to make their union permanent. Holy.

But where did Mara stand on this? On Christmas morning she had taken off her wedding ring, but had she really accepted Todd's death? And what did she want with Brock? Was she testing him? If so, she was doing a great job. As he wedged a rolled slice of beef between two rolls of ham, Brock frowned. This waiting was becoming intolerable.

"Did you remember to buy the eggnog, Brock?" Mara asked as she re-entered the kitchen. "I didn't see it in the refrigerator."

He glanced up, and once again he was thrown a curve by the sight of this woman who had miraculously come into his life. Dressed in a black skirt and a matching black top, Mara had left her blond hair hanging long and loose. Her legs were sheathed in sheer black stockings and velvet high heels. The faint fragrance of a spicy perfume drifted across the room. He grabbed the back of a kitchen chair for support.

"Brock?" she said. "Did you hear me? I asked about the eggnog."

"It's chilling," he replied.

"I hope we have enough of these sausage balls." She pulled open the oven door and bent to look inside. The hem of her skirt swished against her knees. Brock gave up holding on to the chair and sat down in it.

"And these sausages," she said, turning to the crockery pot filled with tiny barbecued links. "If they don't stay hot, they won't be any good."

"I'm no good," he mumbled.

Mara swung around. "What?"

"Nothing."

She smiled. "Brock, would you light the candles in the dining room, please?"

He'd have crawled across the dunes at White Sands if she'd asked.

Brock went through the rest of the evening like a zombie on automatic pilot. Guests arrived. He dipped out eggnog, listened to jokes, made polite conversation. All he could think about was Mara.

She drifted through the clusters of visitors, her black outfit making mesmerizing shadows in his brain. Mara's hair sifted and draped around her shoulders. Her long legs transfixed him with every step.

If Brock hadn't told himself a thousand times he was incapable of it, he would have been sure he had fallen in love with her. He wanted her—definitely. Wanted a lifetime with her. But love? Brock Barnett? No, he didn't have it in him.

Did he?

Mara spent most of the evening apart from Brock as she tended to the guests. He felt he was in a Christmas Eve party rerun. Mara talked for a long time with her friend Sherry. She introduced Sherry to Stephanie, and they seemed to hit it off. Mara moved constantly in and out of the kitchen, carrying trays of hors d'oeuvres or filling bowls with nuts. As midnight approached, she slipped through the crowded room to Brock's side, a shy smile tilting the corners of her pink lips.

"Having fun?" she whispered.

"Now I am." He slipped his arm around her shoulder.

"Ten, nine, eight, seven, six." As everyone joined in the countdown, he folded her into his embrace.

"Five, four, three, two." He turned her toward him and cradled her head in his hands, tilting her chin upward.

"One...Happy New Year!"

As cheers went up and confetti drifted down, he kissed her lips. Her arms slid around him, holding him close. If he could have pulled away, he might have tried. He didn't have a prayer.

"Mara," he murmured against her lips, "we've got to talk. I mean it."

Around them cheers turned to laughter. Music rose in volume. Someone brushed past them. Brock was lost in Mara's arms. And then there was a strange hush.

"Mara?" Brock recognized Sherry's voice.

Catching her breath, Mara pulled away from him. "Oh…is…is anyone going to…uh…refill the eggnog? Well, I guess I should do that."

"Mara?" Sherry repeated.

Brock looked around the room and quickly figured out that he and Mara had unknowingly become the center of attention with their New Year's kiss. Just as the silence was about to become awkward, Brock's friend Joe lifted his glass and shouted, "To the newlyweds!"

"To the newlyweds," the other guests echoed, laughing.

"Did you check the eggnog supply, Sherry?" Mara asked quickly. "I'll see what's left in the refrigerator."

Turning away from Brock without a backward look, she hurried across the room, her heels clicking on the hardwood.

What now? he wondered.

Mara had never been so embarrassed in her life. She could feel her cheeks flaming as she fled into the kitchen and threw open the refrigerator door. She had been smooching Brock like some teenager at a high school party. Sherry had seen. Everyone had seen.

"Mara?" Sherry seemed to be able to say nothing else.

"What?" Mara exclaimed, yanking out an eggnog carton and slamming the refrigerator door. "Do you have something to say?"

"I just…well, Mara…I mean, you and Brock…"

"Listen, Sherry, I'm going to check on Abby. It's past time for her to wake up. Say good night to everyone for me, will you?"

Without waiting for Sherry to agree to the request, Mara left the kitchen and made her way down the long, dimly lit hall.

Oh, she was a fool for the man's kisses. And she'd made an absolute idiot of herself in front of their friends.

She had been so careful to see that no one thought the marriage was anything more than a business arrangement. She had assured herself it was nothing more. But how could anyone believe that after what they had just seen? How could she believe it herself?

Sure enough, Abby was wailing in the nursery. The intercom that broadcast the baby's hungry cries had been drowned out by the party noise. Flooded with guilt, Mara picked up the hot, damp bundle and cuddled her for a moment until Abby's shrieks softened to piteous sobs of relief.

Mara quickly changed the baby's diaper and pulled a fresh nightgown over her tiny head. She half fell into the rocking chair and pulled up her satin blouse. In moments, Abby's contented nursing reminded her that other things in the world were much more important than an impulsive, wayward kiss in front of friends.

All the same, as Mara put her drowsy baby back into the crib twenty minutes later, she wondered if she should go back to the party and find Brock. Maybe it would be appropriate simply to let everyone know that things had changed between her and Brock. Maybe she should smile confidently and tell them that she...that he...

That they what? She didn't know what to say. As she walked across the room, Mara gave up the hope of explaining herself. She didn't know what she meant to Brock Barnett, and she was afraid to admit what he had come to mean to her.

But when she stepped into her room, Mara realized she was going to have to come up with something. Sherry sat in the chair by Mara's bed, her shoes kicked to the floor and her feet curled under her. Her eyes were inquisitive as she rested her chin on her hand.

"Is Abby okay?" she asked.

"She was ravenous, but now she's gone back to sleep. So, is the party over?" Mara hoped her voice sounded light. "I thought Abby was going to nurse forever. I guess everyone's gone to bed, haven't they?"

"What's going on, Mar?" Sherry caught Mara's hand as she passed. "Come on, it's me here. What's up with you and Brock? That was no friendly peck on the cheek I saw a few minutes ago."

"Well…on New Year's Eve…" Abandoning excuses, Mara walked to her closet and leaned on the door frame. She sighed. "I'm kind of embarrassed about it, to tell you the truth."

"Are you okay? I thought you—"

"I'm fine." Mara absently adjusted some hangers. "Really, I'm fine."

"Are you in love with him?"

"Sherry!" Mara swung around, half tempted to laugh at her friend's audacity. "I told you things are fine."

"You're on the rebound, you know. You miss Todd, and you're vulnerable."

"So, when did you get a doctorate in psychology, Sher?" Mara stepped out of her high heels and padded across the room in her stocking feet. "You don't know what's going on here."

"Do you?"

"Yes, I do."

"What?"

"I…admire Brock."

"Oh, please."

"I do. He's good at his work. He cares about the ranch. He's a carpenter, too. I bet you didn't know that."

"I'm impressed."

Mara plopped down on her bed. "Okay, maybe things have heated up between us a little."

"What I witnessed in the living room was an inferno."

"It was a kiss."

"It was love."

"Oh, Sherry, go to bed. Your room's down the hall."

Sherry crossed her arms and stuck out her chin. Her blue eyes sparkled with determination as she stared at Mara.

"Spill it," she commanded.

Mara let out a deep breath and flopped back on the bed. "You drive me crazy. Okay…I'll admit I don't really understand what's happening. One minute I was sure I had done the right thing to marry Brock and take care of the future for Abby. The next minute I was in his arms."

"The next minute?"

"It took a few weeks."

"The last time I visited you out here, we went over all of Brock Barnett's flaws, remember? He's arrogant, self-centered, a perfectionist, stubborn and not at all religious."

"He's loyal, hardworking, funny, strong, high-minded—"

"Oh, no! Mara, you are in love with him!"

"Todd loved him. I'm just seeing the things Todd appreciated for all those years. In many ways, Brock really is a very good person."

"He's bad news, Mara." Sherry moaned and sank down in her chair. "How can you suddenly forget about all those women he's carted around? The man is a bona fide playboy."

Mara stared at the ceiling of her room. "I'm not sure about that anymore, Sher. He's a different man these days. He's kind. Gentle. Almost tame."

"Tame? Are we talking about Brock Barnett?"

"He prays at the dinner table."

"Are you kidding me, Mara? Brock prays?"

"He's changed. He seems very serious about things."

"Things? You're not a thing. Abby's not a thing. Have you thought about how your daughter might be affected by this?"

"Of course I have. You should see Brock with Abby. He's wonderful. He takes her everywhere. He changes her diapers and bathes her. They make breakfast together nearly every morning."

Sherry groaned again.

"And he puts his feet on the table these days," Mara concluded.

"You're nuts. You've gone completely bonkers over the man." Sherry leaned forward and shook her finger in Mara's face. "You're talking about his feet, Mara!"

"You just don't understand. Brock is relaxed with me, don't you get it? He feels comfortable, and so do I. I like him."

Sherry's expression grew serious. "What about Todd? How comfortable do you think he'd be over the notion of you falling in love with his best friend?"

Mara studied the half inch of bare white skin on her ring finger. "Sherry, Todd is gone. He isn't coming back."

Sherry's eyes followed Mara's gaze. "You took off your ring. Mara, do you know what this means?"

"It means I'm letting go."

"It hasn't even been a year!"

"It feels like ten. All these months, I've felt numb. I've been so lonely. Right now, I swear I could almost fly. Sherry, it scares me silly how happy I feel with that man."

Sherry shook her head. "I want you to be happy. If anyone does, it's me, right? The last thing I'd wish for my best friend is to spend her life in misery. But I can't help thinking you're setting yourself up for a fall. Brock is going to use you."

"That's ridiculous. What's he getting out of it? A wife, a baby, extra bills to pay, headaches—"

"A gorgeous blonde with long legs and—"

"I'm a nursing mother!"

"So what? You look beautiful, and Brock can't take his eyes off you. He's a man in lust."

"Lust? Is that what you think this is? You're impossible!" Mara rolled off the bed and stomped across the room. Sherry's comment had hit far too close to the mark for comfort. Mara had wondered if her own feelings for Brock centered on physical desire, and she had no doubt of his longings for her. Were they actually lusting—that enormous biblical no-no? Or were they a married couple denying each other far too long?

"Do you really think this is all just physical?" she asked Sherry. "You know Brock could have any woman he wanted."

"Why should he when you're right here and willing? Have you slept with him yet?"

"That's none of your business." Mara glared at her friend until Sherry looked away. "No, I haven't slept with Brock, but if I decide to, I won't ask your permission. Don't forget, he is my husband."

"Oh, Mara! Don't you see how easily he could take advantage of you?"

"Do you think I'm some spineless jellyfish?"

"I think you're a widow with a two-month-old baby. I think you miss your husband, and you've been scared and lonely. I think Brock Barnett is a man who may be nice enough, but he never learned about love or commitment. He's spent his entire life chasing skirts, accumulating money and heading off on wild adventures. You aren't forgetting Brock was with Todd when he fell off the cliff, are you?"

Mara shook her head. "No," she whispered.

"Does Brock admit he was responsible?"

"We haven't really talked about it."

"Of course not. Why would he want to dredge that up?"

"No, it's my fault, Sherry. Brock has tried several times to tell me what happened. I can't bring myself to hear the details, even though I know it would probably be healing for both of us."

"Mara, are you really getting deeply involved with this man? Are you falling in love with him?"

"I don't know what's happening, Sher. When I try to sort it out, I keep coming back to the same thing. Todd loved Brock for seventeen years. Now I understand why."

Sherry shut her eyes and let out a deep, exasperated sigh. "Todd was a man. Brock is a man. They fished and hiked and camped out together. They were buddies, for heaven's sake. Pals. You're a woman, Mara. That's completely different. We're talking sick babies in the middle of the night, dinner on the table at six sharp, PTA meetings and bake sales, getting old and wrinkled together, brushing his dentures every night—"

"Sherry!" Mara burst out laughing. "Now I know why you've never married."

"That's right. And I sure wouldn't get myself hooked up permanently with a man who had an eye for pretty women and a nose for adventure. Besides, Brock is not a Christian. You told me that when this whole idea first came up. You reminded me that the Bible teaches it's wrong for us to marry someone who doesn't share our faith. It's bad for us, bad for the children, bad for the marriage. If I were you, Mara, I'd put a halt to the whole thing and find a way to make it on my own."

"You know I'm trying to find work. I told you about the situation with the fort project Todd contracted with the Bureau of Land Management. I'm doing my best to keep Rosemond Restoration going."

"Have you found a builder who's willing to work with you?"

"Yes, and he's terrific. He really has a feel for the plans Todd drew up. The man even knows some of the history and understands the ambience I want. He's worked with adobe all his life, so this is right up his alley."

"Sounds great."

"If I can convince the BLM to honor Todd's contract, I'll start working at Fort Selden right away."

"What about Abby?"

"The housekeeper's daughter, Ramona, said she'd love to watch Abby during the day. It's hard to think about leaving my daughter all those hours, but it won't be for long. Once we get the project up and running, I can take Abby out to the site with me." Mara pursed her lips. "Believe me, Sherry, there's nothing I'd like more than to become self-reliant."

"And move out of this house so you can start living on your own."

Mara studied her friend. "I'm not sure about that part, Sherry."

Chapter Sixteen

❧

The first Monday of the new year, Brock picked up his telephone and dialed Washington, D.C. With Mara and Abby in Las Cruces visiting the builder, Pierre puttering in the kitchen and the housekeepers busy cleaning the wings, the house was quiet. A file that included the recent letter tucked under his arm, Brock strolled into the dining room as he asked to speak with the regional director.

When a voice came over the receiver, it was younger and crisper than Brock had expected. "Dr. Stephen Long speaking," the voice said. "How may I help you?"

"This is Brock Barnett in New Mexico. I'm calling in reference to your decision to terminate a contract with the Rosemond Restoration Company."

"Ah, you must have gotten my letter."

"I have it in front of me."

"Good. Then you know the Bureau can't agree to continue the project without Todd Rosemond heading it up."

"And you know that Mara Rosemond Barnett now runs the company. She is expecting the BLM to honor the contract."

"I'm aware of that." His voice hardened. "Mr. Barnett, surely you know your wife is not qualified to carry on with this. We're dealing with seven sites of vital historic significance here. A history teacher and a man with a bulldozer cannot, in the agency's opinion, accomplish a professional restoration."

Brock sat down in his chair and propped his feet on the dining-room table. "Anything else?"

"My position is clearly stated in the letter."

"Dr. Long, when was the last time you looked at the contract you made with Rosemond Restoration?"

There was a moment of silence. "I'm looking at it right now, as a matter of fact. It's signed by Todd Rosemond."

"I see that signature." Brock propped his copy of the contract on his legs. "I also see that the two parties in the contract are the Bureau of Land Management and Rosemond Restoration Company, not you and Todd Rosemond. As I said before, Mara Rosemond Barnett now owns that company. And she's completely capable of restoring those forts."

"I hardly think so."

"I know so. I also think legal wrangling over this matter would create needless expense for all concerned."

"That doesn't concern me. Our legal department is more than capable of handling it. Besides, there's a time limit on the contract, and it's nearly up. I doubt she could put together a legal challenge in time."

"If I were you, I wouldn't put her to the test on that."

"What are you suggesting, Mr. Barnett?"

"I'm suggesting you let Mara Rosemond Barnett supervise the project."

"Look, let's speak frankly here. I received your wife's résumé in the mail. She's obviously educated, and perhaps she did help her husband with the research and plans for Fort Selden. That still doesn't make her a qualified restorationist. You're a businessman, Mr. Barnett. Would you let someone with no experience, no references and few credentials oversee a project of such historical and economic importance to the State of New Mexico?"

"Sure I would. There's nothing to lose and a lot to gain. Mara is the best thing the Bureau has going right now. Read the contract. There's a clause on page three that allows you to inspect the work in progress and terminate if it doesn't meet with your approval. Give Mara a month, then fly out here and take a look at the site. If you think she's doing a good job, that'll save you starting the whole bid process over again. If you don't like what she's doing, shut her down."

For almost a minute, the silence on the line told Brock his suggestion was being weighed. Then Long spoke again.

"Considering your concern about the wording in the contract, and since we would retain oversight, I'm willing to re-evaluate Mrs. Barnett as the potential project director. But even if I changed my mind, it wouldn't do much good."

"Why not?"

"Money. The fort project has lost its base of support. Before the BLM contracted with Rosemond, we promoted the project rather heavily. A foundation in Albuquerque decided to throw some funding our way. It was enough for us to give the go-ahead to the Rosemond company for the first fort. But when Mr. Rosemond passed away and we weren't able to continue with the project immediately, the foundation pulled its backing. We have a little money set aside, but it's not enough to complete the work on even one fort."

Brock propped one foot on the other and studied his boots. "I don't believe that has to be a problem, Dr. Long," he said. "I imagine there are plenty of folks around who are always looking for a tax write-off, especially with the price of oil going up again."

Long fell silent for a long moment. "Well, I can't think of a better place for citizens to put their money than enriching the heritage of the land."

"I can't, either." Brock lifted his focus to the snow melting outside his window. "I'd better be going, Dr. Long. I've got some hungry cattle to feed."

"I'll be in touch."

"You talk things over with Mara next time. She's the boss."

"I'll do that."

Brock pressed the button on the phone and set the receiver on the table. His face softened into a smile. Mara was going to be one happy woman.

"You never used to eat lunch at the house," Mara commented the following Thursday as they sat in the dining room over plates of pasta vinaigrette. "As a matter of fact, you didn't eat supper here very often, either."

"Had no reason to," Brock said.

"The food's the same."

"Different company." He speared a curly noodle. "You beat out old Pierre for conversation any day, and you're a lot better looking."

Mara smiled. Brock had kept his distance since the incident at the New Year's Eve party, and neither of them had brought up the subject of their stroke-of-midnight kiss. All the same, he had eaten every meal at the house, he had come in early in the evenings and he had spent a lot of time with her and Abby. In spite of Sherry's dire warnings, Mara had enjoyed every minute with him.

"Maybe so," she conceded lightly, "but Pierre wins hands-down in the kitchen."

"I don't know about that. These croissants you made are the best I've ever tasted."

"Pierre's a good teacher." Mara fiddled with her napkin, oddly pleased at Brock's compliment. "Unfortunately, I haven't had a lesson in ages. I've spent so much time on the fort project I haven't even worked on the quilt with Ermaline."

"How are things with the builder?"

"Great. I'd like to invite Mr. Dominguez out to the house some evening for dinner. You'd enjoy talking with him. He's read all the plans, and he doesn't see any problem doing the wall reconstruction. He's an older man, and he's spent years building adobe homes. He says all the good jobs these days are going to young men who work in steel and concrete."

"Has he been to the site?"

"Lots of times. He's a serious history buff. His family has deep roots in this area, and he loves combing through museums. He goes to Frontier Days at Fort Selden every year."

"What does he think about working on the other forts after Fort Selden is complete?"

"He's ready to retire from his construction business, and he and his wife want to buy an RV and live at the different sites." She let out a deep breath. "Everything is falling into place, Brock. I just hope I don't have trouble with the Bureau of Land Management over the contract."

"I doubt you will."

"I wish I had your faith. BLM sort of backed away after Todd—"

"Excuse me, Mrs. B.," Ermaline said, stepping into the dining room. "You have a phone call from a Dr. Long. Shall I ask him to call back after dinner?"

Mara frowned. She didn't know any physicians named Long. "Just take his number and tell him I'll—"

"No," Brock interjected. "Go ahead. Take the call."

Mara shrugged as Ermaline handed her the phone. "This is Mara Barnett."

"This is Dr. Stephen Long with the Bureau of Land Management in Washington, D.C."

"Oh, yes." Mara glanced up at Brock and gestured toward the phone. "It's them," she mouthed. As Brock nodded, she returned to the conversation. "What can I do for you, Dr. Long?"

"Well, I'm hoping you can do some work for us."

"I would like that."

"Next Monday I'll be flying into El Paso and then driving up to Las Cruces to begin a tour of several fort sites. I'd like to meet with you for an interview at that time. Would that be convenient for you?"

"Certainly."

"Good. We'll also invite the state monument ranger and the manager of the visitors' center at Fort Selden. They're eager to get to know you. If all goes as I expect, we can get started on the restoration right away."

Mara felt a bubble of elation well up in her chest. "If no one minds, I'll bring Mr. Dominguez. He's my adobe contractor."

"That would be fine." Dr. Long was silent for a moment. "You do understand that your work will be subject to my inspection and approval?"

"Of course. And I'm sure you won't be disappointed, Dr. Long."

"Well, then, I'll see you at about two Monday afternoon in our Las Cruces office."

As Mara placed the phone on the dining-room table, she knew her hand was shaking. Never—not even when she was hired for her first teaching job—had she felt such excitement.

"He wants to interview me," she said in almost a whisper. "Monday."

Brock grinned. "That job is yours."

"I hope so. I want this so much, Brock. At first I felt I had to keep the company going for Todd's sake. It had been his dream all his life. But as time went on, I knew it was something I needed to do for myself. Now I want to touch those adobe walls and breathe life back into the old fort."

"You will, Mara."

She stared into his deep-set brown eyes. "Thank you, Brock."

"For what?" He lifted his cloth napkin to his mouth.

"You believe in me. That means a lot."

He studied her for a moment. "You mean a lot to me, Mara. You and Abby. But you already know that."

She closed her eyes. Wanting to hear more and at the same time wanting to flee, she waited.

"I've kept my distance like I promised," he told her. "But when you kissed me on New Year's Eve, I knew that was no holiday tradition. I'm not going to push you, Mara. But there is one thing I want to know."

She wrapped her own napkin around her hand. "Brock, please—"

"If you take on the fort job, are you moving out of this house?"

She sighed. "I don't know."

"Tell me."

"I don't know yet!" She stood up from the table. "Are you my landlord—wanting thirty days' notice?"

"Mara, you're my wife." He pushed back from the table, rose and walked around to her. "I deserve to know. Mara, we've been tiptoeing around for weeks. I've held back from Abby."

"No, you haven't."

"No? You think all I want to do is change her diaper and give her a bath? I'd like to take her out in the pickup and show her things on the ranch. I'd like the hands to meet her. I'd like to let more of my friends see her. Let them see you, too, for that matter. And I'm not talking about introducing the pair of you as my best friend's widow and their daughter. If I had my way, Mara, I'd stop this crazy game we're playing, and start…start…"

"Start what?" Her heart was beating so hard she was sure he could hear it. "You see? You don't know either. What are we? Acquaintances? Friends? Housemates? Or husband and wife? Every time I think about it, I get confused. I'm scared. You are, too. You don't know what you want. Brock, I'm walking out of this room now, and I'm asking you to please just…just…"

"I do know what I want, Mara. It's the same thing you want. You want me to follow you right out of this room. You want me to take you in my arms and hold you and kiss you until you're shivering. That's what you want. Why won't you admit it?"

"Because I'm afraid," she said softly. "Afraid I won't want you to stop until it's too late."

Dropping the napkin on her chair, she turned away from him once again and left the room.

Mara spent the rest of the afternoon preparing for her interview with Dr. Long. Earlier that morning, Abby had developed a stuffy nose that made her cranky and demanding, so Mara decided to keep her nearby in case she needed comforting. She laid the baby on a blanket on the floor so Abby could kick and play with her rattle, then she picked up a yellow legal pad and began to jot notes to herself. Surely keeping busy would help her avoid thinking about Brock.

Wrong. Brock was far too real to dismiss. He was her husband and her friend and her housemate. Why couldn't he be her lover, too? She tried to remember Sherry's admonitions. They rang hollow. Mara wanted everything about Brock, and he wanted her. Did this mean they should call their marriage real? And if they did, what then? Could she really trust Brock with her future? Did she want to spend the rest of her life with a man who didn't share her faith? A man whose past might easily beckon him again?

Mara looked down at her baby. Tiny feet up in the air, Abby was gazing in fascination at her hand. She turned it first one way and then the other. Mara recalled taking off her wedding ring on Christmas morning. Though her left hand was still bare, she felt very much like a married woman.

"Oh, Abby," she whispered as she stretched out on the blanket beside her daughter. "Do you want Brock to be your daddy? What does God have planned for you, sweet girl? I wish I knew what was right."

Mara stroked her fingers across a cheek so soft she almost couldn't feel the downy skin. Instinctively, Abby turned toward the touch, her mouth pursed. Mara smiled and kissed the baby's forehead.

"All you really want is to eat and sleep and stay dry, don't you?" She dabbed at the baby's damp nose with a tissue. "There, is that better?"

Mara let Abby's tiny, curled fingers wrap around her index finger. As Mara wiggled it, Abby's hand moved in unison. "We're two peas in a pod, you and I. You're ready to nurse right when I'm so full of milk I think I might pop. You fall asleep just when I'm so tired I can't keep my eyes open. I think we're connected, little one. So tell me, what do you think of that guy who likes to make breakfast with you every morning?"

Abby did her best to put Mara's finger in her mouth. Realizing it was futile, she let out a cry of frustration. Her tiny forehead wrinkled and her skin turned bright red. As her mouth opened in the beginning of a wail, Mara chuckled and picked her up.

"All right, have it your way." She sat up and settled Abby on her lap. Lifting her T-shirt, she nestled the baby and let out a deep breath.

The decision of whether to commit to Brock obviously had to be made. Sherry had made her feelings clear. Their pastor certainly would warn Mara of the inevitable peril of giving her heart to a man who couldn't raise Abby as a Christian father ought.

And God? No matter how hard Mara prayed, she couldn't hear Him telling her to run. It made no sense, but more and more, Mara felt that God had put Brock in her life for a distinct purpose. Was she just fooling herself—believing what she wanted to believe? Or was it possible that God could allow, even bless, this strange union?

Mara had no doubt that the Lord she worshiped could take any human tragedy, error or outright sin and use it for His glory. The Scriptures were full of examples. All things—even Todd's death—would work together for Mara's good if she loved the Lord and followed His calling. But that was the catch. Had she been letting the Holy Spirit lead? Or was she listening to her own heart instead?

Frustrated as usual by her uncertainties, she flipped the page on the legal pad and turned her thoughts to the fort project and the coming interview with Dr. Long. The rest of the afternoon, Mara focused on her work and her daughter.

By suppertime, she felt sure she had put everything in perspective. Those were her priorities, after all—Abby and the restoration company. Brock was a confusing, unexpected wrinkle in the tapestry of her life. The best thing to do was stay as far from him as possible until she could secure her job and move out on her own. From a distance, she would be able to look back at the situation and evaluate how she felt about the man. But here—in his house—she was much too close to him to see clearly.

Mara called the kitchen on the intercom and asked Pierre to send a meal to her room. While Abby slept, she took a long bath in lavender oil, then she slipped into her favorite night-gown and fuzzy robe. Curled before the fire in her bedroom, she savored broiled chicken breast and julienne potatoes. She decided she was handling a difficult experience with amazingly good sense.

But in spite of Mara's self-assurance, Abby chose this night to stay awake for hours after what was to have been her final feeding of the evening. Mara wiped the baby's runny nose, gave her the medicine she had gotten from the doctor and worried that what she had thought was a cold might be something worse. She tried nursing her daughter several times, but Abby only grew more distressed. For what seemed like an eternity, Mara rocked and rocked until she was so drowsy she could hardly hold her eyes open. But every time she tried to get up and put her in the crib, Abby burst into tears again.

Worn out, Mara finally checked her bedside clock. Two in the morning. With a groan, she picked up Abby, went into the sitting room, and began to walk her around and around. Instead of calming the child, this made her sob harder. Mara tried singing as she walked, then she tried dancing, then she broke down and started crying herself.

"Abby, please don't do this," she pleaded over the baby's shrieks. "I have three days to get ready for my interview. You need to rest and get well. Let's go to sleep."

As she bounced the howling baby on her shoulder, Mara did her best to quell the frustration welling up inside her. "Abby, what's wrong with you? It's almost time for your night feeding, and you haven't slept at all."

Fear ran its icy course through her stomach. "Abby, what's the matter? Oh, honey, I wish you could talk to me. Where do you hurt?"

"Mara?"

Brock's voice from the doorway stopped Mara's restless pacing. She looked up to find him standing just inside the room. He had pulled on a pair of jeans and a T-shirt, but his feet were bare.

"Is she sick?"

"I don't know," Mara choked out. "It's okay. I can manage."

"Let me hold her."

"No, we're fine."

He walked toward her. "Mara, let me have the baby. You're dead on your feet."

"Brock, I can do this without you."

"I know you can. But I'm here, so let me take her for a while." He lifted the baby out of Mara's arms. "Hey, Abby, what's up?" he cooed. "Why so cranky, pumpkin?"

Mara stood in silence, her empty arms hanging at her sides as Brock settled in the rocking chair with the baby. Still wailing, Abby flung her fists at Brock's chest and jerked her head from side to side. Mara clutched her stomach.

"She was fine this afternoon," she said. "She had a little bit of a runny nose, so I called the doctor and got her some over-the-counter stuff. Now…she seems so sick."

"Shall we take her into town? We could go to the emergency room."

Mara shook her head. "I don't know. I just don't know. I feel helpless."

Brock stood up again and tried walking Abby around the room. As the baby sobbed, he hummed and whistled and jiggled her up and down. Mara collapsed onto the recliner, eyes barely open as she watched Brock doing his best to console Abby.

"When was the last time she ate?" he called over the crying.

"I can't remember. I gave her some medicine a few minutes ago, but…I've lost track of when she nursed."

"Let me check her diaper, and then you can try feeding her again."

Mara followed him with her eyes as he laid the baby in the bassinet she kept in the sitting room. With surprising expertise, he whipped off the wet diaper and slipped a dry one under the baby's bottom. In moments, he had the howling bundle in his arms again.

"Can you bring her here?" Mara asked.

He sat on a chair beside the recliner and laid Abby in her mother's arms. For a brief moment, Mara thought about turning aside in modesty. That lasted until Abby let out an ear-splitting shriek, and Mara swiftly pulled open her nightgown and drew the baby close.

Suddenly, the room fell silent. In spite of her stuffy nose, the baby nursed with deep, ravenous draughts. The only sound was her hungry snuffling.

Mara looked up at Brock. He had leaned against the chair back and stretched one leg onto the recliner's footrest. A tired grin lifted one corner of his mouth.

"I guess she was hungry," he said.

Mara couldn't bring herself to smile in return. "I guess."

"You think she's sick?"

"I'll take her to the pediatrician first thing in the morning." As the baby grew calm, Mara felt the tension ease from her body. She shut her eyes, one arm wrapped around Abby and the other tucked beside her as she dozed off in the soft chair. Drowsy warmth flowed through her veins.

"We're tired," she mumbled.

Brock settled his other foot on the recliner. "I'll wait till she's done and put her back to bed."

"Mmm," Mara murmured.

Brock's hand covered hers, and she slipped her fingers through his. This was exactly right. No question at all.

Chapter Seventeen

✤

Pearly-gray light bathed the room when Brock opened his eyes. Abby lay nestled against her mother, her mouth open and her tiny fingers curled into a comfortable ball. Mara was still sleeping, long lashes fanning against her cheeks and golden hair spread across the cushion.

Brock rubbed a hand across his eyes as a groan of dismay rumbled through his chest. His desire for Mara was still strong, and he had been trying so hard to keep his distance. While his newly awakening prayer life began each time with praises to God and a strong dollop of thanksgiving, Brock realized he spent most of the time asking for divine help in controlling his feelings for Mara.

But it was more than a physical desire for the woman that stirred him this morning. It was the silent, early hour…the drowsy baby…the scent of lavender…the whisper of winter breath against the window…the promise of a crackling fire…and the woman in her robe…his wife, if she would have him.

Sometime in the past weeks of living with Mara, he had felt this change come over him. Maybe it had begun the first time he cooked breakfast with Abby in his arms. Maybe it was the night he held Mara on the snowy roadside. No matter when it started, the change had come swiftly—blindsiding him in its intensity. For the first time in his life, Brock had come to believe in family...and in himself as a successful part of a family.

Not only did he believe in it, he wanted it. He could credit this amazing transformation only to God. His image of a mother as a cynical, embittered woman who could do nothing but flee from her unhappiness had given way to the picture of a blond angel with her baby nestled at her breast and her warm eyes filled with love. The idea of children as unnecessary nuisances to be tolerated but never enjoyed was brushed aside by a tiny baby with pink lips and downy hair who liked nothing better than to be cuddled, hugged and adored. The concept of a house as a place to do little more than sleep and change clothes evolved into the constant refuge of a home—a secure, comforting haven of good food, laughter and conversation.

Fatherhood was no longer the province of men who didn't have anything more important to do with their lives. Nor was it an inconvenience in a real man's quest for power and wealth. Fatherhood became suddenly a place of hope, happiness, delight, surprise and dreams. Without realizing it, Brock had come to crave that role—head of a family of his own—as strongly as he had ever wanted anything.

Gently he scooped up the sleeping baby, pushed himself out of the chair where he had spent the night and deposited her safely in the cocoon of the bassinet. For a moment he studied the unmoving bundle of pastel blankets and plump pink skin. A gritty lump formed in his throat as he drank in the twin arcs of her closed eyes with their wispy lashes, the bud of her nose, the perfect roundness of her cheeks. If the child had been conceived from his own loins, he could not have loved her more.

Yes, he loved the baby.

He couldn't let Abby go. Not ever. There was too much ahead. There were tricycles and trees to climb and drippy Popsicles on hot summer days. There were horses and picnics and swimming holes. There were breakfasts to cook—thousands of them. There were bicycles to ride and wildflowers to gather and dollhouses to build. This baby deserved a father, a living father, who could wipe away her tears and listen to her heartaches as no one had ever done for Brock Barnett.

He reached out a finger to touch the tiny form, and a warm hand slipped over his shoulder. The scent of lavender drifted around him. He shut his eyes and let out a shuddering breath. Mara, his wife. And he was her husband. God had done this thing. Brock knew it.

Within the whirlwind of new images, the profile of *husband* had changed for Brock, too. *Husband* had always been a vague term that involved legal obligation, financial support and parental responsibility. Now it meant deep relationship. A husband was one member of a marriage—a fortress built on a foundation of faith in God. A husband was friend, companion, partner…and lover.

Brock couldn't let go of this woman, either. Not ever. Turning toward her, he saw that she was still half asleep. Was she thinking of Todd? Maybe.

Running his hand down her arm, he nestled her close. He tried to tell himself she was thinking of her first husband. He decided he ought to go check his cattle. Instead, he let his hand slip apart the edges of her gown.

"Mara," he said in a low voice.

"Brock." It was almost a moan. This time her eyelashes fluttered open. Gray-green eyes beckoned him.

"At last," he murmured, his lips touching hers as he spoke the word. He lifted her into his arms and carried her toward her bedroom. "Mara…my wife."

"It's honeymoon time at the Barnett house," Brock announced into the phone he had taken from Mara's bedside table. His eyes feasted on her as she sat curled on the bed, cradling her baby as the little one nursed contentedly.

"Take today and the rest of the weekend off, Pierre," he continued. "And tell Ermaline and Rosa Maria, too. I don't want to see hide nor hair of any of you for three days, got that?"

"*S'il vous plaît,* what about your work? What about the cattle?" The excitable chef's voice registered disbelief. "Surely the men on the ranch will wonder where you are!"

"I'll call them and explain."

"Well…if you think it is best."

Brock could hear Pierre's wife in the background as she uttered exclamations of delight. "Honeymoon? *Très bien!* They are together now, Pierre. Leave them! Put down the telephone!"

"Yvonne!" he growled at her. Then he returned to his amused employer. "What about your dinner tonight?" Pierre asked. "Perhaps you will change your mind concerning this three-day honeymoon? You will become hungry?"

Brock slid his hand down Mara's arm. "Nope," he said. "We can make do with what's here."

Pierre fell silent for a few seconds before speaking again. "Perhaps this happiness *en famille* will mean you do not wish to dine *à la francaise* any longer. Perhaps five-star cuisine and a chef trained with the very finest on the Continent will no longer be necessary for the Barnett household. What do you think? Will everything change now?"

Brock leaned over and kissed Mara's hand. She tousled her fingers through his hair. Things had definitely changed, but not the way his chef thought. "Don't worry, Pierre. Mara's going to start working at Fort Selden next week. She won't have time to cook."

"No?" Pierre's voice brightened. "Perhaps no time to clean house, either?"

"I imagine she'll be busy with other things." He hoped he could keep Mara so happy she wouldn't even have time to run a finger across a dusty table. "And tell Ramona she's on full-time duty with the baby starting Monday."

"Oh, *très bien!* Full-time is good. Give our love to the *cher enfant*. Please tell your lovely wife not to worry, all will be taken care of to perfection. *Au revoir!*"

Brock was smiling as he set down the receiver. He scooted next to Mara on the bed and tucked her against him as she continued to nurse her baby. Abby's eyelids were so heavy she could barely hold them open. All the same, her gaze was transfixed on her mother's face.

"Is everything okay with Pierre?" Mara asked.

"Très bien." He traced Mara's face with the side of his finger. "Is everything okay with Mara?"

"It's hard to think about being apart from Abby."

Brock studied the now-familiar sight of Mara nursing her daughter. He reached down and took one of the baby's round pink toes between his thumb and finger. As he rolled the tiny toe, he thought about what must have gone into her decision to work. "If you take Abby to the fort, you can keep nursing, can't you?"

"Yes," she said, her voice almost a whisper. "I'll do that. And if Ramona comes with us, it will be better. She's wonderful with Abby. Still…it's not easy to think of putting in full days again."

"Mara, you know you don't have to do this for the money. My promise to provide for you is good, no matter what."

"It's not that."

"Are you doing it for Todd, then?"

She lifted her head. "No, it's not for Todd. I want to do this for me."

Brock couldn't suppress the elation he felt at her words. Maybe Mara finally had begun to see her first husband as a memory to treasure, but a memory nonetheless. If she felt Todd was a part of the past, that left the present and the future open to Brock.

Seated behind Mara, he watched her lean over the edge of the bed and nestle her sleeping baby in the bassinet. The night they had spent in each other's arms was everything he had dreamed of—and more. Now she was looking over her shoulder at him as a coy smile lifted her lips. "Did I hear you tell Pierre this was a honeymoon?"

"That's what I said."

She sat down on the bed, picked up her pillow, and hugged it tightly. "Does that mean what happened between us wasn't a mistake?"

"Does God make mistakes? He brought us together, Mara. We married each other for wrong reasons, but God saw what we couldn't. He knew we were meant to be together—not just because of Todd, but because of who we are. We've changed each other. You've made me a better man in so many ways. You helped me see my need for God, and now I've found Him, Mara. I let Him take control of my life, as I should have done long ago. But now I understand this was His plan. You and me. I'm sure of it."

Closing her eyes, she buried her nose in the pillow. When she raised her head, he could see the tears. "I feel alive again, and it's you … you who brought me back. Oh, Brock!"

"Mara," Brock whispered against her ear as she plunged her face back into the pillow. "Look at me."

She shook her head. "I'm afraid to."

"Why?"

"I'm too happy. This has to be a dream. I'm scared that if I open my eyes, you might vanish."

"No, ma'am." He lifted her chin and kissed her eyelids. "I'm not going anywhere. What about you?"

"I'm not going anywhere, either," she whispered.

For three days, Mara was sure she had somehow slipped across the perimeter between heaven and earth and was walking down streets paved with gold. Between nursing and playing with Abby, she and Brock spent hours sleeping, talking, laughing, eating. Oh, they ate.

Late one evening, while stretched out by the fire in the great room, a plate of home-baked chocolate chip cookies beside her, Mara glanced down at her robe and worried aloud that she was gaining back all the weight she had lost after Abby's birth. Brock laughed, handed her a cookie and told her he'd want her no matter what she weighed.

"I wanted you when you were nine months pregnant and your stomach stuck out to here," he reminded her. "I didn't really understand it then, but I wanted you. I want you right now, even with cookie crumbs on your chin. And I'll want you when your hair has turned white and your skin is wrinkled."

Mara stared at his face and absorbed the honesty in his deep brown eyes. But how could this be the carefree, insincere, uncommitted Brock she had known before? "Are you sure you'll want me? Even when I'm old?"

"You and nobody else." He brushed the crumbs from her chin. "I hope you believe that."

She rolled over onto her back and studied the heavy beams in the ceiling. The past three days had been a blur. She had thought about nothing but Brock. Even Abby, who seemed to relish the extra attention of two doting adults, took second place to Mara's desire for this amazing man God had brought into her life. It was as though he had become her entire world, and there was nothing but the present moment. She had relegated the past to memory. And the future...

"Brock, what's going to happen to us?" she whispered. "Job interview, work, the fort, the ranch, church, friends. The outside world is going to start turning again tomorrow."

"And we're going to get back on. Together. I want everyone to know the business arrangement we had is history. This is personal now—a marriage created in heaven, not on earth."

"What will people think? I haven't even been widowed for a year. And you were Todd's best friend."

"Do you care?"

She shut her eyes as he trailed a finger down her arm. "Not really."

"It doesn't matter what anyone thinks. This is between us."

"If we don't let other people pull us apart, the only thing that can separate us is our fears."

"What are you still afraid of, Mara?"

She clutched at her thoughts as they attempted to flee beneath the overwhelming rush of sensation that his touch provoked. "I'm afraid you don't really know me," she said, her words no more than a shallow breath. "And I'm afraid I don't know you."

He bent over her and softly kissed her cheek. "I know you, Mara. I know you inside and out. I know you better than anyone could… We're two of a kind. That means you know me, too. You know who I am, what I do, what I want. You understand how I think. You know me, Mara—you're the only woman I've wanted to let know me."

She slipped her arms around his broad shoulders as his familiar scent drifted around her. "I do know you," she murmured, dangerously, hopelessly lost in him again.

Chapter Eighteen

❦

Mara's interview with Dr. Stephen Long of the Bureau of Land Management could not have gone better. His passion for history was obvious, and she instinctively liked him. His memories of Todd added to the storehouse she was saving to share with Abby one day. In the agency's Las Cruces office that Monday afternoon, he approved her position as director of the restoration project.

A trip to the pediatrician later that day affirmed that Abby was healthy and strong, growing like a weed, developing perfectly. The cold had been just that—a minor sniffle. The next morning, Mara kissed her daughter goodbye, handed Ramona a sheaf of instructions, and climbed into the pickup truck. Brock waved to her from the end of the driveway, and Mara watched him saunter toward the barn, his blue jeans and denim shirt in sharp contrast to his black hair and black boots.

She loved him. That was the clearest thing in Mara's mind as she drove toward Fort Selden. She loved Brock, and she wanted to live as his wife for the rest of her life. But did he love her? He had never said those words—and maybe he didn't feel them.

Again she wondered how well she knew the man. During their short honeymoon, he had said very little about his hopes for their future. He spoke of Abby growing up in the ranch house, but he didn't ask for Mara's opinion on the matter. And even though he had told Mara he wanted people to know their marriage was on different terms now, he had said nothing about their separate bedrooms. He had given her no ring, no words of love and no blueprint for their restructured relationship.

And she knew Brock Barnett was a blueprint kind of man.

But there was little time for worry as she plunged into her first day of work as a restorationist. Dressed in khaki slacks and layers of warm sweaters, she had pulled her hair up into a tight ponytail and laced heavy boots on her feet. Seated in the open air with the melting adobe walls surrounding them, she held her first meeting with Mr. Dominguez, State Park personnel and the fort supervisor.

Even in its dilapidated state, Fort Selden welcomed more than eleven thousand tourists a year. Three full-time rangers conducted tours for individuals, organizations and groups of schoolchildren. Once a year, the fort's Frontier Days featured black-powder shooting, farrier demonstrations, square dancing, races and other competitions, hayrides and a nineteenth-century fashion show. In summer, living history demonstrations were scheduled each hour during the afternoon on Saturdays and Sundays. In the midst of all this activity, Mara would have to conduct her restoration work.

The plans Todd had drawn up called for the work crew to shore up and preserve in their present condition most of the single-story adobe structures in the fort complex. But the two-story administration building, the infirmary and the prison were to be completely rebuilt according to the original blueprints. This meant Mara would need to purchase adobe bricks from a Las Cruces supplier and assemble a crew of skilled carpenters, bricklayers, electricians and even plumbers. Mr. Dominguez would supervise.

After spending the first two days alone at the fort, Mara decided it was time for Abby to join the team. Ramona proved to be the ideal assistant. She occupied the baby when Abby wasn't sleeping, watched over her when she was. And when it was time for a feeding, she brought Abby to her mother. Ramona struck up a friendship with the staff. One in particular—a young ranger named Danny—caught her eye, and the two of them often walked the park trails together while Mara was tending to Abby. Mara organized her time so that she could carry out her work, but see to her daughter's needs as often as possible. It was a perfect arrangement.

Within the first week, Mara had ordered and received her first shipment of bricks—heavy brown twelve-by-eighteen-inch slabs of mud mixed with straw. The blocks looked more like giant bars of chocolate candy than building materials. Adobe, she quickly learned, was actually easy to use in building. Though the heavy blocks were somewhat uneven in size, they mortared well, dried fast and were simple to design with. The ease with which adobe walls went up, Mara discovered, contributed to the ease with which they came down. Under less-than-ideal conditions, and without regular maintenance, adobe structures could disintegrate fairly quickly—as the fort evidenced.

Though she had no experience in construction, Mara absorbed Mr. Dominguez's enthusiasm about building with adobe. Whole walls could be erected and windows cut out later. A pronged tool scraped down the side of a wall provided a trench in which to run wiring or pipe. A quick slap of mortar over the top of the trench safely sealed it away. There was no framing, no insulation, no Sheetrock. Best of all, the adobe buildings were cool in summer and toasty warm in winter.

Late on her first Friday afternoon, Mara stood at the edge of the site with her crew to survey their work. Every muscle in her body ached from the heavy labor. Her clothing was splattered with mud and her boots were caked with it. She was physically more tired than she'd ever been, but Mara felt victorious.

She and Mr. Dominguez worked together like cogs in a smoothly oiled machine. He respected her opinions and her position as director, and she admired his enormous experience and his willingness to teach. Their hastily assembled crew members had proven themselves loyal and eager to succeed in the interesting task. Even the rangers, who had been concerned about the workers' interruption of the fort's routine, had decided to incorporate the reconstruction into their daily guided tours. They urged visitors to return often to "see what will happen as Fort Selden is reborn." And Mara was delighted to explain her plans to the groups of excited students.

"I think we might be able to finish the administration building in two months," Mr. Dominguez said. "But you'd better order some more bricks. The last thing this old, tired body wants to do is build wooden forms and pour them bricks myself. You never knew hard work till you try mixing mud and straw, I'm telling you."

"I'll call in an order right now," Mara agreed. "If we keep the bricks protected from the rain, we can store them until they're needed."

"As long as we don't make them an eyesore."

"True. Dr. Long is coming to inspect the site in a couple of weeks. That'll be our ultimate test. If we don't pass muster, we're out of work."

Mr. Dominguez glanced at the other workers who had gathered for the meeting. "Keep your noses clean, boys, and do what Mrs. Barnett tells you. This has been a good week, but we're just getting started. Next week the work really begins." He took off his battered hat and rubbed a handkerchief over his balding scalp. "Let's go home before we get some more tourists who want to parade through the work site."

"Great idea," Mara agreed. "I'm beat."

"Me, too. Uh-oh, here comes a truck."

Mara started to groan, then stopped short. "Wait a minute, that's...that's Brock!" She slapped Mr. Dominguez on the back. "That's my husband!"

She took off toward the pickup, her blond ponytail bouncing behind her. As Brock's long legs emerged from the cab, her heart soared. The past few days had been so different from the weekend before. Supper had been their only meal together, and the hours of talking and touching were condensed into a few minutes each night. Mara had missed their togetherness, and she was anticipating a weekend of nothing but family— herself, Brock and Abby.

"Hey, boss lady!" he said as she threw her arms around him. "Thought I'd drive out and take a look."

"Oh, Brock, it's great to see you!" She looked into his brown eyes and a wash of emotion poured through her. She loved this man. She loved Brock Barnett...differently, but just as deeply as she had loved her first husband.

Ramona emerged from the visitor center, and Brock lifted Abby from her arms. "Hi there, sweetie pie. How's my Abigail?"

"Come meet my crew," Mara urged. "Mr. Dominguez and the others are just about to head for home."

Brock planted a kiss on Mara's forehead. "I miss you," he murmured.

"Not for long," she returned with a wink. She called out a greeting to Mr. Dominguez who was lumbering toward them. As he shook hands with Brock, the others in the crew gathered to meet their boss's husband.

"You've got to see what we're working on," Mara said, lacing her fingers through Brock's free hand as he cradled Abby with the other. "This has been such an amazing week. It's as if Todd knew exactly what needed to be done to bring the administration building back to life. He was brilliant, Brock, he really was."

"I never doubted it." As he walked beside Mara, he couldn't take his eyes off her. Mara finally had to elbow the man to get him to quit ogling.

She showed him around the site, pointing out the locations of buildings that were now no more than low brown walls, half melted by rain and wind. "This central area is the parade ground...that's the infirmary and there's the post store," she explained. "The fort was originally built to house one company of infantry and another company of cavalry and its sixty horses. After 1879, the commanding officer received word to begin dismantling usable materials for shipping to Fort Bliss in El Paso, and the post was abandoned."

"So that was the end of it?" Brock asked.

"All the buildings were destroyed and left absolutely worthless. But in 1880 the fort was reactivated and rebuilt. This time, though, it could only accommodate one company. During that building phase, Captain Arthur MacArthur came to the post with his family, which included six-year-old Douglas."

"The Douglas MacArthur who became a general?"

"You got it." Mara rewarded him with a grin. "It's another reason we want tourists to visit the site. This fort is one of the cradles of U.S. history. The administration building is our first project. It's complicated, because we have to make sure the structure is strong enough to support a second floor. Adobe buildings are usually on one level."

"Like the old trading post."

"That's right. This is so tricky, but you should see how Mr. Dominguez goes at it. He's amazing." She tapped the roll of blueprints she was carrying. "And Todd has every detail drawn in, right down to the floorboards and nails. The plans are perfectly in tune with this place, Brock. They show exactly where everything has to go. Todd's got such a sense of historical authenticity. He's just amazing."

"Was," Brock said.

Mara glanced up in surprise.

"Todd was amazing," he repeated.

She stared at him. "I know. But it's like I can sense what he was doing here. I feel like I hear his voice talking, explaining things to me. We worked so hard together over these plans, and I know his thinking when I look at them. I understand what he intends with every line."

"Intended."

"Brock—"

"What he intended, Mara. Past tense."

Her fingers tightened on the blueprints. "Brock…"

"Mara, what are you doing? Are you forgetting that he's gone?"

"No, but why should it bother you?"

"You don't have to keep on talking like he's still here."

"Brock, I'm trying to tell you—"

"Mrs. Barnett," Mr. Dominguez's voice interrupted her, and she turned to see the builder waving. "We got another visitor here. It's that Dr. Long fellow."

"Dr. Long?" Mara's heart jolted. "Oh, no. I didn't expect him today."

Without pausing to conclude their discussion, she whirled away from Brock, smoothed down her hair and started across the open parade ground toward the waiting vehicle. Dr. Long wasn't due back for a couple of weeks. Did she have everything in order? Would he be annoyed with something she'd left undone? Only a week on-site! She'd hardly had time to get her feet wet. And what about Brock…and Abby?

She swung around again, focusing on the tall man holding the baby. "I'll be right back," she called out.

"We'll be at home." His voice was clipped.

"Wait, Brock." She watched him turn away. Facing the newly arrived car, she muttered to herself. "Great…just great."

There was no time to reason with Brock. Her stomach in a knot, Mara did her best to paste a calm smile on her face as she heard the sound of his pickup pulling away from the fort. Had she hurt him so deeply with her mention of Todd? Didn't he understand she would always love her first husband—but she had no illusions about the fact that he was gone? Didn't he realize how much he—Brock—had come to mean to her?

"Mrs. Barnett!" Dr. Long greeted her warmly, his hand extended.

"This is a surprise," she replied, dusting off her palms on her thighs before shaking his hand. She wished she'd at least had time to brush her hair and wash the mud off her face. "I didn't expect you."

"I was up north checking on the other forts. Since my flight leaves from El Paso, I thought I'd drop in on you to see how things were going."

"I see. Well, things are going very well. Mr. Dominguez is doing a terrific job with his crew, and we already have our first shipment of adobe. In fact, we began laying bricks this morning."

"Mind if I take a look?"

"I'd be happy to show you around." Mara glanced at the cloud of dust rising from the road as Brock's pickup vanished in the distance. She felt sick inside. How could they have argued over something so small? But was it small? Obviously, Brock cared a great deal how she felt about Todd. After all this time…after their physical and verbal commitment…didn't Brock know what he meant to her?

"My goodness, you have been busy," Dr. Long commented, oblivious to her turmoil. "I don't believe I've ever seen so many adobe bricks."

"The supplier we're using is one of the biggest in the state, and we're fortunate that it's in Las Cruces. The company ships adobe bricks as far north as Albuquerque and Santa Fe. But we'll go through these quickly. In fact, I was planning to call in another order in a few minutes."

Dr. Long nodded as they resumed their walk. "Mr. Dominguez and I think we can finish the administration building in two months. The other structures shouldn't take nearly as long."

They strolled across the parade ground to the ruins of the jail. "Have you thought about what it will mean to your family, Mrs. Barnett, when you start on the other sites? Those forts are certainly not within easy driving distance of your husband's ranch."

She toed a clod of dirt. "I'm focusing on this project right now, Dr. Long. It's difficult to look beyond it at the moment."

"But you have a new baby. And a new husband. What does Brock think?"

"He's been very supportive."

"Your husband mentioned he owns a small plane that you could use for commuting to the more distant sites."

Mara glanced up. "He did?"

"Yes. He seems determined to help these projects move forward."

"You spoke to Brock?"

"About two weeks ago we discussed the future of the restoration company. I assumed he shared that with you."

"No." Mara frowned. She knew that around the time of their hasty wedding, Brock had been in contact with the department. Had he also been talking with them during the weeks she was pitching her proposal?

"Now, this jail should be quite a tourist draw," Dr. Long said, changing the subject abruptly. "People love to look at jails, prisons, courtrooms, crime scenes and battlegrounds. Bring the people in and you suddenly have funds, legislative support, all kinds of good things. Do you have any documentation of the jail's historical use?"

"I'm working on it. I'd like to create artifact displays inside each restored building."

"Good idea. That would complement what's already in the visitor center." He walked beside her around the walls of the old jail. "You know, Fort Craig has three warehouses—each larger and deeper than an Olympic-sized swimming pool. There was once a bakery, a guardhouse, officers' quarters. And that fort was encircled by an earthen wall. Do you suppose we could rebuild that wall, Mrs. Barnett?"

"As I said, I'm taking one project at a time. Fort Selden is the best-preserved of all the sites, and look at the shape it's in. I have detailed blueprints for each of the forts, of course, but I guess everything depends on whether there's money to restore them all."

Dr. Long's eyebrows rose. "The funding looks very strong at this point."

"That's good to know." She brushed back a wisp of hair that had come loose from her ponytail. "As I work on this project, I'll continue to pull together what I'll need for the next one. Mr. Dominguez is willing to move to each site, and I'll speak with my husband about his airplane."

"Good. I'm pleased with the start you've made here, Mrs. Barnett. It looks like Brock was right. You do have what it takes to run your late husband's company."

A little frown tugging at her lips, Mara walked him back to his rental car. "I take it you've spoken with Brock several times?"

"Yes. He's a nice man. Totally supportive of you and this work."

Dr. Long pulled open the car door. "I'll be back to check on things, but don't hesitate to give me a call if you run into any snags. I'll do what I can to smooth your way through the red tape."

"Thank you, sir. I appreciate that."

He started to get in the car, then straightened again. "Oh, and thank Brock again for me, would you? The donation from the Barnett Foundation started us back on track. Then when other benefactors got wind of it, the funding bottleneck opened up." He gave her a warm smile. "And I know your husband is pleased with the good work you're doing—we all are."

Mara's mouth went dry. "Thank you," she mouthed, but no sound emerged.

Dr. Long gave her a thumbs-up as he settled into his car and pulled the door shut. "Thanks for the tour!" he called. "See you soon."

Mara watched him pull away. As his car bounced down the dirt road, a film of dust settled onto her hair, her shoulders, her boots.

Chapter Nineteen

❧

"Donation," Mara muttered under her breath as she drove down the dirt road away from Fort Selden. "Buyoff is more like it."

She shifted gears, turned onto the highway and glared at the yellow line that streaked beneath her car wheels. "He's got a plane you can use," she said imitating Dr. Long's voice. "Oh, he does, does he? How come he never mentioned that to me? And since when have you two become best buddies?"

She tugged the band from her ponytail and shook her hair loose around her shoulders. An airplane? Not that using one was such a bad idea. But what else did the wealthy, well-connected Brock Barnett have up his sleeve? Had he mapped out her whole future with the Bureau of Land Management? Mr. Control Freak.

She could almost hear him talking on his beloved cell phone. "I have resources. I'll see to it you have all the money you need to keep the project going, and you give my wife a job. How does that sound, Dr. Long?"

"Sounds illegal to me," Mara said out loud. "Illegal and unethical and … and manipulative…and controlling…and obnoxious!"

What a low-down thing to do! After all they'd gone through, how could he have failed to tell her what he'd done? What else hadn't he told her? That he owned an island? Or a yacht? Maybe he had girlfriends in every city in America. Maybe he was just biding his time, operating undercover with his old methods, until he grew tired of playing the loyal husband game. Until he grew tired of *her*.

Was the man she had lived with for almost three months just pretending to be common and down to earth—someone who had learned to enjoy the same things she liked? Had he meant what he said about giving his life to God? Or was he really the domineering, selfish stranger she had thought he was in the beginning?

How dare he pull strings to get her that job?

Half choking on repressed, angry tears, Mara pulled the car up the driveway of the ranch house. As she pressed the garage-door opener, she watched his pickup come into view, the infant chair comfortably buckled onto the seat beside the driver. Abby adored Brock.

Oh, Abby! Where was her baby? All Mara wanted to do at this moment was hold her daughter tight and escape from these tangled emotions.

She parked the ranch pickup she was using and shut her eyes for a moment. His vehicle…his house…his money. She had sold out to him, just as Sherry had warned she would. She had trusted him in spite of her better judgment. Worse, she had slept with the man—and not just once. What now? Would he use her and then divorce her, as Sherry also had predicted?

Mara slammed her palms onto the steering wheel and then threw open the truck door. How could she have been so stupid? So weak? He was deceitful, egotistic, bullheaded, sneaky….

"Mara." Hands on his hips, Brock stood just inside the kitchen door as she entered the house. A tower of black hair,

piercing eyes and dusty blue denim, he looked downright me-
nacing. "I want to talk about Todd."

Mara tossed her purse on the counter. "Where's Abby?"

"In the nursery. She fell asleep in the car, and I put her to
bed." He moved toward her, his dark eyes locked on hers. "So,
what's this about Todd?"

"What's this about sending me around the state on an airplane?" She lifted her chin. "You tell me about that."

"I keep a plane in Las Cruces. You can use it."

"And you and Dr. Long have it all worked out that I'm supposed to commute to the other forts."

"If you want to. I've offered the plane."

"You offered it to Dr. Long."

"I'm offering it to you. If it would make things easier, I could
hire a pilot, and you could use the plane to get to work and back."

Mara glared at him. "Why didn't you discuss it with me?"

"What's mine is yours, Mara," he said. "I thought that's how
marriage worked. Give and take."

"Like you give Dr. Long a bunch of money so he'll take me
on? Is that the kind of give and take you're talking about?"

"What?"

"Oh, stop playing games with me, Brock. Dr. Long told me
you donated money to keep the fort restoration project afloat.
That's why he hired me. You pulled all the right strings."

"Wrong!" He pointed a finger at her. "You got that job on
your own merit. And you'll keep it or lose it based on your
performance."

"Or, you could just give another sizable donation to Dr. Long."

"I didn't give anything to Dr. Long. Barnett Petroleum has a
foundation that supports lots of causes. The money does some
good. The company gets a tax write-off."

"Yes, and aren't you Barnett Petroleum, Brock?"

"I didn't authorize that donation in order to influence the
BLM. Dr. Long told me he might be interested in working with
you, but he said there was no money. After Todd died, the
funding had dried up. The fort project was stalled. I stepped in
for one reason—to keep Todd's dream alive."

She stared into his eyes, aching to believe him. "Don't lie to me, Brock."

"I'm not lying, Mara." His eyes narrowed. "Do you think I'd do something illegal?"

"I don't know. I'm not sure I know you at all."

"You know everything about me." He stepped toward her. "What's the problem? You want to see my portfolio? Fine. I'll call my lawyer tomorrow morning, and we'll go over it with you. There's an airplane in Las Cruces, an apartment complex in Albuquerque, a vacation house in Ruidoso, a small plastics company in El Paso, a boat in the Gulf of Mexico and another one in San Diego. I'm part owner of an Indy car team. I've got interests in a white-water excursion company in Wyoming and a mountaineering outfitter in Washington state. I own a hot-air balloon, a hang glider, a dune buggy, a jet ski—"

"Stop!" She covered her ears. "I don't care. You can have all the toys and businesses and real estate you want."

"I want you." He stepped toward her. "I want you, Mara. You're all I want. I'd chuck everything if I could get you to trust me. Trust me? I can't even get you to forgive me. I gave that money to the fort project so Todd's dream could come true. But you won't accept the things I've tried to do to atone for his death. You still haven't forgiven me, have you?"

"Brock, I have. I've tried—"

"No, you still talk about Todd as though he's alive. You tell me you can hear his voice and see the two of you doing things together. You're still holding on to him, aren't you? You're still in love with him."

"I'll always love Todd, but—"

"That's what I thought. And you'll never forgive me for what happened on those cliffs. If you can't forgive and forget, Mara, how can we ever build ourselves a future?"

His eyes were red-rimmed, his jaw clenched with suppressed emotion. Suddenly she wanted nothing more than to feel his arms around her. Nothing mattered but this man and the love she felt for him.

"It's you, too," she said, her voice almost a whisper. "You haven't let go of the past, and you can't forgive yourself. What future does that leave us, Brock?"

Shaking his head, he backed away from her and swung around. He grabbed his hat from the rack by the door and threw his coat over one shoulder. As he pulled open the door, she called out.

"Brock, where are you going?"

"Climbing," he growled.

Mara watched through the kitchen window as Brock loaded the back of his pickup with climbing gear. Ropes, more ropes. Gloves. Rock shoes. Belt. Harness.

She chewed on her bottom lip as tears streamed down her cheeks. She should stop him. She should run right outside and throw her arms around him and somehow find a way to work everything out.

No, she should let him go. If he wanted to climb up the side of a cliff, it was his neck he was risking. She hated climbing! She hated all his crazy recklessness. She hated his money and his stubbornness and his selfishness.

But as his pickup pulled out of the driveway and started down the road, Mara realized that wasn't true at all. She didn't hate him. She loved him. She loved his smile, the sound of his voice, his intelligence, his kindness. She loved the way he put his feet on the table when he relaxed. The way he held Abby against his chest. The way he laughed. The way he touched her.

And that was all there was to it, she admitted, dropping onto a chair by the window. Sherry had been right about that one. Mara was simply a lonely widow on the rebound, and Brock would give her what she wanted until he got bored with it.

Mara stood again and studied the plume of dust that rose high against the setting sun. Let him go. Let him climb away from her, far away until he was back in his world of race cars, parachutes and hang gliders. She had a daughter, a job, responsibilities. Any woman with an ounce of sense would move out of the house, rent an apartment, get as far from Brock Barnett as possible.

With a jolt, Mara knew what she needed to do. She would use her job as a stepping-stone to freedom. For the first time in her life, she could live on her own—fully capable and independent.

In fact, why not call Sherry right now? They could go apartment-hunting in the morning. By Monday morning, she could have everything moved out of Brock's house and be living on her own.

She walked into the great room and picked up the phone. A quick succession of buttons, two rings, and her best friend's voice came on the line.

"Hello?"

Mara tried to speak. Tell me I'm a fool to love Brock. Tell me I'm crazy to want him. Tell me he's no good. Tell me I'll regret it for the rest of my life.

"Hello?" Sherry said again. "Well, nuts."

As the phone went dead in her ear, Mara stared blindly at the side table. She placed the receiver on the smooth wood and thought of the man whose hands had sawed, nailed, planed, sanded and oiled it. Brock.

As her eyes focused again, two little boxes sharpened into view. One was sleek and polished on the outside, perfectly crafted and so fine it made her sigh. The other was lovingly, tenderly made of Popsicle sticks.

Brock and Todd.

Mara picked up the Popsicle-stick box and held it for a moment. She could almost see Todd's freckled fingers carefully gluing the little sticks in place. His tongue would be firmly tucked between his teeth, and his red-blond hair would spill over his forehead as he concentrated on the job.

Mara blinked back tears. She would always love her teddy-bear Todd. He was the man she had married, promised her future to and lived with for nine years. He was the man who had given Abby life. Was it wrong to mourn him? Was it wrong to hold his memory inside her heart?

"No," Mara said out loud. It wasn't wrong.

She ran her fingers over the uneven surface of the little box. Then she lifted the lid. Inside lay a jumble of stones. Brock's rock collection. Some of them obviously had been purchased at a curio shop, machine-polished chunks with dots of glue and paper still attached where they had been pried from their cardboard mounting. Others must have been found in the New Mexico landscape—rose quartz, obsidian, granite, mica.

Mara dug through the stones, lifting each one and holding it to the fading light. Included among them was a piece of hardened rubber tire and a pebble of gravel from the driveway. When she came across a shard of broken glass from a soda bottle, she had to smile. No doubt the little boy Brock thought he had found a diamond.

Then she picked up the smooth box Brock had made her for Christmas. She lifted the lid and gazed at the ring she had put inside it. It was small and rather plain, but she had always loved it. Now her fingers were as bare as Brock's promises on their wedding day.

Did he love her? Did he plan to spend the rest of his life faithful to her? She didn't know. And what about his accusation that she had never forgiven him? She had said the words. She had tried to mean them. But had she really forgiven Brock for asking Todd to climb those cliffs with him? Had she forgiven Todd for dying?

Most important, Mara thought as she shut the lid on her ring, had she forgiven herself and turned loose the root of bitterness in her heart?

Her options stood out as clearly as the two little boxes on the table. She could keep loving and living with the memory of the Popsicle-stick, teddy-bear Todd, and she could view Brock as the slick manipulator who couldn't commit and didn't have the capacity to love or make a successful marriage. She could take her daughter away from this house, use her job to support the two of them, create a life of her own. The voice of sanity and reason instructed her firmly that this should be her decision.

If not, she could take the greatest risk of her life. She could go after Brock and hand over to him her love, her heart, her future—and her daughter's future. She could choose to put

Todd's memory away in his Popsicle-stick box, always loving him but always letting him go. And she could choose to see Brock as the man who cradled her baby, who put his money where his heart was, who told her again and again how much he wanted her. She could believe what the gentle voice inside her whispered—that God had put Brock into her life and that He would bless the marriage He had planned for them.

Maybe Brock didn't love her. Maybe he didn't know how to love. But all the same, she could choose to give her heart to the man who believed broken glass was diamonds.

Mara stared at the telephone. Then at the two boxes.

Chapter Twenty

✤

The moon gleamed like a silver Christmas ornament cushioned in the dusky blue velvet of gathering night. Stars spangled the winter sky, twinkling in the crisp air. Along the road, dry yucca stems rattled as a jackrabbit tore at a clump of brown grass. A barn owl winged across the open plain, its shadow black against the gray ground beneath it.

Mara steered her car down the bumpy road and hoped the rumble of the engine would put Abby back to sleep. She had thought about leaving the baby with Ramona, then decided against it. This was a family matter.

As she drove toward the trading post, she realized her stomach was churning. Had Brock gone to his old climbing place? Or had he chosen somewhere new, somewhere unfamiliar? What if he was halfway up the cliffs? What if he had fallen?

Dear God, please! She chewed on her bottom lip, praying earnestly in the silence of the car. *Don't let him fall. Don't let him die. I love him. Abby loves him… Abby needs him. I need him more.*

Oh, please, please. She swallowed hard as her headlights picked out the smooth brown edges of the former store. With sweaty palms, she steered the car into the open area behind the old building. As she cut the engine, she looked out her window. The cliffs towered above, so high they seemed to touch the moon.

Brock, she breathed as she scanned the vertical face. Please, Brock. Blue denim…black hair…blue denim. Where was he? *God, please show me where he is!*

She glanced at her sleeping baby, then she pushed open the car door. Tilting back her head, she searched every crevice, every outcrop, every slab of flat stone. Her eyes followed the rise and fall of each shadow, each glistening mound. There! A dark form clung to the side of the cliff, legs outstretched. Mara sucked in a breath. Brock!

No, it was a tree with bare limbs and exposed roots that grew from a nook of the rock.

Her hands knotted as she peered into the growing darkness. Where was he? Oh, Brock! She let her focus drop lower and lower, terrified that she would find his crumpled, broken body sprawled at the bottom. She couldn't look. Couldn't.

"Brock…"

He was standing at the base of the cliff, his head bent and his expression one of such sadness and loss that Mara thought her heart might break.

"Brock," she called more loudly.

When he heard her and lifted his head, the tension in his face eased. He straightened, stepped away from the cliff wall and simply said, "You came."

"I couldn't let you go, Brock."

"Mara…I don't want to go up that cliff."

"That's not what I meant." She walked toward him. "I can't let you go, Brock. I don't want to lose you."

"Mara."

As they fell together, he pulled her into his arms and held her tightly, so tightly he knew she could barely breathe. He rocked her back and forth.

"I love you, Mara," he said, his voice rough. "I love you. Everything I've done, every foolish thing I've said is because I love you. And I don't know how to let you know."

"Say it, Brock. Say the words again. Say them every day, a hundred times a day."

"I love you, Mara."

"Oh, I love you, Brock."

He lifted her off her feet and turned her around and around. "Whoa, I feel crazy! I feel free. I'm a man who just got out of prison, Mara. I can say it and mean it and count on it. I love you. I love you."

She laughed through her tears. "Don't let me go!"

"Never. But I would have, Mara. I'd have done anything for you. I gave that money to honor Todd and take care of the people he loved. If I could keep his dream alive, I knew it would be within your reach. I wanted you to stop feeling chained to me." He shook his head. "Instead, I made you think I'd bought you your job."

"It's okay, Brock. I understand now."

"I don't have the power to make you stay with me, Mara. I can only hope you want to. I hoped…and I prayed. Believe me, I've prayed so hard. But tonight I was sure I'd lost you."

She laid her cheek on his broad shoulder and tightened her arms around his back. He was so solid and strong, she wished she could hold him this way forever.

"I want to stay with you, Brock," she murmured. "I don't ever want to go."

He swallowed hard. "What about Todd?"

"What about him?"

"He's Abby's father."

"Todd gave Abby life. He gave her that red-gold sheen to her hair and that funny smile on her lips. But Todd isn't the father she knows. Only one man can be that to her." Mara looked up at him. "You're Abby's father now, Brock. And Todd would want you to be."

He lifted his eyes to the stars as if in disbelief. "I'd do anything for that little girl."

"I know."

"I love her, Mara, and I don't know how it happened. Look at me—I'm not equipped to be a decent father. I don't have the training. But I'll tell you, I'd give my life for her."

"I'm not worried about your qualifications for the job, Brock," Mara declared. "You're a natural."

"You reckon?"

She ran her hand down the side of his face, reveling in the rough brush of his whiskered jaw. "No doubt."

"But what about Todd?" he asked again. "Todd and you?"

Mara let out a shaky breath. "I've been so afraid to let go of him. I've tried to forgive, but I've been unable to let go of my anger, my hurt, my grief. Somehow it seemed like if I kept all that, Todd wouldn't ever really leave. I could keep him real and alive. But he's gone, Brock." She looked at his face through the blurring mist in her eyes. "I want to let him go."

"I'll never forget him," he said, "but I want to let him go, too."

"Tell me what happened. Tell me about that day on the cliff."

He turned away from her and sat down on a fallen boulder. Burying his face in his hands, he was unable to say anything. Only when she slipped to his side and settled on the ground at his feet could he speak.

"It was getting dark because we'd been climbing all day," he began, his voice just above a whisper. "As I told you before, we made the decision to down-climb the cliff without ropes. Rappelling can take a lot of time because you have to secure the equipment or it's not trustworthy. You have to abandon some of your stuff. Todd thought it was wasteful to leave things behind. He never liked to do that."

Mara nodded, picturing the thrifty Todd.

"We checked to see that the route was free of loose rock, and we started down. I'd been there before a few times, so I led. We started down, face-out with our backs to the wall." He paused, shaking his head. Then he let out a breath. "You want me to go on?"

Mara tucked her bottom lip between her teeth and nodded.

"When the angle got steeper, I knew we needed to turn

around and face the cliff wall. I wanted to use a rope at that point, just to be safe. I tossed my rope to Todd. He caught the end of it. We stretched it between us, and he was trying to anchor it"

Waiting for him to continue, Mara could feel the pain of memory racking through his body. For the first time since Todd's death, she became the comforter. She laid her cheek against his leg and kissed his knee.

He didn't speak for more than a minute. When he did, his voice was rough and broken. "He had hammered in a piton, and he put some weight on it to test it. The thing popped out, and Todd started sliding. He cried out to me, 'Brock!' I reached for him, but he tumbled past me too fast. I grabbed for his hand. I missed."

He shook his head. "I missed, Mara. I missed!"

She knew her tears were soaking through his jeans. "Where was the rope?"

"I thought he had it. I jerked at my end to bring him up tight and steady, but he had lost hold of it. I shouted at him, but he kept falling. He rolled and rolled, and I saw him hit his head. When he came to a stop, I was already halfway down to him. I don't know how I did it without ropes. It was like I flew, seeing this blur of rock rushing past me as I scrambled down, screaming at him."

"Oh, Brock."

"When I got to him, I knew it was over. I lifted his head and held it in my lap. He was gone, Mara. Just like that. Gone."

He sat weeping as she stroked his back. "It's okay, Brock."

"I should have put in the pitons myself. I should have reminded him to secure the rope. I've down-climbed cliffs a thousand times, and I didn't warn him! I should have caught him. I should have reached out just that much farther and grabbed him, Mara. Why didn't I? Why?"

"Brock, it's all right." She molded her hands around his damp face and lifted his chin. In the moonlight, she read his anguish. "It's over. It was an accident. I forgive you, Brock. You didn't even have to tell me the story."

He brushed his eyes with his sleeve. "I needed to tell it."

"Brock—thank you. Todd's life was richer for having you as his friend."

"I love you, Mara." He glanced upward, then at her. "And I don't have to climb that cliff."

As his lips met hers, she responded with all the pent-up emotion of the last hours. Peace…the feeling descended over her like a warm cape. She felt at peace with this man, at peace with herself, at peace with their future. His hands caressed her shoulders, and his fingers threaded through her hair. Wanting more of him, she kissed his neck and tasted the salt on his cheeks. He lifted her onto his lap and together they drank in the moment of promise.

"Mara," he murmured, tilting her face into the moonlight. "I love you, you know."

"Keep telling me," she said softly. "Take me home and hold me and tell me again and again."

"I'll show you how much I love you."

They stood and started toward the old trading post. Suddenly, Brock stopped. "Oh, yeah." He unsnapped the flap of his shirt pocket and fished around in it for a moment. "I almost forgot. I've been carrying this thing around for a week."

Mara stiffened as he held out his hand. A circle of diamonds caught the moonlight—so shimmery she felt as though a spell had been cast over her.

"I'd like my wife to wear a ring," he said. "If she will."

"It's beautiful, Brock." She held out her left hand. Gently, he slid the sparkling circlet over her ring finger.

"I'd like a church wedding, too. It's the only way I can think of to let everyone know neither of us is up for grabs. Besides, I want to announce my promise to love you forever so the whole countryside can hear it."

"Forever, Brock?"

"As long as we both shall live." He gave her a quick kiss. "What do you say to that?"

"I say, Amen."

At that, he swung her off her feet and lifted her into his arms. As he started back toward her car, he shook his head. "First we have a pregnancy, then a marriage, then a baby, then a honeymoon, then an engagement, and last of all a wedding. We're a mixed-up pair, you know that?"

"I want the honeymoon again," she whispered.

He laughed. "Oh, yeah!"

They were almost to the car when Mara heard the distinctive sound of her daughter's restless wake-up cry. "Oh, dear," she said softly.

"You brought Abby?" His face broke into a grin.

Brock put Mara down and opened the door of her car. She watched him edge his big shoulders into the open space. As he bent to unbuckle the crying baby, she heard him murmur.

"It's okay, honey. Don't cry anymore. Daddy's here."

* * * * *

Discussion Questions

1. Why does Mara choose to mary Brock? What does she sacrifice in marrying him and what does she gain? Is sacrifice an inherent part of marriage? Of parenting?

2. Is there a moment you can pinpoint when Mara falls in love with Brock? What is the process she must go through to come to terms with their relationship?

3. In Chapter 6, Brock thinks, "Mara was the one who had been wounded, and he wondered if anything could ever heal her." What did it take to heal Mara? Did Brock need healing, too?

4. In Chapter 15, Brock asks himself, "Was I being unfair to Mara by not telling her about the letter?" His answer is no. What do you think? Do you think Brock is certain his answer is the right one?

5. Brock nurses a poisoned cow, which could be seen as a metaphor for his relationship with Mara. How is Mara "poisoned"? Is Brock "poisoned," as well?

6. Was Mara betraying herself, Brock or her faith by marrying Brock for the sake of her child? If a child isn't reason enough to get married, are there any circumstances when it's appropriate to get married for reasons other than love?

7. Does Brock ask Mara's forgiveness for his part in the death of her husband? Does Mara ask Brock's forgiveness? Does she need to? Is it possible to forgive someone who doesn't ask your forgiveness?

8. Mara marries Brock even though she knows he's not a surrendered believer in Jesus Christ. Do her reasons justify her actions? How should a wife behave if she is a Christian who is married to a non-believer? Is it possible to have a truly meaningful relationship in such a case? What does the Bible teach about this?

9. What kind of friend is Sherry? Does she give good advice? What kind of friends has Brock cultivated? Should Christians befriend non-Christians, or is the danger of bad advice or bad influences too great?

10. Why does Brock abandon Mara toward the end of the book? What is he planning to do? Why does Mara follow him? What do both characters learn in this final scene about themselves? About forgiveness? About God? About marriage?

To find out some of what the Bible teaches about forgiveness, read: Psalm 25, Matthew 6:14-15, Matthew 18:21-35, II Corinthians 2:10-11, Ephesians 4:29-32

To find out some of what the Bible teaches about marriage, read: Genesis 2:24, Matthew 19:3-9, Ephesians 5, I Corinthians 7:1-17, Hebrews 13:4, I Peter 3:1-9, II Corinthians 6:14

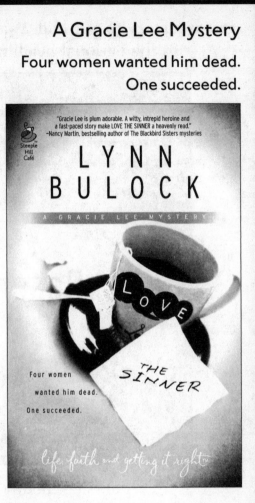

It was a story to put Hideaway, Missouri,
in the national headlines...

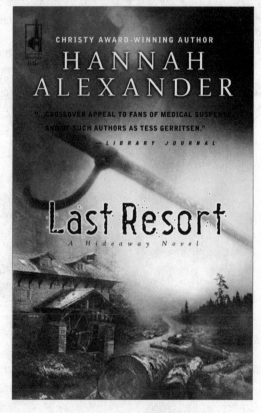

CHRISTY AWARD-WINNING AUTHOR
HANNAH ALEXANDER

"...CROSSOVER APPEAL TO FANS OF MEDICAL SUSPENSE
AND OF SUCH AUTHORS AS TESS GERRITSEN."
—*LIBRARY JOURNAL*

Last Resort
A Hideaway Novel

A missing child...
A woman in crisis...
A man of faith...

PROTECTED HEARTS

BY

BONNIE K. WINN

When her husband and child were murdered,
Emma Perry lost her faith—and her identity. Then
she started a new life in Rosewood, Texas, where the
caring community helped her regain her faith and
introduced her to Seth McAllister, her embittered
neighbor who was also struggling to overcome a
tragedy. Together, Seth and Emma began to open
their hearts to love, just as the still-obsessed killer
picks up Emma's trail….

Don't miss PROTECTED HEARTS
On sale May 2005

Available at your favorite retail outlet.

JOURNEY TO FOREVER

BY

CAROL STEWARD

An eight-day road trip with notorious radio
personality Colin Wright wasn't something
fledgling journalist Nikki Post was looking forward
to. Yet the Colin she met wasn't the immature
prankster she'd been expecting. But when trouble
threatened to end the trip, would Nikki's newfound
role in Colin's life end…or continue forever?

Don't miss JOURNEY TO FOREVER
On sale May 2005

Available at your favorite retail outlet.

A SHELTERING LOVE

BY

TERRI REED

Claire Wilcox sensed there was more to Nick Andrews
than met the eye. The handsome stranger who'd
saved her life twice was running from something.
Claire knew all about running—she'd been a runaway
herself. As Nick helped Claire repair the damages to
the teen center she'd established, he found himself
longing to forge a relationship with Claire…and
the God he'd shut out of his heart.

Don't miss A SHELTERING LOVE
On sale May 2005

Available at your favorite retail outlet.